Help us Rate this book...
Put your initials on the
Left side and your rating
on the right side.
1 = Didn't care for
2 = It was O.K.
3 = It was <u>great</u>

DATE DUE

		AUG 1 1 2014	NOV 2 8 2017	
		AUG 2 1 2014	FEB 0 3 2018	
		SEP 2 4 2014	NOV 1 3 2018	
		OCT - 3 2014	MAR 1 3 2019	
		OCT 2 2 2014		
LR	1 2 ③	OCT 2 8 2014	JUN 1 5 2019	
UM	1 2 ③	NOV 1 3 2014		
nrc	1 2 ③	NOV 2 6 2014		
mro	1 2 ③	DEC 2 3 2014		
Rh	1 2 ③	JAN - 5 2015		
BD	1 ② 3			
mw	1 2 ③	JAN 1 6 2015		
DV	1 2 ③	JAN 2 9 2015		
	1 2 3	FEB 1 4 2015		
	1 2 3	FEB 2 3 2015		
	1 2 3	APR - 9 2015		
	1 2 3	AUG 1 1 2015		
	1 2 3	JAN 3 0 2016		
	1 2 3	FEB 1 0 2016		
	1 2 3	MAY 1 5 2016		

PRINTED IN U.S.A.

Dancing with Fireflies

Center Point
Large Print

Also by Denise Hunter and available from
Center Point Large Print:

A Cowboy's Touch
The Trouble with Cowboys
Barefoot Summer

**This Large Print Book carries the
Seal of Approval of N.A.V.H.**

Dancing with Fireflies

A CHAPEL SPRINGS ROMANCE

DENISE HUNTER

CENTER POINT LARGE PRINT
THORNDIKE, MAINE

This Center Point Large Print edition is published in the year 2014 by arrangement with Thomas Nelson.

Scripture quotations are taken from the New American Standard Bible®, Copyright 1960, 1962, 1963, 1968, 1971, 1972, 1973, 1975, 1977, 1995 by The Lockman Foundation. Used by permission.

This novel is a work of fiction. Names, characters, places, and incidents are either products of the author's imagination or used fictitiously. All characters are fictional, and any similarity to people living or dead is purely coincidental.

The text of this Large Print edition is unabridged. In other aspects, this book may vary from the original edition. Printed in the United States of America on permanent paper. Set in 16-point Times New Roman type.

ISBN: 978-1-62899-080-5

Library of Congress Cataloging-in-Publication Data

Hunter, Denise, 1968–
Dancing with fireflies : a Chapel Springs romance / Denise Hunter. — Center Point Large Print edition.
    pages ; cm
    ISBN 978-1-62899-080-5 (library binding : alk. paper)
    1. Family secrets—Fiction. 2. Large type books. I. Title.
PS3608.U5925D33 2014b
813´.6—dc23
                                          2014004010

Dancing with Fireflies

Prologue

Jade McKinley lowered the stove to medium and returned the chicken breasts to the pan. What had she gotten herself into? She should've agreed to meet him at a restaurant instead of in the tiny apartment she shared with her friend. But it had seemed easier, meeting on her own turf with Izzy in the next room watching the Jane Austen marathon on PBS.

"There's a bottle of merlot in the cupboard," Izzy called. "You can serve it if you want."

The phone rang. "Can you get that?" Jade opened the cabinet and reached for the wine. She hoped it was okay. She never drank, didn't really like the taste.

Izzy entered the kitchen a few minutes later, wincing. "Uh, Jade?"

"He's not coming, is he? That's okay. Seriously, I was having second thoughts anyway." And thirds and fourths. "I didn't even want this date, remember?"

"Chill, girl. That was work calling. They need me on the late shift. Someone's sick."

"Oh."

"I really need the hours."

Jade bit her lip. Nick had been coming to the diner for months. He'd sat in her station every time, and after weeks of his persistence, she'd relented to one date.

"Seriously, girl," Izzy said gently. "You gotta get back on the horse. Aaron's been gone a long time. Give the guy a chance."

A knock sounded at the front door.

"Gotta get dressed." Izzy rushed from the room before Jade could protest.

She checked the table as she passed, then opened the door to Nick, remembering why she'd finally given in. Puppy dog eyes and an easy smile.

"Hey," he said. "You look nice. Like a beautiful gypsy."

She pinched her skirt and dipped in a curtsy. "Thank you. I guess you've never seen me outside the diner? Come on in."

He brushed past her, and his strong cologne filled her nostrils, making her want to sneeze. He wore a button-down and dark jeans. Jade's eyes fell to his shoes just as she caught a whiff of shoe polish. Izzy always said to check out a guy's shoes. Nick's were a brown casual leather shoe. Not that it mattered. One date and she was done.

"Smells good," he said.

"I hope you like chicken Marsala. Make yourself at home. I'll get the wine."

In the kitchen she rooted through the drawer for the corkscrew. She was struggling to open the bottle when Izzy entered in her uniform, grabbing her purse off the counter.

"Here, let me." Izzy removed the cork with ease. "Here you go. Have a nice dinner."

"Wait."

Izzy turned.

Jade lowered her voice. "Do you have to go? Could you hang around for an hour or two?"

Izzy grimaced. "I already told them I was coming. Listen, he's a nice guy. He's been coming into the diner for months, right? Not like he's a stranger."

"That's true."

"It's going to be fine. Mrs. Barlowe's right next door, and Lord knows she'd come barreling in at the first peep."

Jade was just being paranoid. "Okay, you're right."

After Izzy left, Jade took the wine to the table.

Nick rose from his seat as she neared. "I'll pour."

"Perfect."

Twenty minutes later they were halfway through the chicken and still engaged in awkward small talk. Jade finished her last sip of wine, telling him about her family back in Chapel Springs, about her passion for guitar. The wine seemed to have loosened her tongue.

He was a good listener, and he looked attractive with candlelight flickering in his dark eyes.

"I made dessert," she said later when conversation petered out. "You like cheesecake?"

"It's actually my favorite."

It was possibly his longest sentence so far. She grabbed the cake from the fridge. When she returned, she saw he'd filled her glass again.

She did most of the talking over dessert too. She'd used her sister PJ's recipe, and it was divine, topped with a medley of blueberries, strawberries, and raspberries in a tangy sauce.

She was talking too much, and by the time they'd finished dessert, the room had started spinning a little. Sweat had broken out on the back of her neck. The wine. She shouldn't have had the second glass.

"Is it hot in here?" she tried to say, but her words didn't come out right. She should open the windows and let in the spring air.

The table in front of her tilted, and her date seemed to sway the other direction. She blinked hard, trying to clear her vision.

"You okay?" he asked.

"Fine." But her words didn't sound fine. They sounded muffled and distant, like she was inside a tunnel.

"Why don't we sit on the couch?" he said.

She needed a little help getting there. Her knees wobbled, and her feet didn't go where she put them. "I think I had too much wine." She teetered at his side.

"Wanna watch a movie?" he asked.

She sank onto the threadbare sofa and was relieved at the thought of not having to carry the conversation. She actually wished he'd leave but didn't want to be rude.

"Sure. You pick. They're in the cabinet." She didn't think she could make it over there by herself.

He chose one of Izzy's action flicks. He started the movie, but Jade couldn't follow the plot. Halfway through, her eyes grew heavy. So tired. Did alcohol make you tired? She'd never drunk enough to know. Maybe the room would stop spinning if she just closed her eyes a minute.

"Jade?"

A voice was talking from someplace far away.

"Hmm?" she said. And then darkness closed in and everything went quiet.

A twisting in Jade's stomach pulled her from sleep. She drew her knees to her stomach, shivering. She reached for her blanket, but there was nothing to grab. She was on top of the covers. Still in her clothes.

She closed her eyes against the glaring sunlight, trying to remember the night before. Dinner with the guy from the diner. She didn't remember coming to bed, didn't remember saying good-bye. They'd eaten, she'd felt weird. They'd watched a movie.

What else?

Nothing.

She rolled over, her body aching, and pulled her skirt over her legs. Her eyes fell on a scrap of silky lavender at the foot of her bed.

A memory flashed in her mind. Darkness and weight. The overwhelming smell of cologne. The steady creaking of the bed.

She sat upright, her head spinning. Her eyes darted around the shoebox-sized room, the walls feeling tight. Her heart thumped heavily. She gasped for breath.

No. Please no.

What happened? The memories were a blur, separated by gaping black holes.

Her stomach spasmed, threatening release. She raced for the bathroom and retched until her stomach felt twisted inside out. A cool sweat broke out on her forehead. Her throat felt raw. Her eyes burned.

She eased down onto the tile floor, resting her head against the wall. The ache inside spread, consuming her. She trembled with the knowledge of what had taken place.

"Jade?" A tap sounded on the door. "You okay?"

Her eye sockets burned. She opened her mouth,

but nothing passed her chapped lips. How could this have happened?

"Jade?" The knob twisted, and Izzy slipped inside. "You sick?"

Jade pulled her knees to her chest, willing the room to stop spinning. Willing it to be yesterday. Before she'd said yes. Before he'd—

"Honey, what's wrong?"

The tears welled over. Stupid. How could she have been so stupid? This wasn't Chapel Springs, it was Chicago. She knew better. And now she'd been—

Izzy knelt on the floor and felt Jade's forehead. "Can I do anything? Is it the flu?"

Jade shook her head, a shudder passing through her. He'd seemed so nice with his easy smile and big brown eyes. She closed her eyes. She didn't want to think about him. Wished she could wipe his face from her memory. How could he have done this? How could she have let it happen? *God, where are You?*

"Did something happen last night?"

Jade's teeth knocked together, clattering in the quiet. She nodded. Her whole body shook, her own private earthquake.

Izzy's warm hazel eyes settled on her. "Honey, tell me."

"I—I think he slipped something in my drink. I got dizzy, and then I couldn't talk. Couldn't keep my eyes open. I don't remember anything after that. I woke up in my clothes, and my underwear was off. I'm all achy. I'm having these flashbacks—"

"Oh, baby . . ." Izzy pulled Jade into her arms. "This is all my fault."

The memories flashed into her mind, and she closed her eyes against them. The repulsive smell of his cologne. Her limbs weighted and helpless. Sounds, breathing, the squeaking bed, all of it sounding far away. But now it felt all too close, all too real. His hands on her, rough. His smothering weight pressed against her.

Jade broke away, scrambling unsteadily to her feet. "I need a shower."

"Honey . . . you have to go to the hospital."

Jade turned on the water. She had to get it off her. His touch. His smell. She could smell his cologne on her. She couldn't get him off her fast enough.

"I'll take you."

Jade shook her head, pulling the knob on the faucet until the shower sprayed into the tub.

"They'll need to collect samples, Jade."

"I can't." She just wanted to be clean. Just wanted to forget it had ever happened. If she could just forget, it would be almost like it hadn't happened at all. She could put it behind her.

Izzy took her arm. "Jade—"

Jade jerked free. "I can't, Izzy! Leave me alone!"

Izzy gave her a long look. "I'm so sorry. I'll be right outside if you need me." The door closed quietly behind her.

Jade disrobed. A minute later she stood under the scalding water. But no matter how much she scrubbed, she couldn't get clean. She wondered if she'd ever feel clean again.

Chapter One

Jade's foot eased off the gas as she passed the marina, not because the speed limit had changed but because her heart had begun beating up into her throat.

Nearly there.

She hadn't expected to see Chapel Springs, Indiana, for a long time, but it had barely been a year—a year of broken dreams. But then sometimes life took unexpected turns.

The evening sun sparkled on the Ohio River, the pink clouds brightening the water's surface. Spring had wakened the valley, greening the hills and unfurling leaf buds on the trees.

Jade stopped at a light and put down her window, inhaling the fresh scent of a Midwestern spring: rain, river, and pine. Tourists had yet to arrive, and the parallel parking slots on Main Street were empty, the businesses locked up for the night.

Nothing had changed. Same brick storefronts, sun-faded canopies, and ancient streetlamps. On the corner, the Rialto theater's lights kicked on, chasing each other in an endless rectangle. The board listed two movies that had premiered in Chicago months ago.

When the light changed, she pressed the accelerator. Her car gave a reluctant start. She followed the road through town and around a corner that separated her from the river. Her mouth dried as she approached the turn toward her parents' farm.

The fields would be plowed by now, the corn in the ground. Her mom and dad would be snuggled on the couch watching some old black-and-white movie. She suddenly regretted her decision to surprise them.

Her heart thumped heavily against her ribs. She squeezed the steering wheel, her rings cutting into her thumbs. Her foot never found the brake, and she passed the turn, continuing down the winding road.

Ahead on the left, she saw the cement drive. Lined with landscape lighting and turning up a wooded knoll, it was hard to miss.

She headed into the drive and mounted the hill, her pea-green Ford struggling with the effort. Twilight was thick under the canopies of ancient trees. The crickets and cicadas had already begun their nightly chorus.

She pressed on, following the lane down the back side of the hill, sloping toward the river. Ahead, the shingled boathouse was silhouetted against the darkening sky. A lone light shone from the upstairs window through what looked like a thin sheet.

She put her car in park and turned off the ignition. She hadn't been to Daniel's place for years. He was always at her parents' house or hanging around the coffeehouse with his laptop and a ready handshake.

She got out of the car and pushed the door shut, its loud squeak echoing across the water. She stepped onto the dock and followed the stairs that ran alongside the building, suddenly wondering if he'd be upset. She hadn't exactly kept in touch.

When she reached the top, she rapped her knuckles on the pine door and waited. Below her the water rippled against the shore and against the dock. The wind kicked up, and Daniel's boat bumped the wood piling. She wondered if he still took it out on the river when he needed to get away.

The door opened, and there he was. He froze at the sight of her, his lips parting, his blue, blue eyes widening. If she hadn't been so glad to see him, she would've laughed.

"Jade? What are you doing here?"

She walked into his arms and felt his shock ease

as he enveloped her with his solid frame. She already had a big brother, but Daniel filled a spot in her heart she hadn't known existed until Ryan brought him home when they were all still kids.

She heard a voice that belonged to neither of them and pulled away. It was coming from the phone in his hand.

He put it to his ear, stepping aside to let Jade go inside. "I have to go, Mom. I'll call you later." He sighed, not following through. "I guess. I know." He grabbed a scrap of paper and jotted down a phone number. "Fine. Yes, I'll call her. Bye, Mom."

He pocketed the phone and turned to her. He seemed taller and broader. His hair was longer, his bangs dipping down nearly to his eyes—very un-mayorlike. It looked good on him though.

"Sorry to just drop in. It's so good to see you."

She watched his blue eyes go from warm to cool in the space of ten seconds. He'd always had the most mesmerizing eyes.

"You have a minute?"

He crossed his arms. "I'm kind of busy."

She escaped his gaze, scanning the room. A lamp glowed by a leather recliner. His open laptop was perched on the end table along with a bunch of boring-looking forms.

She wiped her palms on her gypsy skirt and flipped her braid over her shoulder. "I'm sorry I didn't call."

"It's been a year."

"I'm sorry."

"I know I'm not your real brother, but—"

She frowned. "Stop that."

"—a phone call isn't asking much. A letter, a postcard, a text—"

"You're right." She'd hurt him. And he probably wasn't the only one. "I'm sorry. Things weren't what I expected in Chicago."

"You had big dreams."

That was the last thing she wanted to talk about. She followed him into the living room, passing a spare room that was filled with barbells and weights. A heavy-duty treadmill stood in the corner, the panel lit with orange numbers. She caught a whiff of sweat and ambition.

Daniel picked up the remote control, and blackness swallowed the political talk show. Silence crept in, filling the room with awkwardness.

He studied her until she felt like an amoeba under a microscope.

"Are you just here for the wedding?" he asked finally.

She shook her head.

An emotion flickered in his eyes, but he turned and headed into his galley kitchen before she could decipher it.

The wedding was less than a month away. Her sister Madison and Beckett O'Reilly. Jade's heart sank at the thought of facing her soon-to-be brother-in-law. The whole secret admirer thing had been one big embarrassment—the reason she'd left. Or the last straw anyway. Deep down she'd been yearning for a fresh start for years.

Jade had thought Beckett had sent her notes and flowers. Thought he'd wanted her. But it had been Madison he'd wanted all along. And now Jade was arriving home just in time for their wedding.

Daniel opened the fridge, pulled out a jug of tea, and poured some into a glass. He added two heaping spoonfuls of sugar and brought it to her.

He gestured toward the brown leather sofa. "Have a seat."

"Thanks." She took down half the glass, then set it on the front section of the *Chapel Springs Gazette*. Her eyes wandered the room and settled on the "curtains"—a white sheet hanging haphazardly over a curtain rod.

"Your folks didn't tell me you were coming."

"They didn't know. Still don't. This is my first stop."

"Why?"

She shrugged. "Impulse." She was beginning to think it had been a bad one. She'd already insulted Daniel by ignoring him for a year. Now she was going to beg a favor?

She was selfish and thoughtless. She should've gone to her parents' or Madison's. She'd at least spared them a few phone calls over the past year. She took another sip of her tea, wishing it were ginger ale.

Daniel cocked his head. "What can I do for you, Jade?"

She hated that he'd guessed right. She didn't want to dive into that yet. She remembered the phone call she'd interrupted.

"How are your parents? That was your mom on the phone?"

He gave her a look—*I know what you're doing*—but settled back in the chair and went along. "They're fine. Mom's found my perfect match again and is determined to set me up when I go there next weekend."

"There" was Washington, DC. Daniel's dad was an Indiana senator. If his parents had anything to say about it, Daniel would one day move into national politics too. At present they settled for town mayor, a post his grandfather had held for sixteen years, but they probably wouldn't be satisfied until he occupied the White House.

She gave him a weary smile. "Maybe she is your perfect match. Mom knows best and all that."

He looked away. Closed his laptop.

"Catch me up on you," she said.

He steepled his hands, resting his chin on his fingertips as he filled her in. Still a volunteer fireman. His job was keeping him busy. Grandma

Dawson was having trouble keeping up with her social obligations and charity work.

"And you, Jade?" he asked when he was finished. "What's going on with you?"

She cleared her throat, thinking of the stressful four weeks she'd just endured. Why did it always seem her life was spinning out of control?

She wasn't going there tonight. "I need a job, Daniel." It was the least of the favors, the easiest one to start with.

"Why?"

"Food . . . shelter . . . clothing . . ."

"That's not what I mean." His blue eyes were like lasers, seeing too much, too deeply.

She looked away, twisting the top ring on her middle finger. "I'm back to stay."

"Why?"

She was sure her family had kept him in the loop while she'd been gone. She'd been living with her best friend, working at a café, playing her guitar at a trendy coffee shop.

And now she was home. Jobless.

"Don't really want to get into it."

Daniel popped to his feet and headed to the kitchen again. He emptied the carafe into a mug and took a sip, his white dress shirt stretching across his shoulders at the motion. The sleeves were rolled up at the cuff, exposing sturdy forearms.

"I thought you might have the inside scoop on who's hiring."

A few seconds later he turned, leaned against the counter. "You could probably get your spot back at the Coachlight. Including your guitar gig. The guy who took your place doesn't compare." His lips turned up before he took another sip.

His smile. That's what had been missing. She wondered if things were as okay with him as he'd said. Or maybe he was more ticked at her than he let on.

The thought of smelling coffee all day made her stomach turn. "I need more than minimum wage. I'm hoping to crash with Madison until the wedding, but after that . . ."

"Don't want to horn in on the newlyweds?"

"Exactly. And I refuse to be one of those twentysomethings eating Cheetos all day in her parents' basement."

* * *

"So can you help me?" Jade's eyebrows rose, disappearing under her dark bangs.

He'd forgotten the magnetic pull of her green eyes. There was something different about her face, though. He studied it, trying to solve the mystery. Same almond-shaped eyes that hitched up at the corners. Same straight, button-tipped nose. Same full lips that so rarely stretched into a smile, he felt like a hero when he made it happen.

"What about your music?" he asked.

She sat up straighter, lifting her dimpled chin. Her rings clicked together as she laced her fingers. "It's time to grow up. I need a real job."

Never thought he'd hear those words come from Jade's mouth. She lived and breathed her music. It had been that way since he'd taught her some basic guitar chords her freshman year. She'd plucked away for hours a day and passed him up within a few months. She'd written songs throughout high school and given lessons to every friend who showed an interest. By the time she left, she'd built a strong base of students.

What had happened in Chicago? She'd always marched to the beat of her own drum. He remembered the first time he saw her, spinning in circles in the McKinleys' darkened backyard, her skirt swirling around her spindly legs.

"What are you doing?" he'd asked, one part scoffing, one part fascinated.

"Dancing with the fireflies," she'd said. "Wanna join me?"

Jade had always done her own thing. But she seemed different now. Like she'd lost her spark. She hadn't really been the same since Aaron's death.

"Daniel?"

He blinked the memory away. "I'll check around. See what I can find."

"I appreciate it." She finished her tea and stood, her long dark braid slipping over shoulder. "I should let you get back to work."

Daniel followed her to the door, wondering

why she'd stopped at his place first. Just the job? Unlikely. There was something she wasn't saying, but he knew enough not to press her.

"The family will be glad to have you home," he said as they reached the door.

She turned and leaned in for a shoulder hug that he longed to make more of. Instead he patted her on the back the way he should.

"It's good to see you again," she said.

"You too, Squirt," he added for good measure.

And then she was slipping out his door, down the steps, and into her car. Slipping back into his life as easily as she'd slipped into his heart.

Chapter Two

Jade rinsed her mouth in Madison's bathroom sink, cleaned up behind her, and headed for the kitchen. Lulu, her sister's border collie, followed, her claws ticking on the hardwood floor. Wedding paraphernalia covered the coffee table, along with a notepad and an empty bowl with a spoon.

Her sister hadn't been home when Jade arrived, so she'd left a voice mail on Madison's cell. ("Guess who's on your front porch? Hope you don't mind if I let myself in.")

She'd called her parents and told them she was home, promising to come by in the morning for tea. After they'd caught up, Jade called Ryan, knowing word would spread quickly through the family grapevine. Her brother was more inquisitive about her return than her parents, but she'd sidestepped his questions and begged off when her stomach became unsettled.

She grabbed a bottled water, washing the acid from her throat. One look at the Burger Barn, one whiff of the char-grilled beef, and she'd pulled through the drive-through, ordering a big, greasy, sloppy burger. It had been heaven. It had also been a mistake.

The front doorknob rattled. The key slid in and the door burst open. Madison rushed in, dark eyes settling on Jade. A smile broke loose, the door whooshed shut.

She charged across the room, enveloping Jade in a rocking hug. "You're home! Why didn't you call?"

Jade couldn't help but smile. "I did."

"I meant before you were on my porch." Madison pulled back, not letting go. "Do Mom and Dad know?"

"Just called them."

"My wedding's not for a month, you know."

"How do you feel about a roommate—just until the wedding?"

"A whole month?" Madison whooped. "Where's your luggage?"

"In the car."

Madison spun, heading outside, already making

plans for the two of them. Lulu trotted behind her, tail wagging, and Jade brought up the rear.

Madison tugged the car door open. Jade's green bathroom rug flopped onto the gravel drive, unrolling. Stuffed into the backseat were her guitar case, her flowered lamp, a bookcase she'd discovered in an antique store in Chicago, two suitcases, and a large box of odds and ends.

Madison turned, brown eyes wide, caution in the line of her slim shoulders. "You're staying . . . ?"

Jade wrinkled her nose. "Yes?"

"Yay!" Madison hugged her again, tighter this time. Jade let out a breath she didn't know she'd been holding.

Madison helped her lug her things into her old bedroom. It looked the same: lavender walls, wooden floor covered by a shaggy purple rug, a high twin bed draped with a faded quilt and piled with lavender, black, and green pillows. Home sweet home. For a few weeks.

Madison set the lamp on the table. "This is . . . interesting."

"Izzy called it my flower child lamp."

"Fitting." She shook the lamp shade, and the green fringe danced.

Jade plopped on the bed, fatigue edging in as they chatted. Madison caught her up on wedding details and family stuff, then shifted the subject to work. Her brainy sister was a veterinarian at the local clinic.

"Have you eaten?" Madison said after a while.

"Yeah." Never mind that the burger was long gone. Food was the last thing she wanted.

"You look tired."

"Long drive."

"Make it an early night. We have lots of time to catch up."

"I think I might. I can hardly keep my eyes open."

"Get in your jammies and go to sleep. We'll chat more tomorrow."

Madison turned at the door. "I'm glad you're back, Jade. I missed you."

"Missed you too."

The door clicked shut. Jade kicked off her Birkenstocks. Her limbs felt like lead. She fell back against the pillows, trying to find the energy to unzip her suitcase and get ready for bed. Instead, she rolled to her side and pulled open the nightstand drawer.

She pushed aside the secret admirer notes, brushing away the twinge of humiliation they brought. Aaron's letters were beneath them. Stacked in the corner, just as she'd left them. She toyed with the idea of reading them again. She'd missed them, had wished for them a hundred times in Chicago.

But no, she was done with all that. Love had a way of taking you fast and sucking you into a delicious vortex of feelings. Then when you thought you were invincible, it grabbed you and held you down until your lungs burned. Until you could only wish for death.

Never again.

Besides, she had bigger things to worry about than love and romance and happily-ever-afters. She pulled the chain on the lamp and rested her hand on her flat stomach. Seven months from now she'd have another person counting on her. And she wasn't about to let him or her down.

Chapter Three

Tiny white lights strung along the porch's eaves twinkled like fireflies in the gathering darkness. Across her parents' backyard, Jade watched Dad and Madison go two-on-two with Madison's fiancé and her brother Ryan. Beckett swept past Madison for an easy layup.

Ryan bumped Beckett's fist while Madison bemoaned the score.

Jade settled on the porch swing, listening to the familiar night sounds build around her. Crickets and cicadas, the wind rustling through the woods. The familiar thumping of the basketball on the concrete pad. She pulled her sweater closed against the chill in the air.

Seeing Beckett again had been as awkward as she'd anticipated. His handsome face had flushed when she'd entered the backyard. But then the normal family chaos had ensued, and the moment had passed. Despite Jade's lingering humiliation over the misunderstanding, it was good to see her sister happy. Beckett was obviously smitten with Madison, and that was all that mattered now.

Daniel sank into the Adirondack chair across from her, kicking out his long legs. The porch light draped a golden cape over his shoulders. When he'd begged off the game, she'd opted out herself. She'd been looking for the opportunity to get him alone.

"Why aren't you playing?" she asked.

"Pulled a muscle." He rotated his shoulder. "There was an accident down on 56 last night."

"Everyone okay?"

"Concussion and possibly a fractured rib. No one we know. Where's Mama Jo?"

"Her back was hurting. I gave her ibuprofen and sent her to bed with orders to stay there till morning." She'd put up a fight because PJ was home from college and Jade was home from Chicago. *All my babies, home and doing well,* she'd said.

Or so she thought.

"Getting bossy," Daniel teased.

"Speaking of bossy, how'd your date with Miss DC go?"

His brow furrowed. "She wasn't bossy."

"I was referring to your matchmaking mom."

That wasn't very nice. True, but not nice. "Sorry."

"Fair enough."

"And the date? Was she hot?"

He made a face. "She's very attractive."

"Intelligent? Witty? A bimbo? Come on, Dawson, give me something."

"She was very nice."

"Nice."

"We had intelligent conversation and things in common. What do you want from me?"

"Men. What's her name? What did she wear? Where did you go? Did you kiss her good night?"

"Courtney, a black dress, Vidalia, and no."

"Fine. Be secretive. Tell me how your job's going. Or is that top secret too?"

"Job's going fine." He told her about the most recent debacle with the housing department involving restoration of homes in the historical district. Daniel had a gift with people. He didn't wear his appeal on his sleeve the way his father did, always talking. But he had a quiet way of working things out. He listened.

"How's the job hunt going?" he asked when his story wound down.

"All right, I guess."

"Nothing panning out?"

"Nope." He'd given her three leads. She'd applied for them all, gotten one interview, but hadn't heard back. She'd also scoured the *Gazette* and put out feelers with everyone she knew.

She'd overestimated the job opportunities in Chapel Springs.

"Something'll turn up. It's only been a week."

"I thought with tourist season almost here . . ."

"Everyone's hired their extra help. I had a lead on a job at the hospital. Administrative assistant. Interested?"

"Sure." It sounded boring, but it probably came with benefits and a decent salary.

"I'll get the info to you tomorrow."

She had no office experience, but she was running out of time. Three weeks to find a place to live, and a bigger deadline seven months away. She'd thought she'd have phase one of her plan wrapped up before starting on phase two. Why had she thought it would be so easy? Since when had anything in her life been easy?

She hated to ask Daniel for another favor, but was it her fault he knew so many people?

Pandemonium erupted on the court as Madison missed an easy shot and cried foul against Beckett.

"That was a legal block!" Beckett said.

"Yeah, right!"

"I knew letting them guard each other was a mistake." Ryan ran his hand through his dark hair.

Dad dribbled the ball. His gray bangs had flopped over his forehead. "All right, you two. Our ball."

Madison scowled at her fiancé. "Cheater."

"What did you call me?" He stalked her play-fully, then charged.

She dodged, swatted his backside as he missed.

He turned, lightning swift, and swooped her over his broad shoulder as she let out a squeal.

"Great, just great," Ryan said.

Jade smiled, watching her dad try to call order. He took sports so seriously. That and corn. She pushed the swing into motion, making the chains squeak. "They seem happy."

"Madison and Beckett? Yeah."

She'd watched them together all night, had watched Beckett especially, and the way he looked at Madison with forever in his eyes. Some people were just lucky in love, it seemed.

"Their lives are about to change drastically," Daniel said. "Seems like they're ready for it, though. They're good together."

She couldn't have asked for a more perfect segue. *Phase two, here we go.* "Speaking of good together . . ."

He turned toward her. She caught a flicker of something in his blue eyes before it disappeared. She wondered if Daniel had secrets of his own.

"I hate to ask another favor, but—" This one was harder than the last. More personal.

"Go on." His voice was deeper than she remembered.

"It's just that you know so many people, what with being the mayor and all. I was going to ask

Ryan, but he tends to be, well, too brotherly, and if left up to him I'm afraid I'd never—"

"Spit it out, Jade."

"I need a man." She winced. *Really, Jade? That's how you ask?*

She curled her fist around the cold metal links. Her face warmed, and she was thankful she wasn't the one sitting under the pool of light.

His left brow hiked up. The corners of his lips twitched. "Excuse me?"

She lifted her chin. "I'm ready to settle down. I'm going to find a job, a place of my own, and I just—that's my next step."

"A man."

"I'm twenty-three, Daniel. It's not unheard of."

He rested his chin on steepled hands, studying her. Those eyes reaching down into her, looking for—what?

She squirmed under the weight of his stare. It was just her guilty conscience. There was no reason for guilt though. She'd tell her dates about the pregnancy early on—she wasn't trying to trick anyone. Just find a willing partner. It didn't escape her that it might be challenging to find such a man in her condition, but she pushed the thought away.

She *could* have a successful marriage built on friendship and rooted in love. She didn't have to be *in* love to get married and have a family.

"I'm sure you know some nice single men . . ."

His eyes hooded and he blinked away.

"I'm not looking for a soul mate or anything. Just a nice, responsible man—here, I have a list." She dug in her jeans pocket.

"A *list?*"

"Just some basic things. Guidelines to help narrow down the field."

He took the list, scowling. "Since when do you make lists? And what's the big rush?"

She shrugged. "Maybe my clock is ticking." It wasn't a lie. Her clock was ticking, and when the alarm went off, her baby would be daddyless if she didn't work fast. That wasn't happening. She wanted for her child what *she'd* had: a mother *and* a father. If anyone could understand that, Daniel would, but she couldn't tell him about the baby yet.

He read from the list. "Over thirty?"

"Men are slower to grow up. I want someone responsible and mature."

"I'm only twenty-eight, and I'm the flipping mayor."

She frowned. "Don't take it personally. You're not exactly typical."

"Good with kids . . . financially secure . . . rooted in Chapel Springs . . ."

"All very reasonable."

"This reads like a grocery list."

She snatched the paper away. "If you don't want to help, just say so."

The swing went silent as it came to a halt.

"I didn't say that." Daniel inhaled. His lungs felt as stiff as iron as they expanded. Great. What could be worse than setting up the girl he loved on blind dates?

And why was she in such a rush to put down roots anyway? Looking for a practical job and a—how did she put it?—a responsible and reliable man. Jade, who lost hours with her guitar. Jade, who lived moment to moment and had been set on finding a way to make a living with her guitar.

"What happened in Chicago? Where's all this coming from?"

"Nothing. Nowhere."

"You've changed."

"I've been gone a year. Maybe I've grown up." She tucked the list back into her pocket. "Forget it. I'll ask Ryan."

What was worse than setting her up on blind dates? Letting someone else do it. "Hang on. You just caught me off guard. A few guys are already coming to mind." There was Lloyd Webster at the nursing home. Couldn't get more mature than that.

"Really?"

"Sure."

Her shoulders fell on a sigh. "Thanks." The gratefulness in her beautiful green eyes made him want to scale Mount Everest for her. It occurred to him that the job might be easier and less painful than what she'd asked of him.

"You know me well, so mostly think about compatibility. And the list."

The list. Of course. All the things he wasn't. Not that it mattered. Wasn't like he could have her anyway. He'd settled that a long time ago, but that didn't mean he wanted to watch her fall into someone else's arms. *Help* her fall into someone else's arms.

"So who are they?" she asked.

"What?"

"The men you're thinking of."

"Oh." Probably best not to mention Mr. Webster. "Ah, let me get back with you on that. Need to make sure they're available."

"Good point. Just . . . you think we could keep this between us? It's kind of embarrassing and, you know . . ." She gestured to the court. PJ had joined the game, helping out Madison and her dad. "They'd never let me hear the end of it."

He couldn't believe he'd been reduced to the role of Cupid. This was really going to blow.

Or was it? He'd be in control of everyone she dated. The criteria were pretty wide—even if he didn't fit them. He'd just have to make sure Jade didn't find exactly what she was looking for.

Chapter Four

Aaron had come into Jade's life the summer before her senior year. He was the new kid in school, his parents moving to the area for his dad's job. Even before school started, he turned the heads of the local girls, but Jade had hardly noticed him.

Until midway through the first day of school. It was just before lunch, and she paused outside the cafeteria doors. The year before she'd left her usual table with her friends to sit with her boyfriend, who'd broken up with her midsummer. She'd saved her weekends for him too, and though she hadn't meant to, she'd let her friendships slip away. She'd been one of those girls.

Now her friends were giving her the cold shoulder. Izzy had barely spoken to her in American history, and Tess had walked right past her after third hour.

Jade faced the lunchroom.

"You look lost."

She didn't recognize the deep voice, but when she turned, the new student stood at her back. Aaron something. They were right. He was a beautiful boy. He was a head taller than she was, with thick black hair and eyes the color of milk chocolate.

"I'm the new one," he said. "Shouldn't I be the one lost?"

She regarded his friendly smile and tried for one of her own, not quite succeeding. "I have lunch next." She eyed the doorway of the cafeteria.

His head tilted back, knowingly. "Ah, the old lunchroom debacle. Who do you sit with?"

"My friends." She remembered Izzy's stilted smile and clipped answer when Jade had asked about her summer. "Except I'm not sure they're my friends anymore."

He regarded her with curiosity. "You want them to be?"

She nodded.

"Well. Let's go sit with them then."

And just like that, Aaron Roberts entered her life. Somehow he'd eased her back into her friendships with Izzy and Tess, and life became normal again. Better than normal. Because for some reason, Aaron was taken with her.

He looked straight into her eyes when she talked about music and her big-city dreams even though he was more cerebral than creative. He made her laugh with his dry sense of humor.

And then one day in the courtyard after lunch, he'd taken her hand, twining his fingers with hers. She'd met his milk chocolate eyes, her heart in her throat. Then his lips tipped up in a smile. Her breaths grew shallow, and the empty spaces in her heart began filling.

By the time they attended homecoming, they were officially a couple. All the jealous girls said it wouldn't last. But after the dance he took her home and, not ready to end the night, they sat on the porch swing.

He took off his coat and wrapped it around her shoulders. It smelled like him, and Jade took a deep breath, curling into his side. They talked awhile, reviewing the best parts of the night, but suddenly it grew quiet. A cricket chirped from somewhere nearby, joining the rhythmic squeak of the swing.

He hooked a finger under her chin, turning her toward him. His eyes were like coal in the darkened corner of the porch, and she felt his gaze on her like a touch.

"I had a great time tonight," he said.

"Me too." Her voice was barely a whisper.

"I always have a great time with you."

He made her want to write a thousand songs. Happy, sappy, gushy ones that would make her brother want to gag. Only she wasn't sure she could put into words what he did to her.

"I love you, Jade." He'd never looked more solemn, and she only had a moment to wonder how she'd gotten so lucky before he kissed her. She melted into his arms, hoping they could stay this way forever.

In the spring they attended prom together, and a rumble of complaint could still be heard echoing the halls of Chapel Springs High. Girls flirted with Aaron, making Jade feel insecure sometimes. They had words over it more than once, but even she had to admit he did nothing wrong. He seemed to have eyes only for her.

They sailed through the end of their senior year together, and people stopped wondering when they'd break up. Her friends called them the golden couple, but Jade knew Aaron was the golden one. She was just lucky.

Graduation came and went, and Jade decided to take a year off from school, working at the coffee shop, while Aaron studied psychology at nearby Hanover College. They spent their free time watching movies and discussing books and music. Jade brought him to family barbecues, and he fit right in with the McKinleys.

His second and third years of college, they began talking about their future. About getting married after Aaron graduated, about settling in Chapel Springs in the new subdivision down by Boulder Creek.

Jade continued working at the Coachlight and began growing a small clientele of guitar students. She played at the coffee shop on weekend nights and applied herself more to songwriting, testing her compositions on her audience. Her performances began to draw a crowd, and she began saving for her own place.

The call came during one of those performances. Her phone vibrated in her pocket, but she was midway through her set, so she let it go. Ten minutes later, Mom and Madison burst into the coffee shop and pulled her boss, Sidney, aside. Jade watched them, dread rising in the pit of her stomach as she played the final chords of the melody.

"Thanks, everyone," Sidney said into the microphone. "Jade's going to take a break now."

She was pulled into the back room, and her mom delivered the news there. Aaron . . . an accident . . . everything they could . . . so sorry.

Jade's legs crumbled under her. Her brain filled with fog, then denial. She wouldn't believe it. It wasn't true. Then they were in the car, and there were screams that seemed to come from far away. They weren't hers, couldn't be hers. Sounds like this had never come from her body.

At the hospital she fought to get out of the car, pushing, trampling. She had to see him. It was a mistake. A cruel mistake. How could they do this to her? She pushed past people in street clothes, people in scrubs. Where was he? She needed to see him. He needed her. She shook off Mom's hands, pushed Madison away.

Someone in a security uniform took her arm and said he'd help her find him. She followed him. They went into an elevator and down a long, sterile hall. At the end Aaron's parents clung to one another, their faces streaked with shock.

They pulled her into their arms, and that's when the truth began sinking in. It wasn't an awful mistake. It was a cruel reality.

But it didn't feel like reality when she opened her swollen eyes the next day to an Aaron-less earth. It didn't feel like reality when she crawled from bed to dress for Aaron's funeral three days later. And it didn't feel like reality when she smoothed her fingers over his beautiful, waxy face one last time.

Where was God? How could He let this happen? Why had He taken Aaron from her? She fell into a black hole and couldn't seem to find her way out. Wasn't even sure she wanted to. But her family kept trying to reach her, wouldn't let her stay in the comforting embrace of sleep. She fought them until she was too tired to fight.

She needed to keep moving, they said. Keep breathing. She went back to the coffee shop. She moved. She breathed. But she didn't live.

She went back to church, and at her parents' insistence counseled with the pastor. His answers all sounded good, but none of it mattered. None of it was real. None of it brought Aaron back or made her happy again.

The fog began to clear, but it had taken her joy with it. She wasn't a stranger to grief. Her brother had died when she was fourteen. It had sent the whole family into a spiral of sorrow.

But this was even worse. She went through the stages of grief, getting lost somewhere between depression and acceptance. Unable to bear the constant sadness on her mom's face, she moved in with Madison and started new routines. She learned to fake a smile at work, pretend to listen at church, and act as if nothing had happened. But something had happened, and she knew deep inside that she'd never be the same again.

Jade managed to find a new normal. Long after the tears stopped, when a welcoming numbness enveloped her, she found the first note on the windshield of her car.

You inspire me, it said. Jade held it in her hands, wondering about the sender. Wondering who could be inspired by her pathetic shell of a life. Nonetheless, she set it on her nightstand and read it every night before bed.

Then the second note came. And a pink rose. The sender left no hint of his identity, and though she and Madison tried to solve the mystery, Jade didn't care. She wasn't interested in discovering his identity.

The notes breathed fresh air into her stale lungs with their kind words and encouragement. Then Beckett had shown up at her door, and she'd believed him to be her secret admirer. For one moment she'd surrendered to the idea of hope. But a humiliating hour later she'd learned the foolishness of that thought. He'd never wanted her, and she should've known better than to try again.

Jade's heart had already been shattered into a thousand pieces, and there was no putting it back together. Even if there were, Jade wasn't interested. Loving Aaron had been like magic, but losing him had been a kind of hell she never wanted to experience again.

Chapter Five

Mrs. Wearly squatted next to the pedestal with her pins. "Just a few nips and tucks, I think."

Jade looked at her reflection in the three-way mirror. The dress was the same shimmering silver as the others, but Madison had chosen a style that suited her personality without making her stand out. The neckline scooped modestly and the skirt flowed past her calves, flaring in an uneven hemline.

"You look beautiful," Madison said.

PJ exited the fitting room, palming her chest. "Okay, I think my boobs shrank."

"Didn't think that was possible," Jade teased.

PJ gave her a mock scowl. "Want some help with those pins, Mrs. Wearly?" she asked with a syrup-sweet voice.

"No thank you, dear."

"Give me a break, PJ," Jade said. "You know

you look like a model. Lucky for you, you're too nice to hate."

Madison fussed with PJ's halter neckline. "It really shows off your shoulders, don't you think?"

"This feel all right?" Mrs. Wearly asked Jade.

The bodice hugged Jade's waist. Already she looked a little bloated. Add another two weeks and—"Maybe a little looser. Room to breathe and all that."

Madison surveyed Jade's reflection. "That color is gorgeous on you."

PJ wedged in between them, frowning. "Why'd she get all the curves?"

"Poor PJ," Jade said. "Those long legs must be such a pain."

"And eating all day, without gaining an ounce," Madison said. "Dreadful."

"I don't eat all day, I cook all day." PJ was in culinary school in Indianapolis. The girl could make pastry like nobody's business. If she ate it all, you sure couldn't tell.

"Are you bringing Brandon to the wedding?" Jade asked her.

Madison snorted. "Brandon was two guys ago. Keep up."

"Was not," PJ said.

"Sorry, three guys."

PJ shot Madison a look. "I'm dating a guy named Josh now. He's a Culinary Management major, and he's very sweet."

Jade found that hard to believe. PJ seemed to be a loser-magnet, much to their mom's dismay. Delinquents, slackers, punks, guys with girlfriends . . . if he was trouble, PJ found him.

"Who's your plus one, Jade?" Madison stepped back to make room for Mrs. Wearly and her pins.

"Uh, not sure yet." Maybe Daniel could set something up. She grimaced. A wedding for a first date? Then again, how better to root out the less serious guys?

"Anyone you're interested in?" PJ asked.

"Not really." She hoped Daniel came through. She wasn't looking for roses and sweet nothings. She just needed reliable, mature, and compatible.

"Maybe one of Beckett's friends. I could ask him."

"That's all right. I'll figure something out. Are you getting nervous?"

"Not nervous, just excited. Can't wait to be Mrs. Beckett O'Reilly."

"How's that, dear?" Mrs. Wearly leaned back.

Jade's eyes went to her reflection where her stomach curved ever so slightly. Feeling her sisters' scrutiny, she crossed her arms over her stomach and stepped down from the pedestal.

"Perfect. Your turn, PJ."

Later that evening Jade curled up on the sofa, trying to convince her stomach to hold its contents. After alterations the girls had headed to

Cappy's Pizzeria, and now they were settled in for a girls' night.

PJ shoved in the DVD, a political thriller, nudging Lulu aside. "Daniel said this was really good."

"Of course he'd say that." Madison turned toward Jade. "He's gearing up to run for the House next year, did he tell you?"

"Really?"

"He's got a campaign manager and everything," PJ said.

Jade felt a prick of guilt. She'd been so caught up in her own problems, she'd hardly asked about him.

An hour into the movie, she began losing track of the plot. Her stomach was twisting. PJ had fallen asleep on the sofa, her long hair fanned across the pillow. Too many late nights at college, Jade supposed.

She took a sip of ginger ale and pulled her knees into her chest. *Please, God.* The only bathroom was right off the living room, within earshot.

A moment later, accepting the inevitable, Jade slipped off the sofa.

Madison didn't tear her eyes from the screen. "Pause it?"

"That's okay."

Jade forced herself to shut the door, making her feel all kinds of claustrophobic. She flipped on the fan and lifted the toilet seat. As if permission was all it needed, her stomach emptied its contents. She tried to be quiet, but even with the noise of the movie, it would be a miracle if Madison didn't hear.

After another spasm, she sat back on her haunches, shaking. Sweat beaded on her brow. The walls closed in. She wanted to fling the door open.

A tap sounded at the door. "Jade? You all right?"

She closed her eyes. She could not tell Madison. Not till after the wedding. It was only two weeks away. Madison deserved to be the center of attention.

"Fine."

"Can I come in?"

Jade flushed the toilet, then stood on shaky legs. "Sure."

Madison frowned as she filled a Dixie cup and handed it to Jade. "You getting sick?"

Jade rinsed out her mouth, and Madison put a hand to her forehead. "You don't feel warm."

She didn't want Madison worrying she'd catch something just in time for her wedding. "Probably something I ate. I feel okay now."

"I warned you about the salad bar."

Cappy's Pizzeria was known for its superb pizza and hangout atmosphere, not its sterile environment. "Guess you were right."

They finished the movie, but Jade's heart wasn't in it. How was she going to keep her pregnancy secret another two weeks with her stomach constantly rebelling?

Chapter Six

Jade wrapped the brown apron around her waist and turned to wait on a customer. Coachlight Coffeehouse wasn't her first choice, but for the time being, it was her only one. She'd applied for the hospital position, but it had been given to someone else.

The wedding was a week away, and Madison had begun moving into Beckett's house. Jade hadn't a hope of affording Madison's rental on coffee shop wages, and her bank account was emptying fast. Health insurance was expensive, and she'd given her last Chicago paycheck to Izzy, worried her friend wouldn't make rent with Jade's sudden departure.

So much for moving up in the world, Jade McKinley. She filled orders like she'd never left the place, inhaling through her mouth because the smell of espresso turned her stomach. The shop bustled in the early morning hours, making time pass quickly.

"Take a break, Jade?" Sidney said when the morning rush ended.

"Sure." She grabbed the baggie of crackers

from her purse and a bottled ginger ale. She'd skipped breakfast, not wanting to get sick her first day on the job. Later in the morning, she'd found, she could handle saltines—usually.

On her way to the break room, she spied Daniel at a table in the corner. Guess he still used the place as his office sometimes.

She removed her apron and sat in the chair across from him. "Didn't see you come in."

He looked up from his laptop, his blue eyes softening. "You got a job."

She made a face and lowered her voice. "Not exactly the one I wanted."

"You want me to keep looking?"

"Oh, yeah. At this rate I'm going to be living in a cardboard box." She bit into a cracker.

"Something tells me there are a few McKinleys who'd have something to say about that."

"I should've gone to college like Mom and Dad said."

"Thought about teaching guitar again? You could call your former students, put up a few flyers around town."

"I need a steady income and benefits. I need a career, which is where the degree would've come in handy."

"It's not too late."

With no money for tuition, no place to live, and a baby on the way, um, yeah, it kind of was. "Any job leads? Please say yes."

"A couple actually. I stopped by the Burger Barn last night. The owner's an old classmate of mine. He's losing his manager at the end of the week. I told him you were looking."

He told her the salary, way more than she was making now. But burgers. Just the thought of the last one she'd eaten made the crackers gel in her stomach. The smell of greasy fries and grilling burgers . . . not happening.

"I don't think that's going to work. What about the other one?"

"Chestnut Farms. They're expanding and looking for extra help."

"Doing . . . ?"

"Horseback trails with tourists, grooming the horses, stable help, basically. The pay's not great, but probably better than here."

She looked down at the half-eaten cracker. She loved animals, but working with horses couldn't be safe for the baby. What if she fell off or got kicked in the stomach? She'd never forgive herself.

"No?"

She shook her head.

His lips twitched, and he took a sip of coffee.

"What?"

He sat back in his chair. "I was thinking of the last time I saw you on a horse."

"Seventh grade. My first annual youth retreat."

Remembering, she pursed her lips. "That horse had a malfunction, I'm telling you."

"Sure it wasn't the rider?"

"They gave me the oldest horse in the stable. I swear he was hard of hearing. And lame. And stubborn."

"Good times, good times."

She shot him a look.

"Fond memories there. Remember the blob?"

It was a huge inflatable in the lake. They used to jump onto it and send people flying off the other end. "It's a wonder we didn't break our necks."

"That's where I finally got serious about my faith," he said.

"On the blob?"

"Funny."

She took a sip of her ginger ale. "Me too. That camp was a special place." Their spiritual journeys had begun simultaneously. How had they wound up in such different places?

"Don't worry," he said. "We'll find something."

"I know it seems like I'm being picky."

"No, you have to live with it. We'll find something more suited for you."

"Speaking of suited for you, I hear you're gearing up to run for Congress next year."

He nodded slowly. "That's the plan."

"Exciting stuff. You have to raise funds and all that?"

"Lots of funds. It's a little daunting, but

my dad hooked me up with a savvy manager."

"Well, you can count on me for support—not the financial kind, though, unfortunately."

"Be careful what you volunteer for. I'll have you stuffing envelopes and going door-to-door."

Jade shrugged. "What else do I have to do?" She sipped her pop, her mind drifting to her date-less status and Madison's upcoming wedding. "So what about our little blind-date project? Sorry, I'm totally interrupting your work."

He gestured at the stack of papers. "The historical society. I should get down on my knees and thank you."

"A simple date would suffice."

He tweaked a brow.

"You know what I mean. Have you talked to any of those guys yet?"

"Sure." Daniel closed his laptop and set it on the forms.

She finished her cracker and zipped the baggie. She was still hungry, but she wasn't pushing her luck.

He picked up a pen and clicked it repeatedly.

"Daniel?"

He pursed his lips, looking down at his hands. They were large and masculine with long fingers tapering down to squared tips. His cuffs were rolled up on his forearms.

"His name is James Geiger. You know him?"

She shook her head.

"He teaches fourth-grade science."

A teacher. "Summers off, kid-friendly. Sounds promising."

"He's unattached and interested. I showed him your picture."

"What picture?"

"The one on my phone. It's old, but you've aged well."

She gave him a mock scowl. "What about his picture? Don't I get to see him?"

"I couldn't exactly ask for a photo, Jade."

"Well, what's he look like?"

Daniel rubbed his neck. "I don't know, average height and build, brown hair . . ."

"That's helpful."

"Well, he's not sprouting warts or anything. He looks"—Daniel lifted a shoulder—"like a science teacher."

"Oh. Well, doesn't matter. I'm sure he's very nice. And he fits the criteria?"

"To a T."

"So what's next?"

"I'll give him your number?"

"Perfect." Maybe he'd be her wedding date.

A line had started forming at the register, and her coworker was looking frazzled. Jade checked her watch, surprised ten minutes had passed. "I have to get back to work."

"Thanks for the break. I'm sure James will be in touch."

Chapter Seven

Jade's feet were killing her. She swayed with James to "Anything But Mine." Across the floor, Madison and Beckett danced, eyes only for each other. Beckett set his forehead against Madison's and said something for her ears only. Madison reached up, kissing him softly.

The wedding had been beautiful, an intimate affair at church, with written vows and personal anecdotes. Madison looked perfect in a simple satin gown that hugged her waist and flared to the floor. After a million wedding party photos, they'd joined the guests at the town hall, which had been transformed into a romantic wonderland of white twinkling lights, draped tulle, and elegant flower arrangements.

Jade tugged at the waistline of her dress. She'd filled it out in the two weeks since alterations. Thank God she'd had Mrs. Wearly leave room. Even so, she'd been worried her family would notice her thickened waistline.

And when she was showing, what then? Who'd want to date her when she was pregnant with another man's baby? Much less marry her. She shrugged the thought away. She was not going to think about that now.

She looked up into James's eyes. "I hope you

didn't mind doing the wedding thing," she said.

"Not at all. It's the event of the year." He had a nice smile and eyes that crinkled when he laughed.

"What are you doing with your summer now that school's out?"

"I'm taking a couple courses—working on my master's. I also do some freelance writing for scientific journals."

Smart, ambitious, and industrious. Not on the list, but all good.

"What about you?" he asked. "You just moved back to town?"

"I was in Chicago for a year with a friend from high school. I worked at a café and played guitar at a coffee shop on weekends."

"You must've missed your family. I love to travel, but I'm always glad to come back home. There's just something about this place."

"I know what you mean. What got you interested in science?"

"My parents bought me a telescope for my thirteenth birthday. We'd take it out in the yard in the summer, sit under the stars. They taught me all the constellations."

She liked the way his voice warmed when he spoke of his parents. "You're close to your family."

"I'm an only child, so yeah, we're close. My mom stayed home, and my dad taught literature at the high school."

She connected the dots. "Mr. Geiger—I had him my junior year. He was tough!"

James smiled. "Don't take it out on me."

"He gave me a D in his class because I was one day late with my final essay."

"Sorry . . . ?"

He did another turn, leading her smoothly to a less crowded spot of the floor. The motion unsettled her stomach. Or maybe it was the food she'd eaten. She'd gone all day without eating, panicked she'd have to hurl in the middle of the ceremony. By the time they'd reached the reception, she was starving. Now she was starting to think that second helping of scalloped potatoes had been a bad idea.

"You have a great voice," James said. "I hadn't heard the song before."

She'd been working on it since Madison had asked her to sing at the wedding. "That's probably because I wrote it."

He backed away, meeting her gaze. "No kidding. You're very good."

"Thanks."

She tried to focus on his words, but her stomach twisted. It wouldn't be long now. With Madison being so busy with moving and wedding details, Jade had managed to hide her morning sickness. *Morning* sickness? Who was she kidding?

Where could she go? The bathroom was probably filled with guests, and it was so small.

She could already feel the walls pressing in, making her even more shaky and panicked.

James was saying something, but she couldn't focus. She became aware of the smells in the dimly lit hall. The garlicky Caesar salad, the cloying scent of flowers, the rich smell of James's cologne, all mingling into one noxious odor. Her stomach spasmed.

The band played the last notes of the song, and before they struck up another, Jade stepped back. "I think I need a breather." She smiled, trying for casual despite the desperation that clawed at her. "Be right back."

She started for the hallway, her feet picking up the pace as the clock ticked down. She wove past dancing couples, her aching feet long forgotten. Maybe the restroom would be empty. *Please, God.*

She turned into the hall in time to see a flash of ivory disappear into the ladies' room. Her mom. She couldn't go in there. She continued down the hall and spied the back door, propped open with a wooden wedge. She swallowed hard against the urge to vomit and pushed the metal bar.

Before it fell shut, she ran to a five-gallon container by the Dumpster and emptied her stomach. She tucked her dress between her legs and hoped for the best. How could one little baby cause so much upheaval? Sweat beaded on her forehead and back, making the dress cling to her skin.

When she was finished, she wiped her mouth with the back of her hand, wishing desperately for a hankie. She set her trembling hands on her knees, catching her breath.

The door behind her swung open, the light from the hall intruding. Jade turned, straightening.

Daniel came out, letting the door fall behind him. "Jade? You okay?"

She tried for a smile. "I'm fine."

He advanced. "I saw you rush out. What happened—" His eyes found the bucket. Lit by the buzzing fluorescent light over their heads, there was no hiding the contents. Or his reaction.

"You're sick." He tipped over an empty box and guided her to it. "Sit down."

"I must've eaten something . . ." How many lies was that now?

He removed his jacket and set it around her shoulders. "Stay here. I'll be right back."

The music grew louder as he disappeared through the door. Great. Just great. What if he brought back PJ or her mom? She should've stopped him. The wedding was over, but this wasn't the way she wanted the announcement to go.

A minute later Daniel returned alone with a damp paper towel and a cup of water. She stood, rinsing her mouth, careful of her dress while Daniel pitched the five-gallon bucket into the Dumpster.

"Better?" he asked when she'd finished wiping her mouth.

She nodded. "Thanks."

"I can get your mom . . ."

"No! I mean, I'm fine now. I don't want to spoil the fun. Besides, I'm supposed to help put the hall back to rights when this shindig's over."

"You should go home and lie down."

"I'm fine. Really." She smiled for good measure. "Whatever I—ate—is gone now." True enough. She turned back to the building. "I should get back to James."

"How's that going?"

"So far so good. You have great taste in men."

He held the door open for her. "Thanks. I think."

One-and-a-half long hours later, James opened the passenger door of his Buick for her. She got in, setting her purse on her lap. Her feet killed her, her throat stung with acid, and she felt like she could sleep for a week straight. But at least her date had gone well. James was the kind of man she was looking for. And bonus: his left-brained wiring meant he was less given to romantic whims and emotional overtures.

They'd seen Madison and Beckett off, the truck decked out with enough flowers and tulle to make Beckett scowl playfully. They were on their way to Louisville where they'd spend the night before flying to the Outer Banks.

"So how are your parents feeling about marrying off their first child?" James asked as he turned the ignition.

Ryan had actually been the first. But things with Abby had ended badly, had ended in their family's first divorce.

"They're thrilled. Mom's already hinting about grandbabies." Little did she know Jade had jumped the gun. Would they be disappointed in her?

"I've already warned my parents not to expect any from me. They haven't given me too much flak about it."

Caught up in her own thoughts, she almost missed it. But the words rewound in her head and played back.

"You don't want kids?" She strove for a casual tone.

"Never have. It might sound crazy, being a schoolteacher and everything, but I can't imagine being a dad. I like having kids during the day and coming home to peace and quiet. There's not much of that with parenthood, from what I hear."

He tossed her a smile. Her own felt stiff. So much for James being her perfect match. Her baby deserved a willing father. And okay, James deserved to get what he wanted out of life too. And that obviously wasn't a kid—much less someone else's.

They made conversation on the short ride to

the house, Jade's thoughts drifting. Madison had paid rent through the middle of the month. After that Jade was moving into a studio apartment on the edge of town. She had between now and then to come up with the deposit. It wasn't her dream home, but it was a step in the right direction. Someday she'd have a real home with a fenced-in yard where her little one could toddle around safely.

As they walked to her door, Jade thought of what she'd say. Might as well end it now. She wouldn't do either of them any favors by stringing him along.

She turned on her porch, glad they had only the moonlight to see by.

"I had a nice time."

"Listen, James."

They spoke at the same time.

He gave a wry grin. "Uh-oh. That didn't sound good."

She hated this. He seemed like a nice guy. It was too bad.

"It's the D my dad gave you, isn't it?" he said.

She smiled at his attempt to lighten the mood. "I'm sorry. You're really terrific. I was totally planning on going out with you again if you asked, but—"

"The kid thing's a deal breaker, right?"

"I'm sorry." He had no idea how sorry.

"I understand."

After an awkward good-bye hug, Jade let herself in. She let Lulu out back and got ready for bed. The house was quiet—too quiet with Madison gone. She was hungry after losing her meal, but too tired to eat. Besides, there was no guarantee it would stay down.

* * *

Daniel settled back on his pillow. It had been hard watching Jade and James all night. The guy had cleaned up better than he'd expected, and Jade looked too comfortable in his arms. Honestly, Daniel hadn't thought they'd connect. Had thought Jade would find him boring.

He remembered her all those years ago, spinning in the yard with the fireflies, skirt twirling around her legs. That girl would've found James boring. Daniel wasn't sure where that girl, the one dancing with fireflies, had gone. He missed her.

He closed his eyes, picturing the way she'd looked tonight. Beautiful. Long hair falling in waves past her bare shoulders, her green eyes sparkling under the dim lights. The silver dress had hugged her curves and swirled around her calves. He'd hardly been able to take his eyes off her.

He'd argued with himself half the night about whether or not to claim a dance. It would be the sweetest kind of torture, having her in his arms. But when she'd smiled at something James had said during the middle of a fast song, he'd made up his mind. Daniel wanted to be the one making her smile.

He'd been right about the sweet torture, though. She felt good in his arms, her delicate hands resting on his shoulders. Her hair smelled like oranges, blending with the exotic, spicy scent she always wore. It teased his senses. The dance had ended too soon.

Later when she'd dashed from the room, frowning, he'd known something was wrong. If James had said or done something to upset her, the man was going to find himself on the wrong end of Daniel's fist.

His phone buzzed with an incoming text.

Much better. Home and in bed. Wedding went great, didn't it? Happy for Sis.

Daniel punched in a response. Yes, good day. How'd date end up?

He doesn't want kids—deal breaker!!!

Relief swelled inside. Daniel chided himself. He should want what was best for Jade. Would he have her go through life alone just because he couldn't have her?

He tapped in a response. What? He's a teacher. Apparently 8 hrs a day is enough.

Sorry! Just assumed . . .

Like you said, not like you can interrogate them. Think you can find someone else?

He scowled. Nothing like getting right back in

the saddle. No problem—who wouldn't want to date you? He reread the text and deleted it. He wanted to tell her the man who was perfect for her was right here, texting her. Sure. Will get back with you soon, k?

He should have been over her by now. She'd been gone a year—how long could a guy carry a torch for someone oblivious to him? Not oblivious. She was aware he existed. Unfortunately he was in the friend zone. No, worse. The brother zone.

He checked his screen. Nothing.

Jade?

He was tired of hiding his feelings. Sometimes he wished he could change them back. Sometimes he wished that he'd just said it on that day all those years ago. Just put it out there and let the chips fall where they may.

She'd been eighteen, and he'd been teaching her to drive a clutch. All the McKinleys had put her off, and Aaron didn't know how. She'd gotten the vehicle for a song, never mind that she couldn't drive it.

The car had stalled again as Jade released the clutch too quickly.

She sighed. "I'm never going to get this."

"Yes, you will. Push the clutch in and turn the key. Okay, now shift into first and ease off the clutch as you press the gas. Good. Easy . . . find the sweet spot."

The car shuddered, then stalled. She hit the steering wheel with her palm. Her jaw twitched as she clenched her teeth and tried again.

This time she made it into first gear, into second, stalling as she tried to shift into third.

"Much better. You're getting it."

"Thanks for doing this," she said as she started the car. "Dad makes me a nervous wreck. I'm surprised there aren't holes in the dashboard from his fingers."

Daniel laughed. "Still does that, huh? Okay, try again. Let's see if we can make it all the way to the end of the street."

Jade shot him a look. She'd recently added a green streak to her hair that matched her eyes perfectly. It was threaded in and out of the braid that fell past her shoulder.

She did make it to the stop sign and only stalled again when she was turning. After that she drove flawlessly around the country block, passing her dad's cornfields and long gravel lanes before arriving back at the McKinleys' place.

At the house she hopped out of the car and pulled him into an embrace. "Thank you, thank you, thank you."

Daniel put his arms around her. He was suddenly aware of her body. Of the way she fit against him. Of the way she smelled, sweet and spicy, the way his hands fit into the curve of her waist.

Not only aware, he thought, as something flared inside of him.

Come on, man. This is Jade. Little Jade. Squirt.

But as she waved good-bye, tossing a smile over her slender shoulder, she didn't look like little Jade anymore. She looked like a beautiful young woman. And in the weeks to follow, he couldn't seem to take his eyes off her. Couldn't seem to stop thinking about her. Until it seemed she consumed his every thought.

It was pointless, he knew that. He was too old for her. She was in love with Aaron. Even if that wasn't the case, Daniel's parents would never approve. They put up with his association with the McKinleys—guilty for not being there to raise him, he'd always figured. But they had his future all planned out, and it didn't include a small-town life or a girl like Jade.

Not to mention the fact that she'd drop over in horror if she knew his thoughts. If she knew he pictured her when he closed his eyes at night and dreamed of a world where he was more than just her honorary brother.

So he looked the other way when Aaron held her hand, when he drew her into an embrace. He took solace in his semesters at college and held his breath when he came home again only to find the couple still madly in love.

As graduation neared, Daniel had thought twice about settling in Chapel Springs, running for mayor, watching Jade start a life with someone else.

Then Aaron had died and all Daniel could do was offer comfort. But after months she didn't bounce back, and Daniel was concerned. The sparkle was gone from her eyes. She was quiet and withdrawn. She stopped playing guitar at the coffee shop, stopped teaching, and moved in with Madison. He rarely saw her unless he sought her out.

After a while she seemed to step back into her life, but something was missing. That's when he'd started sending the notes. It was only going to be one note, just a little encouragement to remind her how special she was. But then he'd left another and another. Her family began teasing her about her secret admirer. He was terrified of being caught. But he'd been careful, disguising his handwriting and leaving the notes only when he was certain he could get away with it.

He missed leaving her those notes and flowers, he realized now. He tried to be an honest guy, and everything about hiding his feelings seemed wrong. The notes had corrected that.

When Jade left town, they'd lost touch. Then last fall Madison had put two and two together and realized Daniel was Jade's secret admirer. She'd promised not to give him away, and with Jade gone, it didn't seem to matter anymore.

But now she was back, and he prayed Madison would continue to keep her word.

He checked his phone, but no new messages appeared. It appeared Jade had drifted off right in the middle of their conversation.

Chapter Eight

"Jade, phone call," Sidney said. "It's your brother, said it's an emergency. You can take it in my office."

Jade handed the empty cup to her coworker. "Americano, three shots, heavy cream." She left the counter, trying to quell the unease in the pit of her belly. Madison and Beckett were flying home from their honeymoon today. Surely nothing had happened to them.

She shrugged off the dark thought. Ryan's car probably gave out or something. Tonight was their weekly barbecue, the night she'd been waiting for since she'd returned. Finally she could tell them about the baby.

The thought of coming clean now far outweighed the dread of her parents' disappointment. She was weary of hiding her illness, her fatigue, her growing belly.

She found the phone on her boss's cluttered desk and took it to the doorway. "Hey. What's up?"

"Sorry to bother you at work. It's Mom. Dad brought her into the ER a little while ago. She had a backache and was sick to her stomach. They think it might be her heart."

Jade pressed her palm against her own heart. "Oh, no."

"I'm at the hospital now. They're running some tests—"

"I'll be right there."

"Dad's with her, and they're not letting anyone else back there."

"I don't care, I'm coming. Have you called Grandpa and PJ and Daniel? Oh, no, what about Madison?"

"Grandpa knows. I'll call PJ and Daniel next. I think we should wait until Madison and Beckett land in Louisville. They can't get here any faster anyway."

Twenty minutes later Jade entered the ER. She wasn't the only one who'd insisted on coming. Daniel was already sitting beside Ryan. They stood as she approached.

"Any news?"

Ryan shook his head. "PJ will be here soon."

Jade sat between the men, toying with the cloth strap of her purse. Time dragged, the minutes on the utilitarian wall clock ticking by in slow motion. In the corner, *Sesame Street* played on the wall-mounted TV.

Ryan's eyes were closed. Probably deep in

71

prayer. Jade stopped to whisper one of her own, memories of her last trip here heavy on her heart.

PJ entered an eternity later, sitting on the other side of Ryan. She kept up a constant stream of babble. Jade's sister cooked when she was anxious. In lieu of rolling pins and whisks, talking sufficed. Jade couldn't focus on the words, so Ryan became the sounding board by default.

Jade couldn't imagine her mom having a heart attack. Her cholesterol was high, but she was otherwise healthy. She was the one who never got sick.

Daniel set his hand on Jade's, stilling it. "She's going to be fine."

"You don't know that."

"She's a strong woman."

Jade drew strength from his steady blue gaze. He looked so sure. *Please, God. I know it's been awhile, but You have to let her be all right.* She couldn't imagine it any other way. Mom was the heart of their family. *Do You hear me, God?*

Remembering something, Jade sucked in a breath, looking at Daniel. "She had a backache last month, at the house. And fatigue, remember? I sent her to bed."

Daniel squeezed her hand. "Jade."

"Those were early signs. Why didn't I—"

"Stop it. Even if it was related, Mama Jo wouldn't have come to the ER. Even this morning your dad had to insist, and she was ready to pass out."

What nobody had mentioned was Grandma. She'd had a heart attack in her fifties. The second one had taken her life.

The ER door opened, and Dad came through. The group met him in front of the vending machines. He looked tired and older under the harsh fluorescent lights. PJ curled against his side, resting her head on his shoulder.

"Any news?" Ryan asked.

"It was a heart attack for sure. We're still waiting for some tests to come back to find out the extent of it."

Daniel's hand settled on Jade's shoulder. "What are they doing for her?"

"They put her on some meds to prevent clotting. I'm not sure where we'll go from here. Depends on the test results, I guess."

"How's she feeling?" Ryan asked.

"Better. The backache and nausea are gone. She's just a little tired."

"I'll put her on the prayer chain," Ryan said.

Two hours later they were still waiting on test results. PJ munched on a bag of SunChips. Daniel talked on his cell, pacing in front of the windows, and Ryan was texting someone.

Jade stared at the TV where *The Andy Griffith Show* played. Each time the door opened, they looked up anxiously, but Dad hadn't returned from her bedside. His texts to Ryan confirmed they were still waiting on test results.

Jade pulled the baggie from her purse and started on a saltine. The waiting room had grown more crowded. A family gathered in the corner, the mom twisting a soggy tissue. A young man waited across from them, holding a bloody dishrag to his hand.

Daniel pocketed his cell and sank into the chair beside Jade. "How you holding up?"

"All right, I guess. It's taking a long time."

"Want something from the vending machine?"

She held up a cracker. "No thanks."

He shifted in his seat, moving closer. She could smell his cologne, a nice clean, manly smell, not too overbearing the way she found most cologne.

"I was just remembering when I came over to your house the first time."

"Sneaked over, you mean." He'd climbed into the basement because it had been a school night, and Ryan had been sure his parents would say no.

"We thought we were being so sneaky. We watched movies all night and went through school the next day like zombies. The next weekend Ryan had me over for supper and asked if I could spend the night. You know what Mama Jo said?"

Jade shook her head.

"She said, 'Sure. This time use the front door.' "

They shared a smile. "It's hard to put one over

on Mom." The main reason Jade hadn't spent much time with her since she'd returned. She felt a pang of guilt. If she'd spent more time with her mom, maybe she would've seen the symptoms earlier.

"What time are we expecting Madison and Beckett?" Ryan asked.

"Their plane lands around three."

Some homecoming it would be for the honeymooners. Hopefully they'd have good news about the test results by then.

As if the positive thought had manufactured him, their dad came through the door. He gestured for them to stay and settled across from them in one of the orange bucket seats, resting his elbows on his knees.

"Mom's resting comfortably. She said to tell you to stop worrying and go back to work."

"Are the results back yet?"

He nodded. "The doctor says Mom needs to have bypass surgery."

Jade covered her mouth. Could it get more major than open-heart surgery?

"Why not angioplasty?" Daniel asked. "Walter Newman had a heart attack last year, and that's what he had."

"I was hoping that would be the plan, but he said there's too much blockage in two of the main coronary arteries. She needs the bypass."

"When?"

"In the next few days. It'll be done in Louisville, and she'll be in the hospital for a week. Recovery is pretty long, a few months he said."

"What about the store?" PJ asked.

"Don't worry about a thing, Dad," Ryan said. "We'll take care of everything."

"He's right," Jade said. "You tell Mom that."

When he left, they huddled together.

"I can take some time off," Ryan said. "Help with the farm."

"Me too," Daniel said. "What about the store?" Mom owned the town's most popular antique store, Grandma's Attic.

"We could hire someone," Ryan said.

"Where would we find someone who knows antiques?" Jade asked.

"I'll take the store," PJ said.

"You can't do that," Jade said. PJ had an internship at a prestigious Louisville bakery. "It took you months to secure that internship."

"She's right," Daniel said. "You'd lose it."

Ryan rubbed the back of his neck. "We can't shut it down. You heard him—a few months—and during tourist season. She makes the majority of profits in the summer."

"I'll take the store." All eyes turned to Jade.

"You just got a job," Daniel said. "I can put in some hours. Maybe Madison and Beckett can help out."

"Madison and Beckett have jobs too," Jade

said. "And you can't do everything, Daniel. Mayor, volunteer fireman, Congress candidate. I can work at the coffee shop after the store closes and on Sundays."

"And when will you sleep?" Daniel asked.

She lifted her chin. "I'm taking the store. I want to do it."

Ryan looked between them. "All right. Daniel and I will handle the farm, and Jade will take the store."

"What about me?" PJ asked.

"You can help out at the house," Jade said. "They'll need meals and laundry and stuff. Madison and I can pitch in too, but I don't want to put too much on her."

"Agreed," PJ said.

"All right," Ryan said. "It's a plan."

Chapter Nine

"Green tea with honey." Daniel handed the cup to Jade. He didn't like the dark circles under her eyes, and it was going to take more than tea to fix that.

"Thanks."

He settled into the waiting room seat between her and Madison and leaned against the wooden rest between them. Beckett's arm was curled around Madison as she flipped through a copy of *Southern Indiana Living.* They'd had a harsh transition from honeymoon to reality.

Across from them, Grandpa McKinley snoozed, his head falling forward every few minutes. Ryan and PJ flanked their dad, whose head rested back against the wall, eyes closed. Probably praying. They'd all done their share of that. PJ's leg ticked off the seconds, and Ryan scrolled through his phone.

"What's taking so long?" Jade said softly.

"They said it could take six hours," Daniel said.

She checked the clock. "I wish they'd give us an update."

"Let me see what I can find out."

"Dad already tried."

Daniel stood. "Well, he's not the mayor."

"That only works in Chapel Springs, Mr. Popularity."

He tossed her a wink as he walked away.

The blonde at the nurse's station gave a flirtatious smile as he approached. He gave her a friendly smile. He was happy to be charming if it would get Jade what she needed.

When he returned, Jade was squirming in her seat and her color wasn't right.

"You all right?"

"Yeah, what'd she say?"

"They're wrapping up the surgery. Eveything's going well, and she should be in recovery soon."

"Great, thank you." Jade excused herself and

disappeared into the restroom, moving faster than a trip to the bathroom should warrant.

When she returned Daniel frowned.

"What?" she asked.

"You're white as a sheet."

She folded her trembling hands under her arms and shrugged. "Just worried, I guess."

Mr. McKinley was speaking to the surgeon at the closed doors in the hall. He nodded as he listened. A few minutes later the surgeon gave an encouraging smile, then disappeared through the doors.

"She's in recovery, still under anesthesia," he told them when he returned. "The surgery went well, thank the Lord. They're going to let me go back when she wakes up."

"Will we be able to see her?" PJ asked.

"One at a time. She needs her rest."

"Whatever's best for her," Madison said.

"We just want her to get better," Jade said.

"I appreciate you kids' willingness to help out around the house and at the store. That'll take a lot of pressure off your mom."

"Of course, Daddy," PJ said.

"Let us know if there's anything else we can do," Beckett said.

"The best thing you can do is help your mom avoid stress. It plays a big factor in reoccurrence of heart attacks. Especially over the next couple months as she's recovering."

"No stress. You got it," Ryan said.

Jade crossed her arms over her stomach, and Daniel wondered about the frown lines creasing her forehead.

* * *

Jade hung up the phone and picked up the dust rag, the bad news ringing in her ears. Madison's house had been rented. There was no extending her stay—she needed to be out today. The manager of the studio apartment wasn't willing to let her in without the first month's rent plus deposit, and it was the cheapest gig in town.

On top of that, she wasn't making enough to pay for rent and keep up her health insurance. And she couldn't drop that. Nor was she going to take money for helping out at the store.

She ran the rag over the antique armoire in her mom's shop, careful to avoid the original brass hardware. What was she going to do?

You could always move back home, Jade.

Mom would be at the hospital another five days or so, but what after that? She'd never be able to hide her pregnancy while living there. And she had to hide it now. She couldn't add to her mom's stress after what the doctor said. Between the vomiting, the fatigue, and the expanding waistline, Mom would have the truth in a matter of days. She couldn't let that happen.

She'd just have to figure something else out. She moved on to a Country French bed, working the cloth into the intricate scrolling of the headboard. Most of her old friends had moved away or married. There was no room for her at Ryan's place, and she sure wasn't moving in with the newlyweds. There was no time to place an ad for a roommate.

She just needed a bed. A sofa even. That's where she'd slept in Chicago after that wretched night. Couldn't bring herself to go back into the closet-sized room. Not only because of the awful memories but because she couldn't tolerate small spaces anymore.

She lowered her hand. She was so tired. She'd hardly been cleaning an hour, and she was already exhausted. She dropped into a French Victorian chair and leaned her head back. She just needed to rest her feet, close her eyes for a few minutes.

"Jade?" The voice called from the fringes of her mind. "Jade?"

Her eyes flew open. She lifted her head from the chair. How long had she been asleep?

Daniel sat on the edge of the antique bed opposite her. "You must be wiped out. Why don't you go home and take a nap? I'll cover."

She straightened and stretched her back. "I feel better now." Besides, she had nowhere to go.

Daniel was looking around the shop, his eyes lighting on all the pieces. "You know, this would be a great source for furnishing your new apartment. I'm sure Mama Jo wouldn't mind you borrowing some pieces."

"You're right. I might ask her." Once she found a place to put them.

Daniel helped her finish dusting, then returned to his office next door. Jade began running the vacuum. What was she going to do? She was out of time, needed something quick. Today.

She moved the vacuum around the chair she'd just napped in. Her eyes caught on the object beside it. The bed.

She scanned the store, an idea rising to the surface. She had a bed right here. Her mom had even made them up with sheets, comfy quilts, and feather pillows. There was no shower, but she could wash up in the sink. Wasn't there a shower at the mayor's office next door? She could find some excuse, or even sneak over and use it. Did Daniel still keep a spare key on the crown molding over the door?

She looked around the store, eyeing the secondhand treasures, and bit the inside of her lip. Could she actually live in a store? She'd seen an old Frigidaire near the office. All she had to do was plug it in, and she'd have someplace to store food. Maybe there was an electric stove or even a hot plate or microwave somewhere in here. She could use her mom's computer to job-hunt. There was no working TV, but she'd rather play her guitar anyway.

It was just temporary. Just until she could return to the coffee shop full time. Maybe she'd even find a better job by the time her mom returned to work. She nodded, turning off the vacuum. Yeah, she could totally do this.

Chapter Ten

Jade rose on tiptoe, feeling along the transom ledge. She clutched a wad of clothing and bag of toiletries in her other arm, her calves cramping as she rose higher. She dragged her hand across years of dirt, spider webs, and—ew—a dead bug. She wiped her fingers on her yoga pants, shuddering, before resuming the task.

At the edge, her fingers nudged something metal. There. She grabbed for it, grasping the key in her hand.

"Yes!"

Her eyes swept the empty street. The brisk morning breeze stirred her hair and pebbled her skin. She unlocked the door and slipped inside, twisting the latch behind her. After two days of washing up in a sink, she was ready for a hot shower. Leaving the lights off, she made her way to the back, breathing in the stale scent of musty files.

Please let the shower work. Daniel's grandpa had installed it during one of his terms. Jade had been young, but even she remembered the fuss taxpayers had made about the luxury.

Entering the bathroom and pulling back the mildewed curtain, the word that came to Jade's mind was not "luxury." Rust ringed the drain and shower handles, and hard-water stains coated the tiled walls. Ribbons of black mold clung to the grout in the corners. The dead spider balled on the floor was just a bonus.

"Ick."

She was cleaner than the shower. Why hadn't she thought to bring cleaning supplies? No time for that now. She'd just have to suck it up.

Grimacing, she flushed the spider and turned on the faucet, backing up when it sputtered brown water. Seconds later it began running smoothly and, thankfully, clean.

* * *

Daniel unlocked the door and stepped into his office. Early morning sunshine shone through the wooden slats, striping the room with light. "Not Gonna Die," the last song he'd heard, played through his head, and he whistled it softly as he set his things on his desk.

Normally he preferred working in the coffee shop in the morning, but he needed copies of the form he'd completed late last night for this afternoon's meeting. He hoped the old printer cooperated—it was a thorn in his flesh. Normally he passed the task to Betty Jean, his assistant. But it was her day off.

He stifled a yawn as he headed toward the old copier, hoping for the best. He'd helped Ryan at the farm for a couple hours the evening before, then he'd been called to an accident at the corner of Beacon and Oak. By the time the paperwork was complete, it had been after midnight.

He didn't think Jade was faring much better. She'd been going from Grandma's Attic to the coffee shop where she worked until closing, only to do it all over the next day. They'd hardly communicated except for a few texts. She hadn't asked about her next dating prospect. Shoot, she probably didn't have time to date. Fine by him.

Unfortunately, he'd already mentioned her to a friend before her mom's heart attack, and now the guy was bugging him about a date.

He turned on the machine, set the paper on the glass, and waited for the old thing to warm up.

A thump sounded at the back of the building. He frowned, listening. The printer started the mechanical groans of waking up. He moved toward the back, wondering if a bird had gotten through the vent again. He neared the narrow hallway. The pipes behind the wall creaked and knocked.

He hoped Betty Jean hadn't left the faucet on last night. There was no water pooling under the door, though. He turned the knob and opened the door. Steam swirled through the space. A pile of clothes sat on the sink.

Someone moved inside the shower, making the curtain billow.

"Who's in there?" he demanded.

Someone squealed. A thump sounded as something heavy fell to the shower floor and bounced a couple times.

A head peeked out, eyes wide.

Jade. Hair wet and sudsy. *What the*—"Holy—"

She had the curtain clutched to her chest. Her bare chest.

He turned and faced the door, heat flooding his face. "Jade, what the heck?"

"I can explain."

"By all means." He stared at the six-panel door, the sharp edges of the molding softened by layers of paint. His heart hammered from the shock. Couldn't have anything to do with Jade, three feet away, nothing between him and her naked body but a plastic shower curtain. The steam grew thick. Moisture seeped through his shirt, making it cling to his torso. The smell of oranges permeated the space.

He swallowed hard. On the sink ledge he noticed her pile of rings and a green towel. "I'll be in the hallway."

He shut the door behind him and leaned against the frame. A few minutes later the shower shut off, then all was quiet. He paced the short hall. What was taking so long?

"I'm waiting," he said through the door.

She huffed. "All right, fine. I didn't have anyplace to shower. I didn't get the apartment, so I let myself in with your spare key."

"What do you mean, you didn't get the apartment? Where are you staying?"

All was quiet on the other side of the door.

"Jade?"

"At the store. I'm staying at Grandma's Attic."

"Your mom's store? Next door? What for?" He was caught in a bad Dr. Seuss book.

"That would be the one. Can we save this until I'm—oh, I don't know—*dressed?*"

"Yeah, sure. I'll be in the office."

Daniel waited at his desk, hands tented under his chin. What was going on with her? Living at the store? How long did she think she could keep that up? He was pretty sure it was a building code violation, not to mention the lack of amenities—though she was proving resourceful.

She appeared five minutes later in a gauzy skirt and loose top, damp hair piled in a sloppy knot. She looked about eighteen with her freshly scrubbed face, clutching her clothing to her chest.

"You can't tell anyone." She lifted her dimpled chin, had that same look she'd had at fourteen when she'd told him she was going to learn "Dust in the Wind" in a week. And she had.

"What happened?"

She leaned against Betty Jean's desk. "I couldn't get the apartment."

"You can't live in a store, Jade."

"It's only temporary."

He frowned at her. He didn't like the thought of her in a deserted building at night. They pretty much rolled up the sidewalks at six, and there wasn't a soul for blocks.

"Between the store and the coffee shop I'm hardly home anyway."

"Do you need a loan? 'Cause I could—"

"*No.* I don't want your money, Daniel."

"Then move back home for a while. Your parents wouldn't mind."

"I'm not moving back home." She gave him the stubborn chin again.

He sighed. This wasn't Chicago, but there was an occasional disturbance. And what if the old building caught fire? Just last year the theater had burned to the ground because of old wiring.

"Don't Beckett and Madison have a spare room?"

"I'm staying at the store, Daniel. Can I trust you to keep it to yourself?"

He met her stare, battling silently for a long moment. Who was he kidding? He was at her mercy the moment he looked into her sage-green eyes.

He released a slow sigh, reached into his desk

drawer, and removed a key. "This is for the back door. Use it from now on."

There'd be all kinds of trouble if anyone saw her coming and going. This was county property, never mind the confidential files.

Her shoulders sank. "Thank you."

"How are you going to eat?"

"There's a working fridge in the store. And a hot plate."

"A hot plate."

"It's just for a few weeks." She stood. "Thanks again, Daniel. I really appreciate it." On her way out she leaned over and dropped a kiss on his cheek.

He watched her go, knowing he'd be feeling that kiss for weeks to come.

Chapter Eleven

"Thanks for driving," Jade said as Daniel opened the door of Baptist Hospital and let her pass. The antiseptic hospital smell filled her nostrils, making her stomach twist.

"No sense putting additional strain on your car."

"You haven't mentioned your date with Courtney." Daniel had met up with her when she'd flown into Indy for a conference earlier in the week.

He shrugged. "We caught dinner and talked business. Her dad used to be governor of

Alabama. She had some good insight on my campaign."

"She's from the South, huh?" Jade set her fingertips on her heart and put on her best Southern belle accent. "Oh, Daniel, I do believe you're the most handsome man I've evah seen. I do declare!"

He rolled his eyes, crowding her as a couple of employees in scrubs passed.

She nudged him. "So, you like her?"

"Sure."

"You going to see her again?"

"I don't know. I guess so."

When they reached her mom's room, Madison and Beckett were there. They found some chairs, making room for Daniel and Jade.

"You look good, Mama Jo." Daniel kissed her on the forehead.

"Madison fixed me up. I was scaring away the doctors." Even hospitalized, Mom was still attractive, with bright blue eyes and dark blonde hair. Her color was better today, though still a bit pale against the white sheets.

"Dad's out getting her a decent salad," Madison said. "She's not impressed with the fare."

"Only a couple more days, right?" Jade said.

"That's what they say." Mom pulled up the sheet, smoothing it out. "I'm tired of talking about me. Catch me up on life outside the sterile walls."

"Well, the store's doing well," Jade said, careful to keep things positive. "I sold the mahogany rolltop desk."

"Who bought it?" For her mom, it was all about passing treasures from one home to another.

"A couple from Columbus. They bought it as a wedding gift for their daughter." She told her mom the story of how the couple had met.

She smiled. "Lovely. I'm so glad they got the desk. And how are you enjoying your new digs?"

Jade's glance collided with Daniel's. "Great shower. You wouldn't believe the water pressure that old thing has. Daniel went on another date with that DC girl. He met up with her in Indy when she flew in on business."

He narrowed his eyes at being thrown under the bus while Jade sank into the chair, relieved that the redirection had worked its magic.

* * *

"See ya," Jade told Daniel as she got out of his car. "Thanks for dinner."

"No problem."

Daniel waited for Jade to enter the rear storeroom door, then continued through the alley. He hated leaving her there. She couldn't even turn on the showroom lights. He'd moved the old fridge for her and loaned her the office microwave. She was all set up. He still didn't like it.

Something buzzed nearby. He stopped at the

end of the alley and leaned over the passenger seat. Jade's phone. Must've fallen from her pocket. It lit up with an incoming text.

Appointment reminder: Dr. Kline Mon June 23 9 am, downtown office

He set the phone aside and backed down the alley. Moments later, he knocked on the solid metal door.

"It's me, Jade," he called. He gave it ten seconds and knocked louder. "Jade. Open up."

He could try the office phone, but she'd probably let it ring through to voice mail.

He knocked again. "Jade!"

He couldn't imagine it taking this long to get to the door. Maybe she'd gone next door for a shower. But she hadn't had time to gather her things and leave.

He was about ready to kick the door in when it opened. "All right already. What's the—"

Her eyes widened, and her lips pressed together. She dashed down the hall. The bathroom door swung shut behind her. The sound of her vomiting propelled his feet forward.

She was leaning over the toilet when he entered, shaking. He pulled her hair back, holding it until she finished. A slick sheen of sweat had broken out on her forehead. He wet a paper towel and set it on the back of her neck.

The text message tickled the frayed edges of his mind. His mind flashed back to the wedding two weeks earlier. Something she'd eaten, she'd said.

A few minutes later she straightened and flushed, wiping her mouth with the towel. Her pallor frightened him as he connected all the dots. The wedding episode, the doctor's appointment, and now again.

"Better?"

She nodded.

"Come on." He wrapped his arm around her waist and helped her to the office, stopping at the fountain where she rinsed her mouth.

Once there, she collapsed onto the antique sofa, giving him a wobbly smile. "Better watch out—you had the brisket too."

"Don't even, Jade." He set her cell on the desk. "You left this in my car. I saw a text about a doctor's appointment, and now I find you like this, just like at the wedding. What's going on?"

She folded her arms, hunching her shoulders. Her eyes studied the floor.

"Jade?"

She met his gaze. "You can't tell anyone."

His gut twisted hard at the fear in her eyes. He swallowed hard. "Are you sick?"

She breathed a laugh, tucked her bare feet under her.

"You're scaring me."

"I'm not sick, Daniel. I'm—I'm pregnant."

"Pregnant?" The word rang in his ears like an

echo at Riverbend Gorge. He stood and walked away. He needed to move. Needed to hide a minute while he collected his thoughts.

He should be thinking about her health, her emotional well-being, her financial situation. But instead all he could think of was Jade with another man. Jade smiling at someone else. Jade in love with someone else. Jade making a baby with someone else. A fiery coal burned deep in his gut.

"Three and a half months."

Three and a half months ago she was with another man. Did she love him still? Where was he? Why wasn't he here, holding her hair while she vomited, helping her find a job, finding a flipping place to live?

"You can't tell anyone."

"You're just full of secrets, aren't you?" He hadn't meant to sound so harsh.

"I keep dumping my stuff on you."

He had to pull it together. She didn't need this right now. Didn't need him to be selfish and jealous. He schooled his features, then faced her. "What about the father?" he asked, careful to keep a neutral tone.

She no longer looked so pale. Blood had rushed north, blotching her cheeks. "He's—he's out of the picture."

He shouldn't feel so relieved. It was pure selfishness. She needed support, financial and emotional. Not jealousy. "You need to tell the family."

"I can't."

"Jade—"

"I was going to. I was going to tell them after Madison and Beckett got back, then Mom had her heart attack and Dad said—"

"No stress."

"You know Nana's second heart attack killed her. I couldn't live with myself if something happened to Mom because of me. I just have to wait awhile, until she's stronger."

"You should tell someone. Madison or Ryan."

"I'm telling *you*." Her eyes met his and held. He felt heady with the knowledge that he was her confidant. It had been an accident, but still. She'd told him. Now she was his responsibility. He had to make sure she was taking care of herself.

"Do you have insurance? Are you seeing a doctor?"

She nodded. "Yes and yes."

Of course. The text. He wasn't thinking straight. She looked so little on that old sofa. Had her face thinned out? Were those hollows under her eyes?

"Have you told your doctor you're getting sick so much? It can't be good for you. Or the baby."

Baby. The word made it seem so real. Jade was having someone else's baby.

"She knows. It's not uncommon, you know.

Otherwise I feel fine, and I have an ultrasound on Monday just to make sure everything's good."

"I'm going with you." Where had that come from?

"What?"

"You need support. If you're not telling anyone else, I'm it."

She tilted her head. "You don't have to do that, Daniel. It's only a couple months. Or as long as I can hide it."

He wanted to know about the father. He wanted to know who he was, if she'd loved him. But of course she had. Jade wouldn't have made love to him otherwise. Not Jade. The thought sliced him wide open.

"It's a relief, actually, telling someone." Then she met his eyes, soothing the ache in him. "I'm glad it's you."

His breath left his body. "Me too."

Chapter Twelve

The paper crinkled under Jade as she settled on the exam table. She lay back, smoothing her shirt over her stomach.

Daniel propped his hip on the table. "Excited?"

"Nervous."

What if something was wrong? What if her body had rebelled against the way she'd conceived? Against the emotional turmoil of discovering the pregnancy? Did the baby know he or she had been unwanted? Maybe that's why she'd been so ill.

And what if the vomiting had deprived the baby of essential nutrients? Maybe she hadn't asked for the pregnancy, but this baby was part of her. As difficult as the last few months had been, she couldn't stand the thought of something going wrong. She rested her hand on her slightly curved belly.

"Will we hear the heartbeat today?" he asked.

"I think so. They can tell a lot with these things, including the due date." Not that she didn't know hers already.

A knock sounded on the door, and the technician entered. "Hi Jade, I'm Maria, and I'll be doing your ultrasound today." The tech had a friendly smile and eyes that were almost black. Her coarse dark hair was pulled into a stubby ponytail.

"If you and Dad are comfy, we'll go ahead and get started."

Warmth rushed to Jade's face. She met Daniel's eyes, then opened her mouth, the correction on her tongue.

He squeezed her hand. "All set."

"Okay then. I'll be taking some measurements, and that'll help with an accurate due date." Maria pulled up Jade's shirt and tugged down the elastic waistband of her skirt. "If I get a good view, would you like to know the sex?"

"No, I don't think so."

The jelly was warm, and Jade was soon transfixed by the image on the monitor as Maria moved the wand. Jade stared at the blurry gray image, trying to find her baby. She should be able to see a three-inch-long baby with developing hands and feet, shouldn't she?

Maria continued moving the wand, watching the monitor, stopping every few seconds. Sometimes she pressed against Jade's full bladder, making her fear she'd drunk too much water in the waiting room.

When Maria stopped the wand, Jade looked hard at the image. There was a big black shadow. Was that her baby?

Maria moved on, adjusting the screen, tapping some buttons. Why was she so quiet?

"Is everything okay?" Jade asked when she couldn't take it anymore.

"Looking good." She moved the wand a bit. "Give me a few more minutes."

Time passed with unbearable slowness. Jade wished she'd at least help her recognize her baby so she didn't feel like a bad mother before her child even left the womb.

A few long minutes later the tech tilted the monitor toward them. "Okay, here we go. Let's call this one Twin A and this one Twin B."

Jade froze as the words registered. She traded glances with Daniel, then stared hard at Maria. "What?"

The tech only smiled at the monitor. "Looks like you're doubly blessed, my dear."

"But—but Dr. Kline only heard one heartbeat."

"That's not unusual." Maria pointed out the body parts of both babies.

Both. Babies. How had this happened? How was she going to take care of two babies on her own? How was she going to support them on coffee-shop wages? *God, this can't be happening! I'm already overwhelmed at the thought of one baby.*

"Shock is normal." Maria was still smiling like she'd delivered wonderful news. "Give it time to sink in. Did you have fertility treatments?"

"No . . ."

"Twins run in your family?"

"My siblings are twins." Or had been. Michael had died at seventeen.

"Well, there you go."

There you go? There you *go?*

Daniel squeezed her hand tightly as if sensing she was about to come unhinged.

"But the babies are healthy?" Daniel asked. "You don't foresee any problems?"

"They look perfect. There are extra precautions with twin pregnancies. You'll have more appointments and need extra folic acid, but Dr.

Kline will talk to you about all that. Sometimes you can tell if they're fraternal or identical, but I'm not seeing the markers, so that'll remain a mystery for now."

Maria kept talking and pointing at the monitor, but Jade couldn't focus. She was having twins. She. Was. Having. Twins.

When Maria left, Jade got off the table in a fog and left with Daniel. The exit doors slid open, and they entered the cool confines of the parking garage. She felt numb.

When he opened the car door for her, she stopped. She couldn't remember what she was supposed to do next. She clutched her purse to her stomach, staring at the vacant car seat. The numbness was leaving, and something else was creeping in.

She was living in a store, had almost nothing in savings. There was no father, no child support, just her, a minimum wage job and . . . two babies.

Her breath felt stuffed in her lungs. Her vision blurred.

"Breathe." Daniel's voice, deep and reassuring, broke the dam. "It's going to be okay."

Tears overflowed, tumbling down her cheeks.

"Hey." He turned her around and pulled her into his arms.

He was warm and solid. A safe place for her. She clutched his shirt in her hands.

"I'll help you. Your family will help too once they know. You'll have all the support in the world. It's going to be fine."

She could hardly hear him through her tears. "How am I going to manage? I'm never going to earn enough to support them. And a partner—ha! Who'd want to marry me, pregnant with somebody else's babies? Two of them! Nobody's going to want me."

"Jade. That's not true."

Twins. Two of everything. Two cribs, two sets of clothing, double the toys and food and diapers. Two *babies.* Twins.

Her eyes snapped to Daniel's. "What if I can't tell them apart? What if I'm the only mom in the world who can't tell my babies apart?"

"You will." Daniel framed her face and tilted it upward. "Hey."

She locked onto his blue eyes, drawing strength from his hands.

"It's going to be okay. I promise."

She could almost believe it when he said it that way. When he looked at her with such conviction, his eyes homed in on her like she was the only woman in the world. How lucky would she be if that were the case?

She blinked away the errant thought.

This was *Daniel.* Practically her brother. Her hormones must be making her crazy. She probably had a double dose.

"Okay?" he asked, holding her captive with his eyes.

Her tears had stopped. She exhaled and nodded. When he released her, she got into the car. He found a Burger Barn napkin in the glove box and handed it to her.

They exited the garage in silence. The sunlight seemed too bright after the darkness of the garage. A few minutes later, he ramped onto 65 and crossed the Ohio River. The sun glinted off the water, blinding her with its white glare. A commercial plane soared across the sky on its way into the Louisville airport.

"What about the father, Jade?"

She pictured Nick, and her skin crawled. She could still feel his iron grip on her arm, his heavy weight pressing her into the mattress. Hear the creaking of the bed. She pushed the memory down deep.

"I told you, he's—he's out of the picture." She twisted her thumb ring, spinning it round and round.

"You're going to need child support, honey— you deserve it. He shouldn't get off scot-free."

He probably thought she'd fallen for some loser. That he'd taken off at the first mention of pregnancy. She should tell him the truth. But somehow the truth was even more humiliating. While she was in Chicago, she'd assured the family she'd been okay, that she was an adult.

That she could handle herself. But she'd invited a stranger into her empty apartment and had ended up pregnant. With twins.

"He can't get away with this. I can help you with the legal stuff. I know an attorney who can handle this and be very—"

"No, Daniel."

"—discreet. He does this for women like you all the time, and he's had a lot of—"

"Women like *me?*"

"—success. I didn't mean it that way."

She looked out the window, her eyes burning. Stupid hormones. Daniel already thought less of her. She may as well get used to it. It wasn't 1950, but they lived in Chapel Springs, Indiana. She may as well prepare herself for the looks, the gossip.

"You know I didn't mean it like that. I just want you to get the financial support you need to take some pressure off. I'll call the attorney when I get back to the office and set up—"

"No."

"—an appointment. Jade, you're being unreasonable."

"I said no, Daniel. I'll figure out some other way."

Chapter Thirteen

Jade pulled the mail from the box in front of Grandma's Attic and took a moment to appreciate her new window display. The coffee shop had been slow tonight, but her mom's store was busy earlier. She'd sold a 1920s oak curio cabinet, a Waterbury mantel clock, and about a dozen odds and ends.

The town was quiet at this hour, only the chirping of crickets and the sound of wind whooshing across the treetops. She unlocked the store and entered the darkened building, walking back to the office.

She'd had almost two weeks to adjust to the idea of twins. She still had moments of shock, moments when fear of the future smothered her. She'd found herself texting Daniel a lot. He had a way of making her believe everything would be all right.

She entered the office, sorting through the mail. Electric bill. Phone bill. Coupon booklet. A letter, just her name on the envelope. She fell onto the sofa, tearing it open. She was so tired. She wanted nothing more than to curl up in her antique bed, but she had to get these bills paid. She'd already put it off too long.

She pulled the paper from the envelope, her

heart racing at the familiar paper, at the note, at the familiar handwriting.

You're as beautiful as a summer sunrise, as desirable as a fresh new day.

Her secret admirer was back. But this time his words didn't make her feel special. She flung the paper away, her pulse racing.

This time they sent a shiver up her spine. He'd been here. Had dropped the envelope into the mailbox, right outside the door. He knew she was working here. Was he watching her? Did he know she was here now? Alone? At night?

She turned toward the office door. Had she locked up on her way in? She made her way through the shadowed store on trembling legs. She bumped a floor lamp. It teetered before crashing to the floor. The sound echoed through the building, making her heart thump harder.

She hurried to the door only to find she'd already locked it. She peered into the darkened night, wishing for blinds on the windows. And thicker glass. The old single-paned windows would shatter with little effort. And who was around to hear it?

A chill seeped into her bones as she turned back to the office. The words reverberated in her mind. It was nothing. Just some guy with a crush. Same as before.

But what if he was a stalker? What if it was Nick? What if it had been Nick all along, and he'd followed her to Chicago? What if he was here now?

She crossed her arms against the shiver that shimmied down her spine. *Stop it, Jade.* She was being ridiculous. Paranoid. Nick was hundreds of miles away. He'd only wanted one thing from her, and he'd already gotten it. The note had come from—

A thump sounded from the back of the store. Jade stopped in her tracks, grasping the nearest object—a weighty candlestick.

The thump came again, three of them. Someone knocking on the back door.

She approached it slowly, swallowing hard. She was being stupid. Her mind knew it, but her heart wasn't buying in. It flailed against her ribs like a bat on the loose.

"Jade? It's me."

She could barely hear his voice through the thick metal door. She palmed her heart, took a steadying breath, then reached for the door.

* * *

Daniel smiled at Jade, relieved that she'd finally answered. He edged past her and down the narrow hall. "Just got back from a fire run. It's not too late? You weren't in bed?"

"I just got off work. Was anyone hurt?"

"No, it was just a little kitchen fire up on

106

Hidden Hollow Road." When they reached the office, he handed her the bag. "It's chili night at the station. Thought you could use some home-cooked food."

"Thanks." She took the bag. "It smells good."

"What's with the candlestick?"

She glanced at it as though just realizing she held it. "Oh, that. I was just—moving it when you knocked."

He might've bought it if her hands weren't shaking as she set it down.

She moved a stack of mail and set the food on the desk. "Thanks. I missed dinner."

"It's still warm. There's a spoon in there too."

She wasn't looking at him. Something had happened. He frowned, walking toward her.

Her eyes slid to the floor near the foot of her desk.

He followed her gaze. A sheet of paper lay crimped on the rug. He recognized it immediately. His eyes darted to her as cold dread shot straight to his heart.

She stepped forward and snatched it off the floor, folding it.

His breath caught in his lungs and turned to cement. She knew. Oh, crap. She knew it was him. That's why she was acting so funny. Why she hadn't looked him in the eye since he'd entered the store. How had she known?

He'd never felt so exposed. He'd only wanted

to reassure her after those things she'd said about herself after the ultrasound. He should've left well enough alone.

She set the paper on the desk, staring at it. Or avoiding him.

He had to say something. Take away this awkwardness. How was he going to do that? He was in love with her, and she thought of him like a brother.

"I need to ask you something."

"I can explain."

They spoke simultaneously. He wasn't thinking, because clearly, he couldn't explain. Not without ruining everything. He was the only one she could depend on right now. The only one who knew of her pregnancy, her living situation.

She picked up the note and handed it to him. "They started again."

"What?"

"The secret admirer thing—remember, from before? I got this a few minutes ago. In the mail-box."

She didn't know. The realization hit him with the pressure of a fire hose.

He took the paper numbly. "The mailbox?"

"The one outside the store. The envelope just had my name. Are you reading it?"

"Yes." His eyes scanned the page, but he knew the words already. Knew them by heart. He couldn't focus on them anyway. Could only thank heaven above that she didn't know.

"Well?" she asked. "What do you think?"

"About . . . ?"

She sank onto the sofa, crossing her arms. "I don't know. This one struck me differently than the others."

"Differently how?"

"It kind of—freaked me out."

He winced. Not the reaction he'd been going for.

"I mean, before I saw them as inspiring or romantic, I guess, but now . . ." She laughed, not sounding amused. "Maybe it's from living in Chicago. Things are—a lot different there. You don't think there's anything 'off' about it? That he knows I'm here at the store?"

"It's Chapel Springs. Everyone knows you're working here."

"I know, I know. It's just—it hit me funny."

The fear in her eyes pinched him hard. "I'm sure he didn't mean to creep you out."

"Well, he did. He put it in my box right outside the store where I'm staying. What if . . ."

Daniel shook his head, hating himself for scaring her. "No. Nothing's going to happen to you." He sat beside her on the sofa. "This isn't Chicago."

"You're right, but I can't help but feel—" She couldn't seem to find the word. "Exposed or vulnerable. What if he's stalking me or something?"

Way to go, Dawson. He put his arm around her. "I'm sure it's not like that. Listen, maybe you'd feel safer if you stayed with your parents until—"

"I can't. The pregnancy, Mom's stress . . ."

"You're not getting sick as much, you said. Maybe she wouldn't notice."

"But my stomach." Jade put her hand on her belly. "Twins, remember? I swear I'm growing by the hour."

He pulled her into his side, loving the soft feel of her against him. "You're right. Besides, there's the glow."

"What glow?"

"The pregnancy glow. You have it."

"I do not."

He nudged her playfully. "You're practically a neon sign."

"Stop it."

Ah, but he'd made her smile. Why did that make him feel like a million bucks? Like he could buy the world twice over with that smile.

Of course, he'd also just scared the tar out of her.

She leaned against his shoulder, stifling a yawn. "I'm so tired."

"I should get going. You need to get to bed." He gave her a squeeze and stood. "You okay now?"

"I'm fine. Just overreacting."

"I don't think you have anything to worry about. I can install extra locks on the door if you want."

"I'm fine. Thanks for coming by." Her gaze darted to the bag on the desk. "For the food."

"Eat something before you turn in. The babies are hungry."

"I will."

"You have your cell phone. I'm three minutes away. You can call me for anything, day or night."

She stood and wrapped her arms around him, pressing into him. He embraced her, set his cheek on her head. She smelled so good, oranges and spice with undertones of espresso. He set his hand on the small of her back. She was so little. Breakable. And she had so much on her shoulders.

Help her, God. She's all alone in this except for me. Help me know how to help her.

"Thanks, Daniel," she whispered into his chest. "I mean it."

He wanted to hold her forever. Wanted to pretend it was a lover's embrace. That he had the right to take her face in his hands and kiss her until the man who'd stolen her heart and left her pregnant was a distant memory.

But she pulled away and gave him a sisterly smile. Then he was walking out the door, his wishes snuffed out like a candle.

Chapter Fourteen

Jade chalked up her cue stick, considering her shot. "Six ball in the corner pocket."

"Dream on," PJ said.

"Don't underestimate her," Madison said. "Remember last time?"

PJ slurped up the last of her Mountain Dew. "Lucky shot."

Cappy's Pizzeria was loud tonight. There was a Little League team in the front, celebrating a big win. The Home Run Derby played on the wall-mounted TV screens throughout the restaurant. The sounds of chatter and boisterous laughter filled the building, while the aroma of garlic and oregano teased their noses.

Jade eased the stick back and hit the cue ball. It kissed the six, which ricocheted off the side, edging past the eight ball, and dropped with a thunk into the corner pocket.

"Somebody's been practicing." PJ made herself at home on a bar stool.

"Haven't played since I left. Three ball in the side pocket." Jade sank the shot. "So where's your other half tonight, Madison?"

"At Mom and Dad's watching the Home Run Derby."

"Ryan's there too," PJ said. "I felt bad leaving

Mom in that testosterone cesspool, but she insisted."

"You need a break," Madison said. "You've been a huge help. Mom said the house would be falling apart without you."

"A gross exaggeration. I think my chatter is about to drive Dad nuts. He's probably counting the days until I go back to college."

Jade missed and nodded to Madison. "Your shot."

"Finally. How's life at the bakery?" Madison asked PJ.

"Sweet."

Jade rolled her eyes.

"I've been decorating wedding cakes this week. Loving that. Gosh, I can't believe what those things cost."

Madison missed her shot. "Tell me about it."

PJ hopped off the stool, her ponytail swinging. "I offered to make yours."

"You had your hands full with the reception."

"Speaking of reception," PJ said, "one of my helpers asked if you were going to give guitar lessons again. Her daughter wants to start back."

"The Etters asked me the same thing," Madison said. "Their boy isn't learning as much from his new instructor."

"I wish I could," Jade said. She missed those kids. Missed watching their eyes light up when they picked up a new chord or played flawlessly through a new riff. "But between Mom's store and the coffee shop, I barely have time to sleep."

"Maybe later when things settle down." PJ made a shot but missed the next. "I'm going for a refill. Anyone want one?"

They handed PJ their cups and returned to the game.

"So married life seems to be treating you well," Jade said.

Madison and Beckett were a sight at the barbecue the night before. They could hardly go two seconds without touching.

"It really is." Madison paused midshot to give Jade a dreamy smile, her dark waves falling over her shoulder. "I mean, there are challenges, don't get me wrong, but it's pretty great. His dad's back in rehab, though—don't know if you heard."

Jade made a face. "I didn't. Sorry."

"It's tough on Beckett and Layla, so hopefully he'll stick with it this time. It's not uncommon to fall off the wagon. He seems to really want to get sober, though."

"Is Beckett's house feeling like your home?"

"Starting to, now that we've got some pictures and stuff up. Sheesh, the place was a blank canvas."

"Men."

"He doesn't even like Tuxedo Cat."

"He doesn't like a painting of a tabby cat playing the piano that you bought at a garage sale? Wow. Go figure."

"What? It's cute."

"Madison, it's tacky."

"Hmm. That's what he said. It got demoted to the hallway."

"Very generous of him."

"Lulu and Rigsby are so cute together. They curl up together at night. It's like they've been best buds all their lives."

Jade leaned over the rail. "Sounds like doggie heaven. Seven in the corner pocket." She lined up the difficult shot, missing by a hair.

Madison chalked her tip, her gaze bouncing off Jade. She opened her mouth, then pressed her lips together.

"What?" Jade asked. "I left you a good shot."

Madison looked into the restaurant where PJ was waiting for refills, then back to Jade, lowering her voice. "I know your little secret."

Jade almost dropped her cue. Her fingers tightened on the shaft until her nails cut into her palm. Heat rushed to her face, burning.

She tugged her peasant top away from her body. "What—what secret?"

"I may be a newlywed, but I'm not completely oblivious." She lined up the shot and made it easily. "I stopped by your new apartment this week with a housewarming gift." She gave Jade a look. "Turns out there's no house to warm."

The apartment. It was just about the apartment. Her shoulders dropped an inch.

"I figured you just found someplace else, and I missed the announcement somehow. But Beckett saw you going into Grandma's Attic late the other night." She turned and fixed her brown eyes on Jade. "Please tell me you aren't staying there."

"It's just temporary."

"Jade, you can't live in a store. Come stay with me and Beckett—"

"No."

"Mom and Dad then."

"I'll be moving out as soon as I go back to the coffee shop full-time."

"I can lend you some money."

"I'm fine. I've never had so much furniture."

"Not funny."

"I have a microwave and a bed, and I'm using the shower next door. What else do I need?"

Madison gave her a fixed look. "Daniel knows?"

"Yes."

Something flickered in Madison's eyes. She bit her lip, looking toward PJ as their sister neared, balancing three drinks. A guy was with her.

"Don't say anything, okay?" Jade said. "It's just a few more weeks."

"Hey, look who I found," PJ said.

"Cody Marquart." Jade set down the cue stick. He'd filled out. His hair was clipped short, and he sported a neat goatee.

Jade accepted a hug from her high school friend. "Haven't seen you since graduation."

He'd gone away for college and hadn't returned.

"Jade, you look amazing."

He and Madison greeted each other. Since there'd been a few years between them, they didn't know each other well.

"Your curls are gone," Jade said.

"It was time for a professional look."

"He works at the hospital now." PJ handed her sisters their drinks.

"Corporate Compliance Officer, my official title."

"Yikes," Jade said. "Is that as boring as it sounds?"

"I don't know." Cody laughed. "You tell me."

"It sounds like a challenge," Jade said.

"It is, and I'm up for it. Now, who's up for a little eight ball?"

Daniel entered the pizzeria, welcoming the air-conditioning. His stomach rumbled at the tempting aromas. He scanned the crowd, spotted Sarah Murray in a corner booth, and headed that way. A reporter for the *Gazette*, Sarah wanted to interview him about the new statue in the city park.

On his way to the table, he spotted the McKinley girls in the poolroom. PJ waved Daniel over and, after greeting Sarah briefly, he excused himself and joined them in the back room.

Cody Marquart greeted him with a handshake. "How you doing, man?"

"Cody. When did you get back in town?"

"Just in time for your Fourth of July speech. You rocked it, Mr. Mayor. Heard you were gearing up to run for Congress. Like father, like son, eh?"

They caught up for a couple minutes while the game continued.

Jade leaned over the rails for the winning shot. "Eight ball in the corner pocket."

Cody's eyes slid south to her denim-encased derriere and hung there for a long second.

Daniel clenched his jaw, fighting the urge to block his view. The black ball dropped into the pocket.

Her sisters groaned as Cody high-fived her. "Way to go, Jade. We make a great team."

Daniel nearly rolled his eyes.

Jade finished her soda, announcing she was done in, and her sisters gathered their purses.

"I should get back to Sarah," Daniel said. "See you all later. Cody, nice to see you."

"You too, man. Let me know if I can help with the campaign."

Daniel turned to leave, but not before he heard Cody's parting words to Jade. "We should go out sometime. Catch up."

Daniel slowed his steps to catch her response.

"Sure, that'd be great."

Daniel could think of all kinds of adjectives to describe the idea. *Great* wasn't on the list.

Chapter Fifteen

"You went to the movies Saturday with Cody?" Daniel took 62 north toward Chapel Springs.

Her doctor's appointment had gone smoothly —all was well with the babies. She smoothed her hand over her stomach. *Her* babies.

"I see the rumor mill's working fine. However, the data is incomplete. We also went to an outdoor concert yesterday in Columbus. How'd your date with Sarah go?" Jade had seen them in a corner booth as she'd left Cappy's. It had bothered her a little at first. But only because Sarah wasn't good enough for Daniel. Not even close.

"It wasn't a date. She was interviewing me about the new statue."

"Yeah, right. She needed to meet you at a restaurant for the two quotes she used in the article."

He shot her a look.

"If she'd been leaning any farther over the table, she would've fallen into her salad."

"It was noisy." He slowed for a car that pulled out in front of him. "So you still want me to hook you up with that friend of mine?"

"Let's wait on that." She'd decided to put the dating plan on hold when she'd found out about the twins. And she hadn't expected Cody to pop into her life.

"Because of the twins or because of Cody?"

"Little of both, I guess."

She felt Daniel's eyes on her. "You think this thing with you two will go anywhere?"

"I don't know. We're going out again this weekend." He was taking her out to eat in Louisville. She hadn't figured out how to handle him dropping her off after the date. She'd driven herself on Saturday, and yesterday she'd had him drop her at the store, saying she'd had some work to catch up on. He'd given her a warm hug and kissed her on the cheek.

"You like him then?"

She thought over the weekend, the easy conversation, the pleasant kiss. "Sure, he's great." She spared Daniel a look. "And he meets all the criteria."

He had a nice family rooted in Chapel Springs. His dad was a widower, and he had two married siblings. He planned on staying now that he'd found a job in the area, and he'd already mentioned his love of his nieces and nephew.

"What about . . . you know, the babies."

"What about them?"

"I don't know, I just—well, you're having twins. Seems like he should know that."

"Well, I can't tell him until my family knows." It wasn't like she enjoyed withholding information. It was hard keeping this from her family, never mind Cody.

"I know, it's just . . ."

"Just . . ."

Daniel shifted. Turned up the air. "It's pertinent information, that's all. If you're dating seriously it seems like—"

"We've had two dates."

"But there's history. Things could advance quickly."

"Because we were friends in high school?"

"You said you like him." Daniel gave a humorless laugh. "And we all know he likes you."

"What's that supposed to mean?"

"Please. He couldn't keep his eyes off your butt at Cappy's."

She gaped at him. "Whatever. Besides, you didn't seem too worried when you were setting me up with James."

"I didn't know you were pregnant then. And what if Cody doesn't want kids either?"

She almost brought up Cody's nieces and nephew, but then . . . James enjoyed teaching children. That didn't necessarily equate with parenthood.

"Very unlikely," she said. Even so, maybe she should feel him out a little on their next date. Or maybe she should slow things down until she could tell him.

"A guy should know about something like this before his feelings get involved—all I'm saying."

Great. He thought she and her babies were like a disease you didn't want to catch. The fact that he had a good point only irritated her more. "You mean he should know he's about to get saddled with two kids who aren't his."

"I didn't say that, Jade."

"It's what you meant."

He sighed, staring straight ahead. "How would you feel if some guy sprang something like that on you after you were crazy about him?"

"I know, I know. One baby would've been hard enough, but now . . . I was going to stop dating after I saw the ultrasound, but Cody just came along, and what do you want me to do? I can't tell him yet."

"I don't know. Maybe slow things down or something."

Maybe she should. She'd be able to tell everyone about the pregnancy in a couple weeks. Dread washed through her at the thought. She wasn't going to tell them about Nick. She was still trying to forget, and she couldn't do that if everyone knew. She'd tell them the father was no longer in the picture. True and easier.

She hated the way that made her look, like she'd hooked up with a random guy. Or like she'd been dumped by some loser. Her parents loved her unconditionally, but they'd be disappointed.

She dreaded seeing her dad's brows furrow, the light snuffed from her mom's eyes. But that was still better than telling the truth. Of having the constant reminder of that night reflected on their faces. Better than stressing Mom out over everything she'd gone through.

Something fluttered inside her stomach, stealing her thoughts.

The doctor had said she'd feel the babies move soon. Was that what she'd felt? She set her hand on her belly, going still. *Is that you, little ones?*

"What's wrong?" Daniel braked for a stoplight as they passed through a four-corner town.

"Nothing," she said softly, waiting for another flutter.

It came a few seconds later. She inhaled, holding still, afraid it would stop if she moved.

He frowned at her. "Something's wrong."

She looked down at the curve of her belly. "The babies are moving," she whispered.

The fluttering continued another few seconds, then stopped. "That was amazing."

"What did it feel like?"

"Like—like a butterfly fluttering around."

She held his gaze, a smile breaking out on her face. The corners of his mouth tipped up.

A car honked behind them and Daniel accelerated.

Somehow feeling them move made them even

more real than the ultrasound had. Made her realize anew she'd better get her act together and soon. *It's going to be okay, little ones. I'll take good care of you. You'll see.*

Chapter Sixteen

Daniel took a bite of risotto and signaled the waiter for a refill. His dad was sharing some fund-raising advice. Daniel traded a smile with Courtney, hoping they weren't boring her to death. His mom had invited her along.

His trip to DC couldn't end soon enough. Something about dinner with his parents made him want to hop on his johnboat and escape to the open water of the river.

He checked his watch, wondering how Jade was faring with Cody. If she was having a good time. If he would kiss her good night.

His heart twisted at the thought. He wondered if the guy had any idea how lucky he was.

"Daniel." He could tell by Mom's tone it wasn't the first time she'd addressed him.

"Sorry, what was that?"

"Darling, where are you tonight? Your dad just had a fabulous fund-raising idea."

"Backyard barbecues," Dad said. "It's all about grassroots these days. You'll capitalize on the hometown mayor, volunteer fireman angle.

People are going to eat that up. You have that down-to-earth quality the constituents are craving right now."

Mom raised her glass. "And don't forget the Harvard education."

Dad chuckled. "My wallet sure hasn't."

"I like that idea, Dad."

"Daddy's always saying that," Courtney said. "You have a great small-town vibe. You should play that up. Between that, your charm, and your good looks, you're a shoo-in."

His mom's blue eyes lit up as they toggled between him and Courtney. He could see the wedding wheels spinning.

The waiter set his refill down and Daniel sipped it, listening as they tossed out ideas. He'd always known what his future held. Dad had followed in Grandpa's footsteps, taking family politics all the way to the Senate floor. When his mom had begun traveling with him much of the time, they'd sent him back to Chapel Springs to live with his grandma.

Daniel had always known he was expected to follow in his father's footsteps, from the Harvard education straight to DC. His run for mayor had been a calculated move on his parents' behalf, but it was a labor of love for Daniel. He loved the town, he loved the people, and he loved being in a position that allowed him to better people's lives.

He loved serving the community, both as mayor and fire fighter. They'd balked on the last one until he'd convinced them it would benefit him politically.

"—Like the McKinleys."

"What?" Daniel said. "Sorry, I missed that."

Mom's perfectly pink lips dipped at the corners. "I was saying that perhaps the McKinleys could host your first local barbecue. They have that sprawling old farmland—just the sort of middle-class image you want to project."

"I don't think so," Daniel said. "Mrs. McKinley's recovering from a heart attack, remember?" He was careful not to call her Mama Jo. The one time he'd let that slip, his mom had snubbed him for weeks.

"Well, it wouldn't be anytime soon," Mom said.

"The McKinleys are farmers," Dad added for Courtney's benefit. "It doesn't get more down-home than that. Your mom's right, son. The farming community is important in Indiana. Get their support, and you've a good start."

"I'm not using my friends to further my career."

Mom chuckled. "Oh, honey, you'd better get used to it."

"If they're friends, they'll be happy to help," Dad said.

"Right," Mom said. "I'm sure the McKinleys would be honored to host. Mrs. McKinley could whip up a big old batch of potato salad or something." Her eyes twinkled.

"Doesn't one of her brood do catering or some such?" Dad asked.

"PJ's in culinary school."

"Perfect." Mom dabbed her mouth with the linen napkin, her eyes lighting up. "And one of them plays the guitar. Bluegrass music, right?" Mom silently clapped her hands. "She could be the entertainment for the evening. I can just see her now, sitting on a tree stump, picking away in a straw hat."

Daniel clamped his teeth together, setting his napkin on his empty plate. "Her name is Jade. And she plays blues, not bluegrass, Mom. You make them sound like hillbillies."

Mom's laugh twittered. "Oh, honey, don't be silly. They're lovely farming folk. Perfect for—"

"Let's talk about something else," Daniel said. "I'm sure Courtney gets more than enough talk of politics."

"How are things going in town with tourism?" Dad asked, not exactly a change of topic. "I know things have been slow the last few years."

"Still slow. I've been meeting with the transportation department. We're considering the idea of a ferry to draw tourists from Cincinnati and Louisville."

"That's a great idea," Courtney said.

"You remember the Allen family?" Dad asked.

"Father and son, representatives from District One in Ohio?"

"Sure. We met at a party last year."

"Their family owns a ferry service on the Ohio River."

"I wonder if they'd be interested in sharing some business," Mom said.

"Not a bad idea, Dad. Too bad it doesn't run to Louisville." Still, one city was better than none.

"Maybe not, but getting in with the Crawfords would be a smart move. Let me do some checking, and I'll get back with you."

Dad swiftly turned the topic to Courtney's job. She was working her way up at Regal, Stallings, and Landry law firm, hoping to make partner by the end of the year.

After sitting at the restaurant until he was stiff, Daniel said good-bye to his parents, finalizing plans for their upcoming visit to Chapel Springs.

When they reached Courtney's door, she turned on the porch. "You know, Daniel, I think you have a bright future ahead of you."

"Think so?"

"You have all the right qualities to go all the way." She tilted her head. "The question is, do you have the support you need?"

"What do you mean?"

"Behind every great politician stands a supportive family, a supportive wife. You're about to embark on a challenging journey."

She ran her hand down his lapel. "I know we haven't been dating long, but I think we make a great team, and I sense something holding you back. Or someone. Either way, some people in your life won't be suitable for the challenge. They won't understand what you're about to undertake." She reached up and set her lips on his. "Those are the people you'll need to leave behind."

"Maybe you're right."

Her words lingered in his mind as he turned toward Dulles where he'd return his rental and fly home. Home. Sometimes he felt so confused after coming to DC. Like he was split in two. Courtney's words hadn't helped matters.

Trying to shake the feeling, he checked the time again, wondering if Jade was back at the store. He hoped she wasn't anxious about her safety anymore. He sure wasn't sending another stupid note.

He thought of Monday when Jade had felt the babies move. He'd itched to set his palm on her stomach. After the doctor's appointments, he felt like he was in this with her. He held her hand during the ultrasound, reminded her to drink water and take her vitamins.

It didn't help that her doctor thought he was the father. A part of him liked it, and God knew, he wished it were true. He could wish all he wanted, that didn't make it so. There was no future for them, not the kind he yearned for. He could hardly count the obstacles.

Even without the problem of his parents, there was his future. He was planning to become the next District Nine congressman, and he knew better than most what that meant. His parents had been gone more than they were home, distracted more than they were present. Jade deserved so much more. Her children deserved so much more. His grandma had been a great surrogate, but no one could replace an absent mom and dad. Not even the McKinleys, though they'd tried.

His future would consist of weeks away from home, publicity, glad-handing, fund-raisers, and interviews. He couldn't see Jade wanting any part of that. Even if she were interested. And she wasn't.

The biggest obstacle of all.

Despite his conflicting feelings, he'd had to be there for her. The problem was that all this extra time with her had only made his feelings grow. Had made him want things he'd resigned himself to never having.

Because if he were honest, he'd begun to tell himself little lies. When she lay on the examination table, he'd let himself imagine she was his wife, that the babies were his. When she looked at him, he'd convinced himself there was more than friendship in her eyes. It had seemed innocuous at first. Just a little make-believe. Just a little pretense to ease the pain of reality.

But somehow the pretense had gotten out of hand. What would Jade think if she knew? She'd be horrified.

He gripped the steering wheel as reality hit him with the force of a head-on collision. He had to stop lying to himself. She'd tell her folks next week, and once she did, he had to let them take over her care and support. It wasn't doing him or anyone else any good to believe the lies.

Maybe Courtney was right. Maybe Jade was one of those people he had to leave behind. Maybe he had to step back, cut ties. Maybe he had to let Jade go once and for all.

Chapter Seventeen

Jade had just finished rinsing her hair when a cool draft entered the shower. The curtain billowed inward, clinging to her wet skin as the bathroom door clicked shut.

She sucked in a breath and her heart shot into her throat.

"Jade," came a whisper.

Daniel. She palmed her heart, then poked her head out from the curtain. "You scared me to death. Do you mind? I'm kind of taking a shower here."

He put his index finger to his lips. "I saw Betty Jean coming in."

"It's only eight o'clock," Jade whispered.

"She's going to hear the water running. I have to make her think it's me."

Jade shut off the water and wrung out her hair. Water gurgled down the drain.

He thrust a towel at her.

"Thanks." She dried off and wrapped it around her. "What are we going to do?"

When she peeked out again, his hands were steepled under his chin. "I'll find a way to get rid of her for a few minutes. You can slip out the back."

"Okay."

"Just keep it down in here."

He slid out the door. Jade dressed as quietly as she could. Her stomach had really popped out this week. She was down to elastic waistbands now and trying to hide behind tables and counters, especially around her family. At the coffee shop she tied the apron loosely and hoped people thought she was eating too many blueberry muffins. Already she'd caught Sidney eyeing her stomach.

She heard Betty Jean greet Daniel just outside the door. His assistant was early because she couldn't sleep, she was saying. She had so much on her mind.

"What's wrong?" Daniel asked.

Jade towel-dried her hair, then cleared a circle of fog from the mirror, wincing at the loud squeak.

"I talked to my daughter last night. She's been feeling so awful. Remember, I told you about that."

"Right, she's been undergoing tests."

"It's multiple sclerosis." Betty Jean's voice wobbled. "They found out yesterday."

"I'm so sorry."

Jade clutched the towel to her chest and leaned against the sink. She remembered Betty Jean's daughter. Poor Penny.

"It's pretty far along. She's a single mom, you know, and I decided last night. I'm moving to Tennessee to help her. I called her this morning and told her, and she sounded so relieved. Daniel, I'm sorry to quit, but I'll give you two weeks, and I'll help find someone else, help with the training too."

"Betty Jean," came Daniel's soothing voice. Jade imagined his comforting hand on her arm. "It's okay. I understand. Do what you need to do, and don't worry about a thing."

"I have to get the house ready to put on the market, and it's such a mess. I never cleaned out Carl's things, and the attic is full of his mother's stuff. Not to mention all my work here to keep up with. So many things I'm in the middle of . . . but my daughter needs me." Her voice caught.

"Here's what I want you to do. Take a deep breath. Now. Take a nice little walk down to the Coachlight and get yourself one of those lattes you love. Have them put it on my account."

"But I have so much—"

"Go. I insist. Take your time. It's going to be fine. I'll place a help-wanted ad today."

"All right. All right, thank you, Daniel. You're a good boy."

Jade listened, her ear turned toward the door. Footsteps sounded, the front door clicked shut.

A tap sounded on the bathroom door. "All clear."

Jade opened it. "Oh, wow, that's terrible about her daughter."

He hiked a brow, turning down the hall.

"What? I couldn't help but overhear." She piled her damp hair on her head and gathered her things, following him. "Sorry you're losing Betty Jean. I know she's been—"

He was losing Betty Jean. The position was well paid. Daniel had fought to raise the salary when he'd taken office, had caught some flak for it. The job offered benefits, regular hours, not to mention a super nice boss.

Daniel sat at his desk and woke up the computer. She stared at him, biting her lip, the thought taking root.

Maybe she wasn't exactly assistant material, but she was a quick learner. She knew the basic computer programs and could learn to operate office equipment. Anyone could answer phones and schedule appointments, right?

"Hey, Daniel?" She waited until he looked at her. "Are you taking interviews for that position yet?"

* * *

Daniel turned to Jade, his mind still on his crowded inbox. He'd ignored it for too long, and now it would take hours to weed through the—

"What?" he asked, her words finally registering.

"I know Betty Jean just quit, but I can do the job, Daniel."

Whoa. Wait a minute.

"I can answer phones and make copies. And I can type. I'm a fast learner and a hard worker . . ."

No.

Oh no.

"The position has insurance and regular hours, and I wouldn't be on my feet all day, which will come in really handy the next few months. Oh, please, Daniel, I promise I'll be the best assistant ever. Better even than Betty Jean."

Hadn't he just decided to limit his time with her? How would he function, trapped in his office eight hours a day with Jade?

Day, after day, after day.

It was a bad idea. Terrible.

But tempting too. Glancing up to catch a

glimpse of her any time he chose. Talking to her on a whim, just because he felt like it. Letting his fingers brush hers as he handed her papers to file. Squeezing past her as she used the copy machine, allowing his chest to brush her back for a fleeting moment. It would be so great.

No. No, Dawson, it'll be awful.

He couldn't do it. "Jade, I—I don't know if that's a good idea."

She reared back as if he'd struck her. Her green eyes widened, taking on that lost look. "You don't think I'd do a good job."

"No. That's not it."

"Then what is it?"

What is it, Dawson? He massaged the back of his neck, willing words to come.

"You don't—you think I'm useless. You think I'm a useless, flaky failure."

"No, I don't, Jade." He stood and paced across the room. He had to put some distance between them. He couldn't think when she was looking at him like that.

"Then what is it? Is it the maternity leave? Because I won't need much time off. I could even bring the babies to work with me—they sleep the first month anyway."

That was the last thing on his mind. "I'm not going to deny a new mother maternity leave, Jade. Least of all you."

Understanding lit her eyes. "It's the friendship.

You're afraid to mix business and personal. It won't be like that. I'd never take advantage of our friendship. What you say goes. You're the boss, Daniel. I'll respect that."

"It's not that."

"Then what? The timing is even perfect. Mom's coming back to work next week, and I'd have a whole week to train with Betty Jean before she leaves."

He'd really backed himself into a corner. How was he going to get out of this? But he had to. He *had* to.

"I'd be a great assistant, and in case I haven't mentioned it lately, I'm kind of in desperate need of a good job . . ."

She's living in a store, Dawson. Cooking in a borrowed microwave and sleeping on a display bed. She'll be on her feet all day if she goes back to the coffee shop full time. While pregnant with twins. Where was she even planning to go after her mom came back to work? She couldn't stay at the store.

"Please?" She gave him that look. The one that made him feel like a dog for even thinking about saying no. How selfish could he be?

Everything softened inside, went to mush. "Okay." Just until she got her feet under her.

Jade threw her arms around his neck. Her rounded belly pressed against him. She smelled so good. He wrapped his arms around her. What was he supposed to do? He had to take care of her. Somebody had to. He could suck it up for a few months. Maybe something better would come along, something more fitting.

"Thank you, thank you, thank you!" She pressed a kiss to his cheek.

He was ashamed of the way his heart responded. Pitiful. Just pitiful. But the twinkle in her eyes was worth every bit of torture he'd face in the coming months. *He* had put that twinkle there.

She pulled away, smiling as she gathered her bundle of clothes. "I'd better go."

"Yeah, she'll be back soon."

Jade hurried down the hallway. "You won't regret this, Daniel, I promise," she called over her shoulder.

Daniel watched her slip out the back door, a knot the size of a boulder forming in his chest. He already did.

Chapter Eighteen

Jade lay on a sleeping bag in the hull of Daniel's boat, staring up at the stars, listening to the cicadas and the rippling of the water.

"Thanks for having me over," she said. "This is the most peaceful I've felt in weeks."

He'd made pasta for supper. She'd scarfed it

down like a starving woman only to look up and find Daniel's amused gaze on her.

She watched a firefly float around the edges of the boat. "Look. A firefly." It danced away over the water.

"Every time I see one, I think of you," he said.

"Really? Why?"

Daniel slid the oars into the water, propelling the boat gently forward. "The first time I saw you, it was in your folks' backyard. There you were, right in the middle, spinning round and round."

She chuckled. "I was? Why?"

"You said you were dancing with the fireflies."

She smiled. That sounded like her. The old her. So much had happened since then. She felt the smile drooping.

"That's who you are, Jade. Who you've always been."

Awhile later they came in off the water and settled in Daniel's living room. Jade squirmed until she was comfy, then tucked her toes into Daniel's couch cushions and channel surfed. "Contrary to popular opinion, antique sofas aren't that comfortable, especially on a pregnant woman's back."

"I'm just glad you got a night off."

"Yeah, I've been working some crazy hours."

Daniel settled on the other end of the sofa. "Not for long."

She lowered the remote control. "Oh, I've missed this show. So you're going to Indy tonight?"

"Yeah. I'll be back tomorrow in time for the barbecue and your announcement."

Her mom had her strength back, and the doctor had given her permission to return to her regular schedule. Jade's days of hiding behind countertops were almost over. She'd been avoiding her family for a week.

Daniel's boathouse felt like home after living in the store the past month and a half. She'd forgotten how much she loved the luxuries of TV and home-cooked meals, not to mention the waterside ambiance.

"I didn't know you liked scary shows."

"It's not scary, just kind of tense." Her favorite female lead was scouring the beach at night for her lost diamond ring. The flashlight made wide sweeps across the darkened sand. The creepy music started.

"Who brings expensive jewelry to the beach?" Daniel asked.

"It's a long story, and I've missed—" A darkened shadow appeared. The music swelled.

"I still think—"

"Shhh!"

Daniel chuckled. "I think I'll go pack."

The darkened shadow turned out to be the character's boyfriend, and a romantic interlude proceeded before they cut to a commercial.

Jade muted the TV, catching the pink glow of the sunset through the window. The last light of the day reflected on the surface of the water, turning the river periwinkle. Daniel had a beautiful view here on the water. Below, the dock and his boat were darkened silhouettes in the fading light. Outside, the insects had begun their nightly chorus.

She was so tired. She leaned back, sinking into the cushions, and let her eyes drift shut, just for a minute.

It was dark and quiet. She was alone.

A bed creaked, the sound running like an electrical current up her spine. It stole the moisture from her mouth. Her hands began to tremble. Her heart palpitated.

The weight of his body fell on hers. Her limbs were numb. That horrible creaking wouldn't stop. She was dizzy and helpless. Everything was dark and heavy and smothering.

She smelled him. That repulsive mix of cologne and shoe polish. Her heart quickened, and with each breath, her lungs seemed to fill with it.

She heard him grunting, smelled the wine on his breath, his mouth too close to her face. Her stomach turned.

He touched her shoulder. She pushed at him, but he wouldn't budge. She struck him on the face, then again. But he leaned away, reaching for her again.

"Jade."

She swung without aim, struggling for air.

He grabbed her wrists, capturing them in his iron grasp.

Panic rose hard and fast. A scream crawled up her throat.

"Jade, stop!"

That voice. She dared to open her eyes. Was blinded by tears. Her heart punished her ribs. Her breaths came hard and shallow.

"It's me, honey. It's just me."

Daniel, standing over her.

Not *him*. Not her apartment in Chicago, but Daniel's place. Safe in Chapel Springs.

She closed her eyes again, wishing she could shut out the last minute. Make herself disappear. What was happening to her? She was losing it. She was some kind of freak.

"You're okay." His hands stroked her shoulders. "It was just a dream."

His voice, his touch, beckoned her. Fear sparkled in his eyes. His brows drew tight, those two dashes forming between them. Of course he was worried. She'd just flipped out like a complete psycho.

A red blotch bloomed on his cheek where she'd struck him. Repeatedly.

She covered her mouth with a trembling hand. "I'm sorry. I'm so sorry." She'd never struck anyone in her life. Her eyes burned, threatening to flood again.

"What's going on, Jade?"

She couldn't tell him. She only wanted to forget. It was the only way she could move forward. She shook her head.

"Did someone hurt you?"

"No." She answered too quickly.

He sank to his knees on the floor, his hands dropping to her knees. "Then what? What was that about?"

"I just . . ." Her mind spun for excuses and found nothing. She had to get out of there before he made her say it. Daniel had a way of making her talk. And she couldn't talk. Not about this. Talking made her remember, and she didn't want to remember.

"I don't want to talk about it. I should go."

"You're not going anywhere."

"Get out of my way!"

"You're shaking."

"Leave me alone, Daniel." She pushed him aside and collected her purse.

When she reached the door, he blocked her way again, his jaw set. "I'm not letting you drive like this. Sit down a minute."

He was a foot taller and broad as a barn. She crossed her arms and glared at him. She was tired of having no control. First Nick, then the pregnancy, then her mom's heart attack, and her crummy living conditions. Life was steam-rolling her, and all of that helplessness was directed at Daniel right now because he thought she couldn't make it two inches without him.

"*Move.*"

"Fine, we'll have the discussion standing right here. Who hurt you?"

She clenched her jaw, felt her nostrils flare. Her stomach turned.

"You can tell me, Jade. You can tell me anything, and it won't change the way I feel about you. I want to help you."

"I just want to forget it!" It was out before she could censor the thought.

His brows pulled lower. He stared at her, and she swore he could see all the way to her soul. She looked down, shutting him out.

"Please, Daniel." She couldn't seem to manage more than a whisper. "Please let me go."

"Is that how—" His words came to a strangled end, as if someone had closed a fist around his throat. "Is that how you got pregnant?"

His tone begged her to say no.

And she should. The lie was right there on her tongue. But something thick and heavy had swelled in her throat, choking it off. Her tongue was heavy and wouldn't seem to move. Her eyes burned and filled. Her mouth worked soundlessly.

"I—" she finally choked out. "I have to go."

Daniel pulled her into his arms.

She stiffened. Her straitjacketed arms pressed against his stomach. She wasn't going to do this. Wasn't going to go there. Never wanted to go there again.

Forget. Just forget. Think of something else, anything else. Think of being out on the water, staring up at the stars. Peace. Calm.

He set his palm against her face. "Oh, baby. I'm so sorry."

At his words, his touch, something broke loose inside. It rose up from down deep. She tried to push it back, but she couldn't. It bubbled to the surface, spilling out.

Daniel's arms tightened even as her own loosened from their grip and stretched around him. She burrowed into the softness of his shirt, seeking safety.

Was there such a thing? Would she ever feel safe again? Every night, lights out, her eyes searched the shadowed store for movement. As she lay in the dark, willing sleep to come, the flashes came. She pushed them down, but even when sleep finally came, she jumped at every noise. When the air kicked on and off, when a truck roared past. Safety seemed like a childish fantasy.

But now, tucked into the warmth of Daniel's arms, face pressed into his soft shirt, safety didn't seem so elusive anymore.

Daniel was going to kill him. He didn't care who it was, he was going to track the monster down and kill him with his own bare hands. The thought of someone violating his girl made him want to—

He clenched his teeth together, swallowed hard. He had to get a grip. Maybe he felt like busting a hole in his living room wall, but Jade didn't need that right now. He drew in a deep breath, then another.

She shuddered on a cry, and his heart cracked in two. *How could You let this happen, God? She didn't deserve this. No one does. I don't know how to help her. I don't have a single clue.*

He tightened his embrace. She felt so small in his arms. So tiny and helpless. He wanted to protect her, but it was too late for that, wasn't it? He hadn't been there when she needed him. It was irrational, but a seed of guilt wedged in anyway, sprouting roots.

Focus, Dawson. Think.

She'd faced that nightmare alone. Discovered she was pregnant. No wonder she'd come home. She needed her family. She needed him. She was carrying that monster's baby.

Babies.

How had she come to grips with that? How had she carried this secret for almost five months without a whimper of complaint?

No wonder she hadn't wanted to talk about the father. No wonder she hadn't been eager to tell her family.

And yet he recalled the way she stroked her belly when she thought no one was watching. The way her eyes lit when she heard the heartbeats. The way she'd frozen in joy when she'd felt them move the first time. Somehow she'd worked through the pain and decided to give them life, to raise them on her own. She'd found a way to love those babies despite the circum-stances. Was it any wonder he loved her?

When her sobs turned to sniffles, he stroked his thumb along her cheek, wiping the remnants of tears. He set his chin on her head and sighed.

"Can you talk about it?" he said softly. "Did you report it?"

She shook her head, to which question he wasn't sure.

"I was so stupid," she whispered. "I invited him over. Izzy was supposed to be there, but she was called into work. I should've cancelled or met him somewhere, but I didn't. And like an idiot, I let him refill my drink. He must've slipped something in it and—"

He framed her face, holding her gaze firmly. "This was not your fault."

"I was so stupid."

"Not. Your. Fault."

A tear slipped out and ran under his thumb. Her lower lip trembled.

"There's only one person to blame. Understand?"

She gave a little nod, stilling her lip with her teeth.

"Who was he? What's his name?" He worked for a neutral tone even as he swore he was going to hunt him down and make him pay.

She shook her head. Had she read his intent?

"Nick something." Her face crumpled. "I didn't even know his last name. So stupid!"

"Don't." He wished he could laser the truth into her heart.

Her fingers curled into his shirt at his waist. "When I found out I was pregnant . . ."

She must've been devastated. He hated that she'd been so alone. "Did you tell Izzy?"

She nodded. "I couldn't keep it from her. She really held me together. I was a mess for a while."

Of course she was. She'd been raped. A lot of women would've had an abortion. Or she could've given the babies up for adoption and never told anyone.

"You're so strong, Jade. You're amazing."

She shook her head. "I was so afraid. I still am."

"And you've gotten through it anyway. That's called courage."

"I lie awake at night, scared he's going to come

back." Her voice quivered. "I know that's stupid. He doesn't even know where I am. That's why I freaked about that note in my mailbox."

The note. Daniel gritted his teeth. He wanted her to know it was harmless. That the sender would sooner cut off his own arm than harm her. But he couldn't do that without telling her the truth. And she had enough on her plate without adding to it.

"I know the notes started a long time ago," she said. "And it's absurd to think he's been sending them all along. But these days, I'm feeling a little crazy."

"You're not crazy. You suffered a trauma. You need to talk about it, maybe even to a professional."

She jerked back, looking up at him, fear in her eyes. "You can't tell anyone, Daniel."

She was carrying too much. "Secrets lose their power when they're shared, Jade. You need to—"

"No, Daniel. Mom'll have enough stress dealing with the pregnancy, twins no less. I'm afraid the rest of it would be too much for her right now."

"It's so like you to worry about others." He sighed. "I don't like it. But it's your decision. I won't tell."

"Promise."

"I promise."

Her shoulders relaxed, her face softened.

"But you're going to have to deal with it eventually. These things have a way of creeping back up. You can always talk to me. Or Izzy."

He brushed the remaining tears from her face. Even with her eyes swollen and her wet lashes clumped together, she was the most beautiful woman he'd ever seen.

She smoothed his dampened T-shirt, her eyes following her hand.

He felt the touch down to his toes. His muscles clenched.

"I'm carrying his babies, keeping them." She met his eyes, and he thought for the millionth time that God had invented that shade of green just for her.

"Is that crazy? What if every time I look at them, I see his face? What if I can't love them?"

He touched her cheek. "You already do."

Her brow smoothed, her lips softened. "Yeah, I do. I know that sounds impossible."

"It sounds amazing, just like you."

She pulled back with a little smile. "You're sweet, and I slobbered all over your shirt."

"What's a little snot?"

She gave a wobbly smile, wiping the remnants of makeup from under her eyes. It only smeared. "I should let you go. It's getting late, and it's a long drive to Indianapolis."

He didn't want her driving when she was upset. Hated that she had to go back to that cavernous store and worry herself to sleep. Or did she?

"Stay here tonight."

She looked at him.

The thought grew on him. "The bed's comfy, I have a TV, and God knows it's secure enough." Grandma had insisted he arm the place like Fort Knox once he'd become mayor. Because Chapel Springs' politicians had to worry about being assassinated and such.

"Really?"

He shrugged. "Why not? Bed's just going to go empty all night. I have a top-of-the-line mattress, and there are bacon and eggs in the fridge. You need a good night's rest—big day tomorrow."

"That it is." Her eyes drifted across the room as if weighing her options.

He suddenly wanted her to stay more than he could say. Wanted to know she was safe and secure tonight. Wanted to lie in his hotel bed imagining her curled up in his bed, his scent on the sheets.

When he returned, his pillow would smell of her. Bonus.

"All right," she said. "I'll stay. Thanks."

Chapter Nineteen

"You gonna eat that?" PJ eyed Jade's plate from across the picnic table. She looked gorgeous in the golden light of the sunset. Of course, PJ always looked gorgeous.

Jade handed over the burger. "Have at it." Though her morning sickness was long gone, her stomach had been churning since she arrived at her parents' house.

"Must be nice," Mom said.

"No kidding." Madison forked a bite of salad. "I'll have to run five miles tomorrow to work this off."

"Wait'll you're our age." Dad patted his almost flat belly. "You'll have to run ten."

Beside Jade, Madison groaned.

Beckett whispered something in Madison's ear, making her giggle.

"It starts after the first pregnancy and gets worse from there," Mom said.

"Thank you, Debbie Downer," Madison said.

Mom shrugged. "Just saying."

"And we're eagerly anticipating that first pregnancy," Dad said, eyeing Madison and Beckett.

"Thomas!"

"Well, we are. Not trying to rush you, but grandchildren are the only thing left on my bucket list."

Jade's eyes bounced off Daniel's beside her. Little did Dad know she'd be the one helping him reach that goal. She should say it now, while they were on the subject. Her heart rate accelerated, her tongue dried. She tried to draw strength from Daniel, from the warmth of his arm, the solid length of his leg against hers. She opened her mouth, the words on her tongue.

"A bucket list is supposed to include things you can achieve on your own," Ryan said.

"What do you think the hints are for?"

PJ scooped a forkful of corn. "Smooth, Dad."

"Where's Grandpa?" Ryan asked.

"Went fishing with his friends."

"So you're headed back to work on Monday, Mom?" Madison asked.

"Doctor gave her the go-ahead this week," Dad said.

"I am so ready. I miss my antiques."

Her moment was gone. Jade closed her mouth. She met Daniel's gaze, and he gave her a reassuring wink.

She'd slept so soundly in his bed last night. It was soft, and the smell of him had comforted her. She didn't even remember falling asleep and had slept through her alarm. This morning she'd made a hearty breakfast, frying the bacon to extra crispy just the way she liked, and washed it down with a large glass of Tropicana.

Beckett scraped the last of the baked beans from the Pyrex bowl. Supper was winding down. She needed to tell them soon. She'd popped out so much this week, there was no missing the bump under her loose top. She'd been hiding behind the picnic table since her arrival. She didn't dare get up or her body would make the announcement for her.

"Jade?" Mom said.

She blinked. Everyone was staring. "What?"

"PJ was saying you'll be working for Daniel?" Mom said.

"When did that happen?" Dad asked.

Daniel pushed his plate back. "Just Monday when Betty Jean gave notice."

Mom gave a sad smile. "I was sorry to hear about her daughter."

Madison nudged Jade's shoulder. "You even know how to type?"

"As a matter of fact, I do. This job is perfect for me."

"Except for the whole tyrant boss thing." PJ stuck her tongue out at Daniel.

"You're a fast learner," Madison said. "And you're neat and tidy. You'll hardly know she's there, Daniel."

Something flickered in Daniel's eyes. His lips parted and closed. Jade wondered if he regretted offering her the job.

What offer, Jade? You begged for the job.

Under the table, Daniel nudged her leg. "I was surprised by Betty Jean's announcement, but it'll be okay. Sometimes what initially seems like bad news can be a gift in disguise."

Perfect segue. All she had to say was, *speaking of announcements* . . . Then Dad's face would fall, Mom's forehead would furrow, and chaos would break loose.

"Betty Jean has to pare down her belongings," Mom said. "She's giving the church a ton of things for the rummage sale."

PJ kicked Jade under the table. "You should come. There'll be a lot of furniture."

"Your apartment must be half-empty," Dad said.

Completely empty was more like.

Mom tilted her head. "I'm sorry we haven't been by to see it yet."

"It's fine," Jade said around a mouthful of beans. She felt Madison's eyes on her.

Thankfully, the conversation moved on to the play Madison was rehearsing for. The historical theater had burned to the ground last year and wasn't yet rebuilt, so they were using the church. The conversation shifted to the River Sail Regatta. Madison and Beckett were entering again, but after winning last year, the bar was high.

Mom set her napkin on her plate and rested her elbows on the table. Almost everyone had finished eating. Jade was running out of time. In seconds Mom would stand, and everyone would follow her into the house with plates and empty bowls. Then most of them would meet on the court for a competitive game of HORSE.

Except Jade. She couldn't go anywhere until she told them.

She felt Daniel's eyes on her.

I know, I know.

Mom stood, gathering the dishes, and Dad joined her.

Jade's heart beat up into her throat, throbbing. "Wait!"

Her parents looked at her expectantly. Everyone stilled at her tone, looking her way.

Jade swallowed hard. "Mom, Dad, could you sit back down? I—I have something I need to tell you."

Oh, God, give me words. I don't want to do this. Look at them. They're going to be so disappointed.

Under the table, Daniel found her hand, grounding her.

Madison's gaze dipped down, catching the gesture.

"I don't know how else to say it, so I'm just going to say it." She pulled in a breath and let it out. One of her babies chose that moment to do a little flip. "I—I'm pregnant."

Daniel's hand tightened around hers.

She couldn't stop her eyes from drifting around the table. Mom first, for signs of stress. Her brow was furrowed. Was she okay? Was she flipping out? Not that Mom ever flipped out. She kept it inside, but that was even worse, right?

Dad's arm settled around Mom's shoulders. Jade avoided his gaze.

PJ's lips had parted. Ryan's expression went unchanged. Beckett stared at his empty plate.

Beside her, Madison's eyes met hers, softening. Her gaze darted over Jade's shoulder to Daniel, her lips pressing together, then back to Jade. What was that about?

"Well." Mom tucked her short blonde hair behind her ear and tried valiantly for a smile. "Honey, this is . . ."

"A surprise," Dad said.

PJ twisted her napkin. "I didn't even know you were seeing anyone."

"Congratulations." Madison squeezed her other hand.

Jade clung tight to Daniel. She wondered if he knew how heavily she was leaning on him right now.

"I know it's a shock. But I'm okay, and everything's going to be fine. I have a good job now, and everything's on track."

"What about the father?" Dad said.

"Thomas."

"Well, he has some responsibility here."

She leaned into Daniel, needing his solid strength. Madison shot him a look that he missed.

"The father's out of the picture. I'm doing this on my own."

"Well, that's not fair," PJ said.

Mom gave PJ a look. "Let's save that for later."

"How far along are you?" Madison asked.

"Five months." Jade smoothed her hand over her rounded stomach, wondering at Madison's frown.

"My goodness!" Mom said. "So far! I thought I noticed a little weight gain, but I thought—why didn't you tell us?"

"I was going to after the wedding, then you had the heart attack and . . ."

"Oh, honey. You were worried about my stress? I wish you'd told us. I hate the thought of you going through those months alone."

"Daniel figured it out early on. And Izzy knows. I haven't been alone."

Mom gave Daniel a smile and stretched her arm over the table, clasping Jade's hand. "We love you, and we're behind you all the way."

"I'll babysit when I'm home from school," PJ said.

Madison gave her a smile. "We all will."

Dad looked at Mom. "We're going to be grandparents," he said as if it just dawned on him. "We're having a grandbaby."

"Um . . ." Jade glanced around the table,

wishing she could brace them for the next news. Then again, she'd had no warning either. "Actually . . . I'm having twins."

Someone gasped, then all movement, all sound stopped. The crickets ceased their chirping, the breeze stilled, and the evening clouds seemed to freeze in the sky.

"Did you just say—?"

She winced. "Yep."

Everyone started talking at once, asking questions, making comments, and the chaos was officially underway.

* * *

Daniel plugged in his cell and flopped into bed. He'd been nervous for Jade all day, and he'd only been more nervous when he'd shown up at the McKinleys' and seen her pale face and trembling hands.

She'd done it, though. The secret was out. He'd wanted to talk alone afterward, maybe follow her to the store, but her sisters and mom kept her until the moon had risen high in the sky.

She had other people to lean on now. It was what he'd wanted. Right?

He flipped over on his pillow and caught a whiff of Jade's spicy perfume. He nuzzled into the pillow and inhaled again, filling his lungs with her.

Was she really okay? Her family seemed to take the news well, but he'd been on the court with the guys after supper, so he'd missed some of the conversation.

He grabbed his phone and punched in a text. You okay? I thought it went well.

He sent the text and waited. Maybe she was asleep already. He remembered what she'd said about her difficulty sleeping, her fear. Was she staring into the darkened shadows of the store, afraid?

A text dinged in. Me too. Thanks for being there.

Welcome. Mama Jo seemed to handle it well.

Hard to tell. Wouldn't let me know if she was stressed.

You worry too much. She'll be fine. What were you girls talking about after supper?

Wouldn't you like to know.

You were talking about how hot I look in my new Armani shirt, weren't you?

Thought you didn't care about designer labels, Mr. Moneybags . . .

Gift from Mom. Gotta keep up the image.

Very important for a future congressman.

Don't think it escaped my notice that you didn't deny it.

Deny what?

That I looked hot.

Oh, brother. Fine, yo were hot. Happy?

Ecstatic.

Is there an eye-rolling emoticon? :) How'd the Indy thing go?

Okay. Dad set it up. The man's loaded and ready to contribute. Too bad he's kind of a schmuck.

There's a lot of those in politics.

Gee, thanks!!!!

Present company excluded! Sheesh, I'm supposed to be the hormonal one. Thanks for letting me stay last night. Best sleep in weeks!

Welcome. My pillow smells like you now.

Sorry! Shoulda washed your sheets. Bad, Jade! :(

Wasn't complaining . . .

He sent the text and reread it, wincing. How would she take that? He wished he could recall it. Her reply dinged.

Okaaaay . . .

What did that mean? He didn't even know what to say. Obviously, she hadn't either. He'd better shut this down before he blew it.

Should let you get to bed. Working at the coffee shop tomorrow?

Bright and early. Last weekend.

Hurrah!

I heard my new boss is a tyrant though.

Lies!

Ha. We'll see.

Get some rest.

Night.

Chapter Twenty

"What's this?" Jade took the slip of paper from Daniel. She tucked her bag under Betty Jean's desk, still trying to wake up.

"Your first paycheck."

Jade handed it back. "It's my first day on the job. I haven't even answered a phone call."

Daniel crossed his arms, his biceps bulging. "It's an advance. Go get your apartment, Jade."

She eyed the check. Her mom was back in the store today. Jade had covered her tracks, washing her bedding at the Quick Spin and returning Daniel's microwave. She'd come early this morning and piled her belongings into the storage closet at the back of Daniel's office. Now she needed a nice long nap.

"You saw all my stuff, didn't you?"

"I don't care about that. It's just an advance. Is it enough to get you in?"

If she combined it with her piddly savings. "Yeah."

"Take care of it at lunch. I'll help you move in tonight. Deal?"

Her own place. Her own bed. Her own shower! She couldn't say no. She gave a grateful smile. "Thanks, Daniel."

"Don't thank me yet. You haven't met Tyrant Daniel."

"I'll bet he's a pain in the—"

"Hey now . . ." He nudged her leg. "I'm signing your paychecks, you know."

Betty Jean hadn't arrived yet, so Daniel showed Jade around. He acquainted her with the phone system, pointed out the minifridge, and introduced her to the ornery copy machine.

"Jade, meet Methuselah. Methuselah, Jade. I hope you have better luck than I do." He gave the ancient beast a sideways glance. "Betty Jean has a special way with him. I hope she shares her secret with you."

He unlocked the door to the walk-in closet. "This is keyed the same as the back door, and I'll get you a key for the front door."

He opened the closet door. "You'll find all the files and supplies in here—whoa!" He caught the door as it swung shut behind her. "Rule number one: the door locks automatically." He nudged a wooden wedge into place under the door, then explained the file system. "We lock the closet at night but keep it propped open during the day."

The faint smell of his cologne teased her nose in the small enclosure. He always smelled so nice. Like soap and leather. He pointed out the supply of ink for the printer at the back. His sleeves were rolled at the cuff, displaying strong forearms and a thick-banded wristwatch.

"Paper for the copier is on this side, and down here"—he squatted down—"is the all-important supply of coffee with filters and cups, et cetera." His movement pulled his shirt taut across his shoulders. They were broad and tapered down to a trim waist, enhanced by a brown leather belt. As he stood, her eyes fell over the rest of him.

When he left the closet, she followed him back into the office. A text dinged as she approached her desk. She checked it, then silenced her phone.

"Sorry about that. The family won't leave me alone. I swear, since Friday I've gotten about a hundred texts a day between the five of them."

"They're worried about you."

"Everything's fine."

"They have five months of fussing to make up for."

She settled into Betty Jean's chair. "They're making up for it, believe me."

"Your doctor's appointment is in the morning, right? I had Betty Jean reschedule my meeting with the transportation department."

"Oh—yeah. Actually, you're off the hook. Mom and the girls want to go. I'm having another ultrasound and—" She stopped at his crestfallen look. "I can't tell you how much your support has meant. But I know you're busy. I've already taken up too much of your time."

"You haven't taken anything, Jade. My time is my own to give."

"I know. I just—I'm sure you have better things to do than sit around a waiting room with a bunch of pregnant women." She chuckled.

He smiled. She wondered if she'd imagined his disappointment. "Yeah, no problem. I'm sure they're dying to see the babies." He sat in his chair across from her and woke his computer.

"They are."

He was already checking his e-mail, so she left him alone. The clock on the wall showed four minutes until Betty Jean's appointed arrival time. Jade's eyes drifted over her future desk. Stacks of papers, files, and framed photos covered the top, and an HP monitor sat front and center. The system unit hummed quietly from a cubby by her leg. She was going to clear off the desk or at least find some organizers to clean it up.

Daniel's desk was worse. Papers fanned across the top of a black blotter, barely visible, in no apparent order. A colorful bouquet of pens and pencils bloomed from a mahogany canister in the corner. A photo of his parents and grandma perched beside it, and a calendar, filled with penciled-in appointments, was tacked to the wall next to him.

Her eyes slid to Daniel. His fingers did a fast hunt-and-peck across the keyboard as his brows furrowed. The glow of the screen lit his face in the inadequately lit room. He had a nice profile. Long dark lashes that swept up and down as he typed, the perfect sized nose, a strong jaw, freshly shaven. His lips were nice too. Gently rounded peaks, set far apart. His lower lip was generous. Good kissing lips. He pursed them now.

Jade jerked her eyes away.

What are you doing, Jade? That's Daniel. She'd never noticed his nose or his long lashes, to say nothing of his lips—or had thoughts of kissing them.

It was the hormones. They were doing weird things to her. Making her think crazy thoughts.

Thoughts that need to stop. Good grief. Maybe she needed another date. She'd been putting off Cody for a couple of weeks, feeling guilty about withholding the pregnancy.

Now that she'd told her family, she could tell him and potentially resume the relationship—if he was still interested. Word had spread already. Once she'd stopped trying to hide her stomach, folks noticed. She wondered if Cody knew already. She hadn't heard from him since . . . she thought back. Thursday or Friday. He'd asked her out Saturday, but she was working.

She should've called him. He'd probably gotten wind of the news. That was why she hadn't heard from him. Why had she thought any man would want her in this condition?

The front door swung open, and Betty Jean entered, all swaying hips and poofy hair, saving Jade from the depressing thought.

Chapter Twenty-One

Jade placed the pillar candles on the wall shelf next to the family photo and frowned. She moved them to the end table and gave a satisfied nod.

Her new apartment had filled out a bit, thanks to the church rummage sale. Her mom had let her pick from the leftovers, and she'd scored two ugly but serviceable sofas, two end tables, a decent bed, and other odds and ends. Her eyes drifted around the room. Mom had donated an old TV from the store, and Dad had installed a cheap set of curtains in the living room. They weren't her style, but they covered the window and blocked the stark view of the parking lot. The view from her bedroom was better. Once the trees shed their leaves in the fall, she'd be able to see the river.

She'd gotten a first-floor unit, and unfortunately there were some active children upstairs. She'd hoped for the quiet and security of the second floor, but at least the door came with a thumb-turn lock, a sturdy dead bolt, and a chain. Plus she could tromp around as her pregnancy advanced without worrying about disturbing anyone. Not to mention the coming pitter-patter of toddler feet.

You will not be in this dingy apartment by then. You'll have your cozy home, complete with fireplace and fenced-in yard.

She took a deep whiff and scrunched her nose. She'd almost managed to rid the apartment of the musty odor by airing it out, vacuuming with a deodorizer, and setting out bowls of white vinegar—her mom's suggestion. The remaining odor would probably disappear when she could afford to clean the carpets.

She fanned herself with the novel she'd started the day before. The air conditioner never seemed to keep up with demand. After she'd cooled a bit, she walked down the hall, scowling at the brown carpet, and entered the soon-to-be nursery. A box of baby stuff from the rummage sale sat in the corner. The stark white walls begged for a coat of fresh yellow paint, and the bare window awaited gauzy white curtains.

A knock sounded at the front door. She checked the time as she went to see who it was. Almost eight. Her stomach released a loud growl as if reminded it was past suppertime. A trip to the grocery would have to wait until her next pay-check. For now it was mostly rice, yogurt, and apples.

She checked the peephole and caught Daniel's profile. She smiled, sweeping open the door. "Really? You don't get enough of me at work?"

He held out a sack from the Burger Barn. "I come bearing food."

"In that case." She moved aside, letting him past.

He took about two strides and entered the kitchen-slash-dining room. "Hey, you've been busy."

"You may as well come back in here," she said, stopping by the sofa. "No table."

"Living room, it is."

"How'd you know I hadn't eaten?"

"I heard your stomach growl from the coffee shop. They're missing you, by the way."

"Well, my feet don't miss them." She emptied the bag, inhaling, the delicious aroma of grilled cheeseburgers and fries making her as giddy as a ten-year-old at Six Flags.

He handed her a jumbo-sized drink.

Chocolate shake. Her favorite. "I'm going to get fat."

"You're eating for three. Besides, the babies wanted chocolate."

"Oh, really?"

"They told me earlier today."

She rolled her eyes and tucked into her burger, settling back on the couch. Daniel took the other end, scanning the sofas. "They match your car."

"The color is an insult to greens everywhere, say it."

He grinned. "Maybe it'll come back in style."

"It's the color of canned peas," she said around a bite of burger.

"It's comfortable, and it's in good shape. It feels like springs too. Quality stuff."

"Who knew rich people had such bad taste?"

"You got curtains up. And a TV." He frowned as he stuffed fries in his mouth. "Does that thing really work?"

"Ryan put a cable box or something on it. The picture's like looking through gauze, but it's better than nothing."

"We should start hitting up some garage sales to fill out this place."

"My funds have kind of dried up. I have the basics. I need to focus on the nursery. I'm kind of on a deadline, in case you hadn't noticed." She smoothed her hand over her stomach.

"They moving much today?"

"Like a couple acrobats. They like the shake, by the way."

"What'd I tell you?"

Their conversation bounced from work to family and to what they were reading and who was going to be in the World Series. When they finished eating, Daniel picked up her guitar and started picking, eventually drifting into "Love in Vain."

"Nice chops. You've been practicing."

When he finished the song, he handed it to her. "It's the master's turn."

"Listen to you. *You* taught *me* to play."

"And you passed me up in about three weeks."

She shook her head as her fingers found their places on the strings. She played a new riff she'd been working on. "My belly's getting in the way. In a few weeks there'll be no room for the guitar."

"How are you sleeping?"

"Good."

She caught his skeptical look and shrugged. "Lots of new sounds to get used to." The foreign noises still woke her. When her neighbors closed their entry doors, her own door shook in the frame. The noise had her bolting upright in bed the first time it had happened.

"I'm not used to the elephants yet," she said.

He lifted a brow.

"My neighbors upstairs. They must be out tonight, otherwise you'd hear them practicing their handstands." She moved her fingers over the strings effortlessly, enjoying the familiar strains.

Daniel settled against the sofa back, tapping his foot to the tune. "Nice. A new one?"

"It's called 'Pregnancy Blues.' " She shifted from a C to a G7.

"I want to hear the lyrics."

"No you don't." She looked up in time to catch his smile, then finished with a G chord. "That's all I got."

She plucked out a few of the songs she'd written in Chicago, settling into a groove. Playing had always relaxed her. She hadn't had much time since she'd arrived in town. She hadn't realized how much she missed it until now. Her fingering improved the more she played, but she'd lost some of her calluses, and her finger-tips were starting to burn.

"You're so gifted," he said when she set the guitar aside. "You should be playing concerts with crowds of adoring fans instead of working in a stuffy office with a tyrant boss."

She smiled at him. "He's not so bad. Any-way . . . I tried the music thing. It didn't work out so well. So I'm playing for me now. It's more fun anyway."

"You should start teaching again."

"When am I going to have time for that after the babies are born?"

"Good point."

He checked his watch. It had gotten late, and it was a work night. Even so, she didn't want him to go. The apartment was lonely, and she knew she'd lie awake for hours, her heart thumping at every bump and creak.

He stood. "I brought you a little house-warming gift."

"Daniel. You didn't have to do that."

"I'll be right back. Don't move." He left the apartment, turning the dead bolt behind him so the door didn't quite shut.

She hoped he hadn't spent a lot. He'd already

done so much. He was so generous. Sometimes she wondered how he'd escaped the privileges of his childhood without becoming entitled or spoiled. Somehow his grandma had grounded him. Heaven knew it hadn't been his parents' influence.

His head poked through the door. "Close your eyes."

She rolled her eyes but did as he said.

The door whooshed shut. His feet shuffled across the carpet. "No peeking."

"Wouldn't dream of it."

Everything went quiet. Not even the air stirred around her. She waited another minute. What was taking so long?

"Daniel?"

"Keep them shut." He was nearby.

She felt his hand on her elbow. "Come with me."

"Where?" she asked, standing.

He turned her toward the TV. "You're not peeking, are you?"

"Never."

His hands on her shoulders, he guided her. "Keep going."

She shuffled slowly. "I'm going to hit the TV."

"You're nowhere near the TV. Have some trust, woman."

She kept going, enjoying the solid weight of his

hands on her shoulders, the clean scent of him nearby.

A moment later, he stopped her. "Okay, open your eyes."

They were in the nursery. Her eyes fell on a new object in the corner by the window.

"A rocking chair!" It was mission-style, stained a dark, rich brown.

"If you don't like it—"

"I *love* it."

His hands fell from her shoulders as she moved forward. She ran her fingers over the smooth wood. She'd planned to look for a used one once her funds grew. There was nothing used about this one. Not a single scratch marred the beautiful finish. Tags hung from the arm, though the price sticker had been stripped away. She had an idea how much it had cost. She'd initially looked for baby furniture online, a reality check.

"It's too much."

"No it wasn't. I promise."

"Are you sure?"

"Positive."

She pushed it, watching it glide silently back and forth. He'd done so much for her. The emotional support and doctor's visits, letting her use the office shower and microwave, giving her a job, the advance, and now this. Way above and beyond.

She turned and embraced him, squeezing tight.

His arms went around her, settling on her lower back. She was so lucky to have him in her life. He was a rock. An anchor.

She gave him a final squeeze and backed away, planting a kiss on his cheek.

Except he turned at the last minute. Her lips missed their mark, landing firmly on his mouth. And clung there a beat too long. His lips were soft and responsive. Nice.

She jerked away.

His eyes widened. His lips—just on hers!—parted.

Holy Toledo. She'd just kissed Daniel. She'd kissed *Daniel*. On the mouth. Just now.

A bubble of laughter rose in her, but she caught it before it escaped. She touched her fingers to her lips.

She wondered if her eyes were as wide as his. Wider. "I'm sorry."

He blinked, and his eyes shuttered. "My fault." He stepped back, palming the back of his neck.

Her face burned in the awkward silence. She couldn't think of a thing to say. Not a single thing.

Not. A. Single. Thing.

"I should go. It's late and—I should go." He backed from the room.

She found her tongue. "Thanks for the chair. And supper."

He couldn't seem to meet her eyes. "Yeah, ah, no problem. I'll let myself out."

"See you tomorrow."

"Lock up behind me?"

"I will."

* * *

What had he done? Daniel turned the ignition and pulled from the parking lot. He couldn't get out of there quickly enough. Jade had meant to kiss his cheek. His *cheek*. He was sure of that.

Had he turned on purpose? Some pitiful subconscious excuse to collect a kiss? He wasn't sure. It had happened so fast—her lips were on his. He'd returned it, no more than a quick brush. Then she'd jerked away as if she'd touched a hot plate instead of his mouth.

Then he'd heard that gurgle of laughter before something had choked it off. Probably horror. He'd finally kissed Jade—sort of—and had to apologize for it. Not exactly the moment he'd always dreamed of.

Chapter Twenty-Two

"I have a favor to ask," Daniel said as he hung up the phone two weeks later.

Jade gathered the paper clips and dropped them into her new drawer organizer. Now that

Betty Jean had left, Jade had spent the morning rearranging things to her liking.

"What's that, boss?" The awkwardness of the accidental kiss had faded as they settled into a new routine.

"Grandma asked me to invite you to dinner tomorrow night."

She'd only seen the woman twice since she'd returned. She felt a twinge of guilt. Mrs. Dawson had always been so good to her. "Sure, I'd love to come."

He gave her a look. "My parents will be there."

"Oh."

"You don't have to."

She didn't want to be rude. They were his parents. But she'd always felt awkward around them. Not awkward. More like a pair of Birkenstocks in a closetful of Pradas. Plus she always felt angry around his parents. They were supposed to love Daniel more than anyone, but they'd abandoned him, and they pressured him all the time.

But his grandma had invited her. "Is it like a dinner party with lots of people?" Where she could blend into the background and avoid talking to his parents?

"No, just us. It's okay, I get it."

"No, no. It's fine. Nice of your grandma to think of me. What time?"

"I can pick you up at seven?"

"Sounds good."

Heaven knew she had no other plans. She hadn't heard from Cody since word had gotten out about her pregnancy.

Jade had nothing to wear. Half her closet was strewn across the bed. Everything was either too small or too casual for an elegant dinner party.

She finally settled on an empire-waist dress in a bold print. Too bohemian for the occasion, but her options were limited. She slipped it over her head, then frowned into the mirror. The bodice was tight on her enlarged breasts. The filmy material draped over her rounded belly, falling to her calves in an uneven hemline. It would have to do.

She removed a few of her rings and took off all of her earrings except the pair her parents had given her for her birthday. Her one pair of nice heels were tight on her swollen feet and sported a small scuff mark on the toe. But she squeezed her feet into them anyway.

She only had a few minutes to fuss with her hair and makeup before Daniel arrived.

"Wow, you clean up nice," Daniel said when she opened the door. "I like your dress."

"Thanks." She immediately felt better about her choice. The bright colors looked good on her. Her hair had behaved, so she'd left it to fall around her shoulders in loose waves.

She settled into the passenger seat, watching Daniel round the car. He wore khakis and a pressed button-up, sleeves rolled to his elbows. She admired his broad shoulders and trim waist. His brown belt matched his shoes, she noticed when he entered the car.

"You look nice too, Harvard Boy."

He shot her a wry grin. "Thanks."

She rested her arms on her slouch bag. "Why are your parents in town? You just saw them recently, didn't you?"

"Dad had an event in Bloomington, so they swung over, mostly to see Grandma. They're flying out tomorrow night."

"Quick visit."

"Sometimes that's best."

Daniel gave another crooked grin, drawing her eyes to his lips. His jaw looked as smooth as granite, and the clean scent of aftershave filled the car's interior.

Her thoughts went back to their accidental kiss, as they had many times already. It should've disgusted her. At least a little. He was like her brother. After all, if it had happened with Ryan . . . ewww. She shuddered.

"Cold?" Daniel reached toward the thermostat.

"A little." No way was she admitting the real cause of her shiver.

Daniel hadn't seemed too shaken by the kiss, but then, he came from a different world. People in his circles kissed on the mouth in passing, didn't they? At least they did on TV.

She wondered if that's the way he greeted Courtney when he traveled to DC. Maybe their kisses had progressed to the more passionate variety. They'd had, what, three dates? The thought settled under her skin like a barb.

What is wrong with you lately, Jade?

A few minutes later, Daniel pulled into the long winding drive of the Dawson mansion. The night darkened as they mounted the wooded knoll, passing the manicured lawn. Porch lights splashed against the brick façade and pooled on the welcoming veranda.

As they climbed the porch steps, Jade shifted her faux leather bag, wishing she'd left it in the car. It had seen better days.

"Jade!" Daniel's grandma opened the massive wooden door and drew them inside, giving them delicate hugs. A filmy pantsuit the color of champagne hung on her tall, lean frame, and her silver hair shimmered under the light of the enormous chandelier.

"Hi, Grandma." Daniel kissed her on the cheek.

"Such a handsome boy. And Jade, you look lovely."

"Thank you. I like your suit." Jade's heels clicked across the marble entryway as she followed his grandma.

When they entered the sitting room, the

Dawsons rose to greet them. Daniel had inherited his stature and dark good looks from his dad.

Mr. Dawson embraced Daniel, then he shook Jade's hand. "Nice to see you again, ah . . ."

"Jade, Dad," Daniel said.

"Of course!"

Mrs. Dawson turned her cheek for Daniel's kiss, then gave Jade a nod with her foreboding chin, her eyes bouncing off Jade's stomach. "Jade. Lovely to see you."

Her stilted tone said more than her words. She was long and lithe, where Jade was short and curvy. But now she only felt like a big pregnant lump.

"You too," Jade said, dredging deep for a smile.

She and Daniel sat on the sofa across from his parents while Daniel's grandma excused herself to the kitchen.

"Can I help?" Jade asked, hopefully.

"No, dear, you just relax. I just need to assist Mrs. Pierson with the finishing touches."

Jade hid her bag at the side of the sofa. Mrs. Dawson took a seat. She wore a red pencil dress with a scooped neckline. A ruby necklace lay against her porcelain skin. Her brown hair was perfectly coiffed. Her makeup was impeccably applied, a touch of rosy blush where her cheeks would bunch if she were smiling.

"How was the event in Bloomington, Dad?"

Mr. Dawson nodded. "Not bad, not bad." He

traded a look with his wife. "We were able to see the Chandlers while we were there."

"Friends of my parents," Daniel explained to Jade. "Mom's known Mrs. Chandler since their college days."

"They spent the day shopping," Mr. Dawson said. "My wallet has yet to recover."

Mrs. Dawson folded her hands on her lap. The setting on her wedding ring was the size of a guitar pick. The diamonds sparkled under the Tiffany lamp.

"Sounds like you had an enjoyable visit," Daniel said.

His mom nodded once. "Very much so."

She was being awfully quiet. She'd hardly looked at Jade since they'd arrived, not even when they'd greeted each other.

Jade twisted the sole ring on her finger. A silver band engraved with daisies, a gift from Madison.

"When did you get into town?" Daniel asked.

"Around noon," Dad said.

"You should've called. I would've set up a tee time."

"I had some business to take care of. And Mother needed some help with financial matters."

"We stopped by the country club," Mrs. Dawson said, finding her tongue. "We ran into the Flannigans and the Whitfields."

Mr. Dawson gave her a look. "The Flannigans

are buying a winter home in Phoenix. Six bedrooms, an indoor pool, the works. The pictures were stunning."

"They have grandchildren there, right?" Daniel asked.

"That's not the only news we heard," Daniel's mom said.

Mr. Dawson fixed her with a look. "Victoria."

"It has to be addressed, Allen."

"Now is not the time."

Daniel stiffened, looking between his parents. "What's going on?"

Jade shifted. She shouldn't have come tonight, not if they were going to talk about family matters.

She inched forward on the sofa. "I should go help your grandma."

Mrs. Dawson narrowed her eyes at Jade. "Perhaps you shouldn't, as this concerns you."

Jade shrank back into her seat. Her skin heated. The flesh under her arms prickled.

"Mom, what's this about?"

"It's just a rumor, Victoria. For heaven's sake, give them a chance."

"What rumor?" Daniel's eyes found Jade's. Her look must've convinced him she was clueless, because he was looking back at his mom now.

"That *she's*"—Mrs. Dawson's eyes flitted to Jade—"carrying *your* child."

"What?" Daniel said.

Jade palmed her heart, which thumped like a jackhammer. "Oh no." She hadn't heard any rumors at all. But then, the person at the center of the rumor was usually the last to hear.

"I'm so sorry." Jade's eyes went back and forth between the Dawsons and Daniel. "It's not true."

"Of *course* it's not true," Mrs. Dawson said.

"Mother."

As if her son would never be so stupid as to conceive out of wedlock. Jade shrank into the cushions, wishing she could melt into the chestnut-colored leather. Jade couldn't even disagree. It was true.

"I'm sorry."

He set a hand on her balled-up fist. "You have nothing to be sorry for."

Daniel's grandma poked her head into the room. "All right, dearies, dinner is served." And then she was gone.

Mrs. Dawson's red lips pressed into a tight line as she stood.

* * *

They filed quietly through the foyer, the tension palpable. Daniel surveyed the dining room, seeing it as Jade might. The formal table was set with so many plates and bowls that the burgundy tablecloth virtually disappeared. In the center, silver candelabras flanked a fresh flower arrangement. On each of the five plates sat a slab of prime rib, a perfect circle of potatoes, and an artfully arranged bouquet of asparagus. The air was thick with the smell of beef and horse-radish. His stomach twisted hard.

"How lovely," Mom said as if she hadn't just dropped a bomb into the conversation less than a minute ago.

Daniel pulled out Jade's chair, and she sank onto it. She wouldn't even look at him. His palms grew damp in anticipation of the coming conversation. It wouldn't come over the meal— his mother's manners would never allow that.

They joined hands, forcing Jade to take Mrs. Dawson's across the table. After his grandma said grace, Daniel squeezed Jade's hand before releasing it.

"Smells delicious, Mom," Dad said.

"I'll tell Mrs. Pierson you said so. I can't imagine what I'd do without her."

The sentence was punctuated with the sound of silverware scraping fine china.

Daniel cut into the tender beef, grateful for something to do, something to look at. He was glad for the dimmed chandelier. Maybe it would hide the flush of anger that had crept up his neck.

"Mmm. Delicious," Jade said. She'd probably rather be eating rice and yogurt in her dingy apartment, and he didn't blame her. Had he known an ambush was coming, he never would've brought her.

"Daniel, have you met with the Crawfords about the ferry?"

He was happy to talk about anything besides the rumor. "I have. They're eager to work out an agreement. It seems business isn't what they'd wish."

"So you'd be doing them a favor," Dad said. "And they in turn will do a favor for you. Those boys have a lot of pull in DC. You're working smart. I'm telling you, son, between your grassroots campaign and the Crawfords' support, you're on your way to the top."

"Unfortunately they're not willing to let the ferry go into Louisville, which is a potential problem for us."

"How so?" Mom asked.

"A lot of locals work in Louisville. A ferry would save them time and gas and allow some families to scale back to one car instead of two."

"Well, you can't back out of the deal with the Crawfords," Mom said. "There's a lot more than a few gallons of gas on the line here."

"We haven't come to a deal yet, but I'll let you know how it goes." This was a matter for the transportation department. He wanted what was best for the community, not what was best for his political future, but his parents would never see it that way.

Daniel's grandma and mom picked up the conversation. Jade was being so quiet. Was she angry? His mother had been inexcusably rude in the sitting room. He looked at Jade, but her eyes were on her plate, her cheeks pink.

She swallowed and began coughing immediately. Daniel reached for her drink and handed it to her, and she took a sip. Linen napkin over mouth, she coughed again. The conversation continued over her coughing fit, punctuated by frowns from his mom.

Jade gave a final hack. "I'm sorry."

Daniel touched her arm. "You okay?"

She nodded, taking another drink of her tea. Her face was red, and Daniel wanted nothing more than to get her out of there. But respect for his grandmother kept him rooted to the seat.

The conversation turned to the uncommonly mild summer, and the charity his mom had founded in DC for disabled veterans.

Daniel choked down the rest of dinner and forced himself to finish the chocolate mousse with raspberry garnish. By the time he spooned the last bite into his mouth, he was full and tense, dreading the conversation to come.

Finally Daniel's mom rose from the table. "I'll help with the dishes, Mother Dawson."

"Nonsense. I have nothing but time on my hands. Go relax in the sitting room while I start the coffee. I'll wash them later."

The sitting room was the last place he wanted to take Jade, but he clung to the hope his mother would drop the subject. He set his hand against the small of Jade's back as they walked.

Mr. Dawson patted his flat stomach. "I'm stuffed."

Jade settled into the sofa corner. Daniel sat closer this time, his thigh pressed against hers. He wanted her to feel his presence and know he was in her corner.

"We need to discuss the rumor circulating about town," Mrs. Dawson said, picking right up where they'd left off.

"There's nothing to discuss, Mom. It's not true."

"Be that as it may, we all know unsavory rumors can destroy a political career."

"I'm afraid your mother's right." Mr. Dawson shot Jade an apologetic smile.

"What do you want me to do—take a paternity test? Rumors fade."

Mrs. Dawson set her chin. "Or they catch like wildfire, spreading and wreaking havoc on one's political aspirations."

Daniel's jaw twitched. "It's not *true*. Just do the math." She'd been two months pregnant when she arrived in town, for heaven's sake.

"It doesn't have to be true, son. It just has to be believed."

"You have to separate yourself from *her*, and furthermore you must—"

That was enough. "*She* has a name, Mom."

Daniel stood, pulling Jade with him. "And we've had enough."

"Sit down, Daniel," his mom said.

"We have to be going." He gave his parents a final look. "Have a safe trip home."

They swung by the kitchen and said good-bye to his grandma. He took Jade's arm as they walked outside. In the car she crossed her arms.

Daniel started the car, turning off the air-conditioning. He snapped off the radio. He couldn't believe his parents. How could they be so rude? So demeaning to his guest? He'd taken Jade in there like a lamb to slaughter. *Idiot!*

His jaws clenched. His hands clamped the steering wheel, the bones of his hands spreading like rigid fans.

"I'm so sorry, Daniel."

His hands tightened on the wheel. "Don't you dare apologize."

"It's my fault. We've been spending too much time together. I let you go to all those doctor's appointments. Someone must've found out and drawn their own conclusion. Or maybe they saw my car overnight at your place. I begged my way into your office, and now they probably think—I should've been more careful, and now you're paying the price. Your mom's right, we should—"

"Stop it." He braked at the traffic light. "We didn't do anything wrong, and if anyone should be apologizing, it's me." He palmed his neck. "I shouldn't have brought you tonight."

"You couldn't have known." She watched him as he accelerated through the green light. His nose flared. Something flickered in his eyes.

Jade frowned. "You didn't know about the rumor. Right?"

In the distance a train whistle sounded. A car whooshed past. Daniel's grip on the steering wheel continued. His lips pressed together.

"Daniel?"

"I heard someone talking at the coffee shop last week."

Jade blinked. "And you didn't tell me?"

"It's just a rumor. I don't care what anyone thinks."

"You're a politician, Daniel, you'd better start caring. If your parents are right, this could ruin everything."

"Even it were true, it's not a crime. People conceive out of wedlock every day."

"Well *you* didn't! This isn't DC. This is Indiana. People care about things like family values and integrity."

"Then they shouldn't be spreading false rumors."

She turned to the window. "You're impossible."

Maybe so, but he was right. "Just put it out of your mind." He knew that was going to be easier said than done.

Chapter Twenty-Three

"Hi, Jade," Cody said. "Thanks for meeting me."

"No problem." Jade sat.

Cody had scored a relatively quiet booth in the back corner of Cappy's Pizzeria. The after-church crowd was mellow, and the TVs were muted. Cody was tapping out a text on his phone.

"Sorry I'm late," Jade said. "Church ran a little over." She scooted across the bench, glad to hide her pregnant belly under the table, away from curious eyes.

He smiled, his brown eyes kind and calm. "I just got here myself. We had a missionary this morning, so our service ran a little over too."

She asked about his job, and they made small talk until after the server took their order. He'd texted her last night and asked to meet for lunch, giving no indication of his agenda. But he'd been short and to the point, leaving her no doubt he had one.

When his phone buzzed, he picked it up and read. His thumbs went to work, then he set it back down a moment later.

She might as well get this started. She squeezed her hands tight in her lap. "I owe you an apology, Cody."

He held his palm up. "Jade—"

"No, I do. I—I should've been honest about the pregnancy. I wanted to, but I hadn't told my family yet and—"

"Jade. You don't owe me anything. We went out on a couple dates. I had a great time. But I'm glad you brought that up. It's why I asked to meet you. I heard something about you and Daniel . . ."

She shook her head.

"You're not dating Daniel?"

"No. We're not—"

His phone buzzed. He tapped out a text and set it down.

"We're not like that. The babies aren't his."

He shook his head as if to clear it. *"Babies?"*

Great. This was going great. Her heart sank. "You didn't hear that part. Yes, twins."

He blinked. Fingered his beard. "Wow. I mean I heard about the pregnancy, but not that."

She wondered again why he'd asked to meet her. He'd wanted clarification on Daniel's role in her life. Had he been interested in dating her again despite the pregnancy?

If so, the script had changed now. He had plenty of reasons to walk away. He didn't even need the Daniel thing. Obviously the whole twins thing wigged him out. Could she blame him? She set her hand on her stomach as one of the babies kicked. She was starting to feel like the last one picked in gym class.

She set her elbows on the table, unearthing a

smile. "Look. I'm glad I had the chance to apologize and clear the record. I hope we can still be friends."

He looked away. To the silent TV, to the empty salad bar, then back to her. He had nice eyes. Brown and warm. She could sit across the breakfast table from that every morning. Too bad he didn't feel the same.

"So you're not dating Daniel."

She frowned. "No. He's like family." She remembered the stray thoughts she'd been having lately. The way she noticed his lips. The way she kept rehashing their accidental kiss. She shook the thoughts away. Hormones.

Cody was staring at her like she had pizza sauce on her face. But they didn't even have their pizza yet.

"What about—the father . . ."

She shrugged, looking down at her chipped nail polish. "He's not in the picture. He'll never be in the picture. I came home for a fresh start, to be near my family."

The server set down their drinks and left the table. Jade unwrapped her straw and stuck it in the water. When Cody's phone buzzed again, she took a deep drink, waiting until he responded.

She wished they'd had this conversation over the phone. Then she could say good-bye instead of waiting for a pizza and flailing around in the awkward silence.

When he finished the text, he unwrapped his straw. "I heard there's a blues concert in Louisville this weekend."

Small talk. This she could handle. "Robben Ford. One of my favorite contemporary bands. He rarely makes it to the Midwest." Too bad Jade couldn't afford tickets.

"Would you like to go?"

"Of course I'd—" She met his serious gaze. He was asking her out. "Oh."

"I know things are complicated right now. But I like you, Jade. I have fun with you. I'd like to keep seeing you."

"You're not—" She cleared the squeak from her throat. "You're not totally freaked out by the whole twin thing?"

He gave a little laugh. "Not *totally* . . ."

Who was she kidding? *She* was freaked out. She smiled, gazing into his kind brown eyes and said the only thing left to say. "I'd like that a lot."

Chapter Twenty-Four

Daniel put up a shot. It sailed through the air, hit the rim, and bounced off. Shoot.

Beneath the net, PJ caught the ball. "That's an E for you, sonny boy."

"You're done, dude." Ryan slapped him on the back.

"First one out too," PJ said. "So sorry."

Daniel darted toward her, picked her up, and threw her over his shoulder. "Oh, yeah, Peewee? How sorry?"

She squealed, thumping his back. "Sore loser! Mom, he's being a bully."

"Fight your own battles, children." Mama Jo didn't even glance up from the newspaper.

"It's a little hard from this angle." She smacked Daniel on the backside. "Get your big shoulder out of my gut. I can't breathe."

"Aren't you going to help her?" Cody asked Jade. "Sisters and all that?"

Jade shrugged. "I'm six months pregnant— she's on her own."

"Thanks a lot, Sis."

Daniel set her down and darted away, but not fast enough.

PJ walloped him on the back of the head.

"Ow."

"Bully."

Daniel settled on the picnic table across from Mama Jo. On the corner of the court near the azalea bushes, Jade and Cody were having a private conversation. Daniel felt the smile slide from his face. Cody held the ball under his arm and leaned close, an annoying grin curling his lips.

They'd been going out the last two weeks. Daniel wondered if the rumor about Jade and himself had dissipated, but couldn't bring himself to care. He didn't like the thought of Cody making her smile, or worse, holding her in his arms. It was hard enough just knowing she was with him. Tonight was the first time he'd seen them together. He wasn't a fan.

"We gonna play or what?" Ryan asked the couple.

"Your turn, Jade." PJ tapped the ball loose.

Daniel tore his eyes from them.

Mama Jo opened the *Chapel Springs Gazette* to the Living section. Madison and Beckett had begged off tonight to practice for the regatta one last time, and Thomas had taken Grandpa out to look at one of the tractors after supper.

Mama Jo was looking better in recent weeks. Now that she was working again, her color was back, and she seemed her happy self. She'd never taken kindly to lying around the house. He knew her recovery had been hard on her.

"Nice shot, Jay-Jay." Cody gave Jade a high five.

Jay-Jay? Really? Wasn't it a little early for pet names? Turning to look, he noticed Jade didn't seem to mind.

Cody tossed the ball to Ryan and draped his arm across Jade's shoulder. Daniel fought the urge to go knock it off. She smiled up at Cody. The look she gave him cut right through Daniel.

He took in Cody's scruffy goatee, his office

attire, his slight build. Was that the kind of man who appealed to Jade? Daniel could take him down with a breath. Plus the guy always had his flipping cell phone in his hand. And he reeked of eau de hospital: disinfectant and rubbing alcohol.

Daniel clenched his jaw, looking away. But it wasn't a contest, was it?

What was wrong with him anyway? He wanted Jade to be happy, didn't he? She'd been through a lot. She deserved that much. If she wanted Cody, Daniel needed to suck it up. Cody wasn't a bad guy. He just wasn't Daniel.

"Lucky shot, bro!" PJ caught the ball as it swished through the net and tossed it to Cody. "Let's see what you got, fancy pants."

"Oh, I got plenty, Peej. I got plenty." Did the man have a nickname for everyone?

"How's it working out with Jade at the office?"

Daniel's eyes swung to Mama Jo. "What?"

"You and Jade getting along okay at work?" Her blue eyes perused his face, seeing too much.

"Sure. You know Jade. She can do anything once she puts her mind to it."

Mama Jo nodded. "That's my girl, all right." She flipped the page and scanned the articles, her bifocals low on her nose. "I guess you heard the rumor."

So the family had gotten wind of it. He'd wondered. "I did. Guess some folks struggle with basic arithmetic."

She gave the barest of smiles. "People are going to talk."

His eyes drifted to the court where Cody helped Jade with a shot. He was behind her, arms around her, holding the ball. Please. Jade had been shooting hoops since she was old enough to toddle.

But she wasn't protesting. She was smiling over her shoulder as though he held the golden keys to the basketball kingdom.

Daniel was losing her again. It never got easier. He'd lost her to Aaron for four heartbreaking years. He'd felt guilty when Aaron had died. As if his own jealousy had somehow caused the tragedy. Watching Jade suffer had been unbearable. He'd wished a thousand times he could bring Aaron back. Watching helplessly while she grieved was a hundred times worse than seeing them together.

He needed to remember that. Remember all Jade had been through. Remember that her happiness was all that mattered.

"When are you going to do something about those feelings of yours?"

His eyes darted to Mama Jo. Her blue eyes studied him over the ridge of her bifocals.

Heat rose on his neck. "What do you mean?"

She pinned him with a look. "I think you know what I mean."

There was something in her eyes that made the blood rush to his face.

Cacophony erupted on the court as PJ sank another shot, the others groaning. Daniel watched them blindly, his heart in his throat. First Madison, now Mama Jo. His secret wasn't a secret anymore.

His heart raced. "How long have you known?"

"Since about five seconds after your feelings changed."

He scratched his neck, wishing twilight would fall faster.

"I understood why you held back at first." Mama Jo flipped another page. "She was so young. She was with Aaron, and they were so—"

She stopped before saying the hurtful words. He'd stayed away a lot during those four years. It was too hard seeing Jade so in love with someone who wasn't him.

"The secret admirer notes." She looked at him over her glasses. "They were from you?"

His lips parted as his eyes shot to her. This was getting out of hand. "Please don't tell her."

She removed her glasses, folded them, and set them on the paper, looking down. "At first, when she came home, I thought maybe the time was finally right. That you'd finally tell her how you felt." She waved her hand. "I know I'm butting in here." She looked toward Jade and Cody, then back to him. "But I see things moving forward, and I worry you're missing your open window. Maybe the last one you'll get."

He knew it was true, that this was the way it had to be. But that didn't stop the cold terror of his lonely, Jade-less future from shooting straight up his spine.

He reminded himself of all the reasons. His political aspirations that would take him from Chapel Springs. From any family he'd one day have. He'd rather be a permanent bachelor than subject his wife and kids to the life his parents had offered. He'd been so low on the priority list, and from what he'd seen, that wasn't uncommon in politics. Your country was your wife. Your constituents your children. There was room for little else.

Jade—and her babies—deserved so much more.

He didn't say all that, though. He went for the easy answer. "Jade thinks of me as a brother."

Mama Jo's brow arched. "Does she?"

He remembered the accidental kiss. The movement of her lips on his, for just the briefest moment. Had he imagined it? He'd relived it a hundred times. Maybe it was only wishful thinking. It probably was. He'd gotten pretty good at lying to himself.

His eyes swung to the court where PJ was trying for a three-pointer. Jade's hand rested on her stomach. Cody reached out, and she placed his hand on her belly, looking up at him expectantly.

The moment sliced him in two. Daniel had yet

to feel the babies move. She hadn't offered, and he hadn't asked. Gravity pulled the corners of his mouth.

Mama Jo set her hand on his. "Don't wait too long, honey. Open windows have a nasty way of closing."

Chapter Twenty-Five

Jade couldn't sleep. She wanted to blame it on her growing belly or her swollen ankles. It wasn't her body that fought the darkness, though—it was her mind.

She'd gotten caught up in a TV movie, not realizing until too late that the main character was going to be attacked. She'd grabbed the remote and shut it off. It wasn't so easy to shut off the memories.

She turned to her side, wishing she could lie on her stomach. The clock's red numbers glared back at her: 11:52. She had work in the morning. Had to get some shut-eye.

One of the elephants crossed over her head, making the ceiling groan. Someone else couldn't sleep either. She gave up a few minutes later and grabbed her phone off the nightstand. She'd planned to text Cody, but when Daniel's name appeared below his on the screen, she clicked on it instead.

You up? she tapped out, then hit Send. He was

probably fast asleep like she should be. She should've texted Cody. Things were going well with him. He was fun, engaging, a good listener. He didn't pry or ask too much of her. The idea of twins hadn't scared him away, and he'd even asked to feel the babies move last week. She hadn't expected that. He was a little too attached to his cell phone, but everyone had his faults.

A text came in. Can't sleep? Jade propped up on her pillows.

I miss sleeping on my stomach. Big belly, swollen feet . . . ARGH!

Need a bedtime story? Once upon a time . . .

Ha. Tell me one about politics. Will put me right out.

I think you just called me boring.

Who me?

Good time to remind you I'm your boss. AHEM!

Don't let it go to your head. I have all kinds of dirt on you, and I'm not afraid to use it.

Please.

You cheated on Marcie Lewis.

I was in 7th grade! And it was only a kiss on the cheek.

You hold Barbie dolls hostage and charge little girls a candy ransom.

Let it go, Jade.

You drove illegally.

What? When?

Your freshman year. My dad's truck.

From your house to the barn? That's not illegal.

Says you. It's all coming out, I tell you.

That's nothing. I got a friend pregnant with twins two months before we were even together . . . Uh sorry—didn't sound right . . .

Immaculate conception, round two. :)

I think that rumor's fading, btw.

Let's hope.

Mom made a bigger deal than it was. Just a handful of busybodies with too much time on their hands.

Still . . . I'm sorry . . .

Stop that.

It does seem to have died down. Helps that I'm out with Cody a lot these days.

That's not why you're dating him . . .

What? No. I like him. He's great. Snuffing the rumor is just a convenient side effect.

You two getting serious?

It's only been 3 weeks . . . Well, plus the few weeks before.

Looked pretty cozy at the regatta. ;-)

Great job on the speech btw. I don't know how you do it, off the cuff, find just the right things to say.

It really does help to picture the audience naked.

ACK! I was in the front row.

I saw nothing. Promise.

Whew. Too bad Madison and Beckett didn't win.

Share the love. Third place isn't bad.

Jade stifled a yawn. Finally her body was ready to give up the fight. She sent Daniel a couple more texts and lay back down, content. Daniel had a way of chasing away the dark thoughts.

His question about Cody lingered in her mind. Were they getting serious? He'd kissed her a couple times. Nothing too deep or heavy. His kisses were pleasant and comforting. The relationship was easy. Enough, but not too much. She liked him. She could learn to love him, she thought. Not be *in* love with him, but love him. If he felt the same, she could see the potential for a long and lasting relationship.

Chapter Twenty-Six

"Could you believe that guy?" Cody turned into Jade's apartment complex.

Jade smiled at the indignation on his face. He'd taken her to a French restaurant in Louisville. Afterward they'd meandered through Waterfront Park, watching the boats on the river, holding hands. Despite the poor service, it had been a good night.

"What guy?"

"The waiter. He was such a jerk. Did you hear

him mumbling under his breath in a foreign language?"

"Um, he was French, Cody."

"He was probably complaining about us."

"He was repeating our order so he didn't forget."

"Oh. I knew I should've taken French in high school." Cody turned into the empty space beside her car. She'd forgotten to leave her porch light on. Her burgundy door looked muddy brown in the darkness.

Cody put his Camry in park, wearing a sheepish smile. "I guess I probably should've tipped, then."

"You didn't leave anything?"

"Now I feel like a jerk."

Jade wished she'd known. She would've left a tip herself. Having been a server, that one hit close to home. Jade unbuckled her seat belt and glanced at the car's clock. It wasn't late, and neither of them had work tomorrow. She should ask him in for coffee. She wouldn't mind extending the evening.

She waited while he responded to a text, looking at the darkened stoop. A shiver passed over her. She hated coming home to an empty, dark apartment. But she hated even worse the thought of letting a man into that space with her. When was she going to get past this?

He opened the car door, and she followed suit

before he could come around. They paused at her front door while she unlocked it. She was being silly. Cody was a great guy. He was gentle and easygoing. He'd never hurt her. She opened her mouth, the invitation ready.

But nothing came out. The words stuck in her throat. She swallowed hard as she unlocked the second lock. Her mind knew he was safe, but her heart wasn't ready to trust. She glanced at him from beneath her eyelashes and saw him waiting expectantly.

She pulled her key from the door and turned. "Thanks for dinner, Cody. I had a wonderful time."

"Me too. I always have a great time with you." His easy smile relaxed her.

He touched her chin and lowered his lips to hers. They met softly. His lips were yielding, and his scent was inviting. He kept space between them and didn't pressure her for more.

When he drew away, his lidded gaze was trained on her. The easy smile was gone, and in its place was a serious look she hadn't seen before.

His thumb swept over her chin. "I have a confession to make." There was a serious note in his voice, a somber look in his eyes.

"Uh-oh," she said lightly, bracing herself.

"I know we haven't been going out long, but I feel like we've known each other forever.

These past couple months have been great, and I wanted you to know . . . I think I'm falling in love with you, Jade."

No. No, no, no. This wasn't supposed to happen. They were supposed to keep it light and easy. That's why Cody had been so appealing. He was safe. She worked to keep the rising panic from showing on her face.

"I hope I haven't scared you off, but I—I just wanted you to know."

She looked into his eyes and felt like scum. This was so unfair to him. He had a right to feel that way. Had a right to pursue that kind of love. But that's not what she was looking for. She should've been honest. Now his feelings were involved, and she was going to hurt him.

He straightened, put his hands in his pockets. "It's too soon. I shouldn't have said anything."

She touched his arm. "No. You should have. It's just . . ."

"You don't feel the same." His flat voice cut right through her.

"It's not you, Cody. I'm just—I'm not looking for serious right now." *I'm not looking for love, just for a husband and a father for my babies.* She closed her eyes. What a crock. Why had she thought that was even possible?

"You've got a lot going on." He looked down at the ratty welcome mat the previous tenants had left.

"I do, I just—I can't go there right now." Or ever. She wasn't living through the horror of love and loss again. Nothing was worth that.

"We can still, you know, keep going out." He gave a hopeful grin. His phone buzzed, and for once he ignored it. "I promise I'll keep my over-wrought emotions to myself."

A little piece of her heart broke. It would be pointless for her and painful for him. He needed to move on, find someone special. It wasn't her.

She squeezed his arm. "I—I don't think that's a good idea, Cody. I'm really sorry. This is my fault. I never meant to—"

He held a palm up. "No, I get it. Really." He turned his hand over, extending it. "Friends?"

She took his hand in hers. "Sure."

He kissed her on the cheek, and with one last easy grin, he turned and got in his car.

Jade entered her apartment and locked it behind her. She flipped on the light and leaned against the door, remembering the hurt on his face. She felt like a dog.

You did the right thing.

Even if she were open to loving again, she didn't think she'd ever love Cody the way he loved her. And she couldn't help that. It had been the right thing to break it off. How else would he find that someone special? Still, it didn't erase the memory of the hurt on his face. Jade closed her eyes and let out a sigh that came from her toes.

Chapter Twenty-Seven

Daniel glanced at Jade. "You've been quiet today."

She was stuffing envelopes at her desk. The mundane task must've been boring her silly. She hadn't smiled once all day despite his efforts to cajole her from her bad mood.

"Twelve hundred envelopes won't stuff themselves." Her hair was pulled back in a ponytail today. Several pieces had fallen out and brushed the sides of her face. Her purple top skimmed her pregnant belly.

He remembered Cody's hands resting on her stomach and fought back a growl.

She arched in the chair, rubbing her lower back. She'd been doing that a lot lately.

"Everything okay with the babies?"

"Yeah. I had a doctor's appointment last week."

"You should get up and stretch more. Would it help to put your feet up?"

She pulled the last few envelopes from the box. "I'm fine, Daniel."

"Something's wrong."

She shot him a look as she slid her finger under the flap. "Ow!" Frowning, she sucked her finger.

Daniel rolled his chair to her desk and took the envelope from her hand. "Take a break.

Boss's orders." It was nearly quitting time anyway.

She sat back in her chair. The twin commas between her brows and the pouty lips were adorable. "Stupid paper cut."

"It's more than a paper cut. Talk."

She folded her hands on her stomach and fixed him with a look that made him squirm in his seat.

"Are you unhappy here?" he asked. "You want to look for another job?"

"No. I love it here."

He found that hard to believe. "Then what is it?"

She looked down at the rings on her fingers. Started twisting the braided silver one. "I'm just in a funk." Her eyes bounced off his. "I broke it off with Cody on Friday."

Relief swelled inside. It was immediately squashed by the weight of guilt. "What happened?"

She started on the thumb ring. Her cheeks filled with color. She squirmed in her seat, avoiding his eyes.

An uneasy feeling started beneath his ribs and pushed outward. So help him, if Cody touched her—if he harmed one hair on her head, he was going to lay the guy flat out.

His cell phone on his desk vibrated.

"Your phone's ringing."

"I don't care. Did he—Jade, did he hurt you?" There was no hiding the intensity of his tone.

Her eyes flew to his. "No. No, Daniel, he'd never—he'd never do something like that. He was . . ."

"What?"

She scowled, pressed her lips together until they were a flat line.

"He was what?" Daniel tried unsuccessfully to read the look on her face.

"Falling in love with me, okay?"

All the air left Daniel's body. It was like a sucker punch to the gut. He reminded himself of what she'd said before. She'd broken up with Cody. It was over. No reason for his knees to start knocking now.

"That's a bad thing?" he asked.

She sighed. Her rings clicked together as she messed with them. "I don't want serious."

He tilted his head. "Four months ago you were looking for a groom."

She glared at him. "I do want a husband."

"But not love?"

Jade's eyes fell to her fingers.

What was she thinking? "They kind of go together, Jade."

"I do want love. Just not—*that* kind of love."

He shook his head, trying to clear it. Or maybe hoping the motion would jar some pieces into place, and he could figure out what the heck she was saying.

"I want someone safe and dependable and

considerate. Someone who'll be a good partner, a good father. I told you all this."

"No guy's going to want that, Jade."

She met his eyes, and her shoulders slowly slumped, all the fight seeming to drain from her. Her eyes teared up. He felt like a jerk for making her cry.

"It was a stupid idea."

He pulled her chair until their knees connected. Her chin wobbled, her lip trembled. *Way to kick her when she's down, Dawson.*

Why didn't she want love? It was a natural, healthy desire. Something wasn't right here. Had the attack changed her? Was she afraid of men? Afraid to trust?

"So what's with the boycott on love?" He'd hoped for a smile but didn't get one.

She shrugged. "I don't want to go there again."

"Why not?" He wasn't letting her off the hook. Not even when she narrowed her eyes at him.

She didn't say anything for a while, so he waited her out.

"I haven't exactly been a raging success in that department," she said finally.

He wasn't sure what she meant. The rape? That wasn't her fault. And she'd had a good relationship with Aaron. Of course it hadn't ended so well. His death had sent her spiraling into a . . .

He fixed her with a look. "This is about Aaron."

Her Adam's apple bobbed as she swallowed. She caught her trembling lip between her teeth as her lashes swept down. "I don't want to do that again. Ever."

His heart cracked open. He'd been there. Granted, on the outskirts. She'd hardly let her mom in, let alone him. She'd been like the walking dead for months.

"Honey, that won't happen again."

"You don't know that."

"It was a freak accident. The chances of losing somebody like that again are one in a million."

"Everyone dies eventually."

"But you can't—you can't just give up." Was he really trying to talk her into loving someone else? He was a glutton for punishment.

"I'm not giving up." Her voice wobbled. "I'm just making an adjustment."

The kind of adjustment no man would ever accept. It was impossible to be close to Jade and not want all of her. He knew this better than anyone.

He looked at her face, at the remnant of pain from loving Aaron, and knew a moment of insane jealousy. The man was dead, and he still had the power to make her weep. Aaron was gone, but he was still holding her back.

Daniel palmed the back of his neck. This wasn't Aaron's fault. Much as Daniel had hated seeing them together, he'd been good to her, had loved Jade as much as she'd loved him.

"Aaron wouldn't have wanted this for you."

That got her attention. She nailed him with a look. "This has nothing to do with what Aaron wanted. It's about what I can handle. And I can't handle loving again, Daniel. I *won't*."

He didn't like seeing her riled, but it beat sad any day of the week. "So you broke up with Cody just because he was falling in love with you."

"Yes, I did."

"And you're going to break up with every other guy who has the misfortune of falling for you."

Her lips fell.

"I didn't mean it like that."

"Thanks, Daniel." She stood, her chair spinning backward as she walked toward the back.

"Jade . . ."

She disappeared into the supply closet.

Way to go, Dawson. For a politician, you sure do have a way with words. He banged his head against the chair back. Once, twice, three times. Maybe he could go down to the nursing home next and pick a fight with one of the elderly women.

He heard a grunt from the closet, then a loud clattering sound. He sprang from the chair, darted across the office, and blasted through the doorway. Hundreds of envelopes fluttered to the floor around Jade. Reams of paper smacked the floor as the towering shelf tipped. Beneath it, Jade ducked her head, arms outstretched.

Daniel nudged Jade out of harm's way and caught the shelf. He pushed hard. The heavy-duty shelf settled back in place just as the closet door banged shut.

Chapter Twenty-Eight

Jade's pulse raced. The shelf had nearly squashed her. Her toes throbbed. A ream of paper had fallen on her foot.

"Are you okay?" he asked.

"Yeah. Thanks. I couldn't reach, and I stood on the lower shelf—thought it was bolted to the wall." She bent over and started picking up the mess.

"Where's your phone, Jade?"

"In my purse. It's going to take forever to clean this up." She was ready to go home. She wanted to crawl under her covers and take a nice long nap. Her stomach let out a growl. After dinner. Something quick and microwavable. Or maybe a salad. She should probably have a salad.

Daniel stepped around her, moving toward the door.

"I could use a little help here," she said, hearing the edge to her voice. A box of paper clips had fallen too. Hundreds of them. "Great."

"We have a problem."

She looked up at his serious tone.

Daniel ran his hand over his face.

She noted the closed door and remembered. "We're locked in."

"I left my phone on the desk."

"What happened to the—" The wooden wedge lay at his feet.

"I must've knocked it loose when I ran in."

She dropped the stack of envelopes and stood. Not good. Not good at all. The closet was small. Seemed even smaller with the door closed. Her lungs seemed to deflate, refusing to fill. *Get a grip, Jade. Breathe.* She turned so he couldn't see her panic.

"Maybe—maybe someone will come in," she squeezed out.

"Were you expecting someone?"

Deep breaths. In. Out. "No, but you have a five thirty at the coffee shop with Sarah from the *Gazette*, remember? I set it up this morning. Maybe when you don't show she'll—"

"She had to change it. She's calling tomorrow instead."

Jade looked away. The walls were closing in. She couldn't breathe.

"You okay?"

"Maybe someone'll see the lights on later, when it's dark."

"Maybe."

Who was she kidding? The town shut down after dark. No one was going to wander by the mayor's office and check the doors.

She inhaled deeply and walked toward the back of the closet, a whole four steps. A chill passed over her, and she looked up at the ceiling. Who'd had the bright idea to put a vent in here? And why had she never noticed it was freezing cold?

Maybe because you never faced the prospect of a night in here.

No. They were not spending the night in a closet. There had to be something they could—

"Mom," she mumbled. Grandma's Attic was right on the other side of the wall. Mom's office was about this far back.

She raised her hand to the wall and pounded. "Mom!"

She stopped to listen, but there was nothing from the other side. She pounded and yelled again. The more she yelled, the harder her heart pounded, the more desperate she was to be heard. The harder her heart beat, the smaller her lungs felt.

"Mom!" She kept pounding. Her fist felt bruised. She switched hands.

"Jade."

"Mom!" No one was expecting Jade tonight. Daniel lived alone. No one would even miss them, much less come looking.

"Jade, she's not there."

Her hands sore, she began kicking the wall with her good foot.

Daniel took her arms. "Jade. She's gone home for the day."

"No, she hasn't."

"Yes, she has. Calm down. Come on, don't freak out on me. It's going to be okay."

She turned on him. "We're stuck in a closet, and no one's coming to get us."

"I have a meeting with Bill Hollis at seven thirty to talk about the ferry."

She spun, hopeful. Why hadn't he said so? "Tonight?"

His face fell. "In the morning."

Over twelve hours away. Dread sucked the moisture from her mouth. She needed out of here. Now. "I don't like—" She couldn't make herself say it. Felt stupid. It was a closet—and a pretty big one at that. Normal people were not afraid of closets.

"It's going to be okay. If no one comes in, we'll just sleep here. Nothing bad's going to happen."

"Sleep here?" She couldn't fathom her heart settling enough to allow for sleep.

"The floor'll be a little hard, but we'll make do."

A new thought hit. "How am I going to go to the bathroom? Hello, I'm pregnant."

"Well. There's nothing to drink anyway."

Thankfully she hadn't had anything to drink in

a few hours. "Or eat," she said. As if making the same realization, her stomach growled.

"Maybe there's a granola bar or something. Betty Jean used to keep the office stocked with those. We'll be fine. Have a seat while I get this cleaned up, okay?"

She tried to draw strength from his calm eyes. He wasn't freaking out. Then again he didn't have a pregnant bladder or a fear of tight spaces.

He squeezed her arm, and she squatted down. Might as well help. Not like she was going anywhere, and she needed a distraction.

When everything was back in place, she checked her watch. A whole ten minutes had passed. How was she going to make it for hours? While Daniel rummaged through the shelves, she palmed her aching back and walked toward the door. Maybe . . .

"There's no way to pick it. Or remove the hinges. If there were a way to get you out of here, I would, Jade."

She pulled on the knob and shook the door in its frame. It barely budged. This couldn't be happening. Other than the bathroom and her doctor's appointments, she hadn't been in a small room with a closed door since that night. And she'd had to do deep breathing to get her through those.

"Look, a Nutri-Grain bar." Daniel stood and blew the dust off the wrapper, then wiped it with

the tail of his shirt. "Come on. Come sit down."
He tossed a jumbo package of generic toilet tissue
against the back wall and slid down beside it.

Jade lowered herself onto the package, her back
braced against the wall.

Daniel handed her the Nutri-Grain bar, giving
her a wry grin. "Bon appétit."

"What about you?"

He set his head against the wall. "Had a huge
lunch. I'm still full."

She ripped off the corner, the cellophane
rattling loudly. "You sure?"

"Positive."

Soon the breakfast bar was gone. Now she had
nothing to distract her from the narrow enclosure,
no wider than a hallway, maybe ten feet long. She
dragged in a lungful of air and found her lungs
stiff, unyielding. Maybe if she couldn't see it.
Maybe she could pretend she was someplace else.

She shut her eyes. Darkness closed in, thick
and suffocating. Her heart hammered in her
chest. Her eyes popped open. She shook with
the adrenaline that coursed through her veins.
Despite the chill in the air, her palms grew damp.

How much longer? She checked her watch and
sighed.

"Tell me about the babies," Daniel said.

"The babies?"

"How big are they now?"

She turned her head and met his warm gaze,

soaking in some of his calm. "A pound and a half each—twelve inches. Fully developed hands. They can even touch each other."

He smiled. "I'll bet they're already saying 'He's touching me, Mom.' "

She drew in a long, even breath and blew it out. "Probably. They can hear too."

"Like, womb sounds?"

"That, but also us."

"They can hear us? Right now?"

"Right now."

His gaze fell to her tummy. "Hey, little Nugget." He said softly. "You hear me in there?"

"*Nuggets* you mean. Two of them, remember?"

"The other one is Peanut. I was getting to her."

Jade smiled. "Her?"

He shrugged. "That's just the way I think of them."

It warmed Jade that he thought of them at all. "And Nugget—is Nugget a girl or boy?"

"Both girls. They're going to have their momma's green eyes and musical flair."

"Wouldn't that be something? Maybe they could form a band when they're older." The thought made her smile.

One of the babies moved, and Jade set her hand on her stomach. Soon they were both flopping around. "I think Nugget woke up Peanut."

He watched her belly for movement, a funny look coming over his features.

"Do you—do you want to feel them moving?"

His eyes locked with hers. Blue had never looked so warm. "Sure."

She took his hand and placed it on the side of her stomach, pressing his fingers into the movement. Would he think her belly felt gross?

One of the babies moved.

His eyes darted to hers, widening. A smile lifted the corners of his mouth.

"That was like an elbow or something."

"An elbow, a knee, a heel . . . they poke me with all their limbs."

He kept his hand there while the babies squirmed and poked, a look of wonder on his face. His eyes narrowed in concentration, waiting for the next movement.

When it came, he smiled again. "Nugget or Peanut?"

"Your guess is as good as mine."

"Have you thought about real names? I mean you're welcome to Nugget and Peanut, but—"

"Yeah, maybe something a little more meaningful." She gave a wry grin. "I think something old-fashioned. And I don't want them to sound too much alike."

"No Haley and Kaylee?"

"Uh, no. I'm already worried about telling them apart." The babies hadn't moved for a while. "I guess they're falling asleep again."

"Thanks." He pulled his hand away, taking his warmth with him. "That's amazing."

Jade crossed her arms against the sudden chill. She was going to freeze in here tonight. There was nothing to cover up with unless she wanted to mummify herself with toilet tissue.

"Cold?"

"A little."

He unbuttoned his pinstriped shirt and leaned forward as he tugged it off. A white T-shirt hugged his beefy shoulders and well-defined chest. If there were a local fire fighters' calendar, he'd be on the cover.

Jade looked away, shook her head to clear it. What was wrong with her? She was looking at Daniel like he was a man.

Uh, Jade. He is a man.

He handed her the shirt.

"Thanks." She slipped her arms into it, avoiding his eyes. The shirt swallowed her, and the cuffs, rolled to the elbows on him, fell to her fingertips. She burrowed into the Oxford. It was still warm from his body, and it smelled like him.

She took a deep whiff, wishing for bigger lungs. "Won't you get cold?"

"Nope. Warm-blooded."

His arm did feel warm against hers. He was a virtual furnace.

She settled back against the wall. She was

adjusting to the small space. If she kept her mind off it, maybe she wouldn't freak out again.

Daniel asked about Madison's birthday. The three sisters had gone for manis and pedis at Sassy Nails to celebrate. Jade waved her glittery purple nails at him, and he admired them.

They talked about work and the upcoming ribbon cutting for a new car dealership. He kept her mind busy, the conversation flowing, and the next time she checked, it was almost nine.

"How's the fund-raising going?" she asked when there was finally a lull in the conversation. Daniel had a lot of local support, and his family's connections helped matters, but campaigns were expensive.

He shrugged. "Okay, I guess."

"You're about to run for Congress. It's a big deal, Daniel."

"I know. I don't take it for granted. It's just overwhelming sometimes. People are so disenfranchised, so skeptical, and you can't blame them, you know? It seems like a long uphill climb to Washington, all the glad-handing and speaking and kissing up. I'm tired just thinking about it."

"But you want it, right?"

She didn't expect the pause and looked at him.

He rested his forearms on his knees. "I want to have a positive impact on our world. Politics is the best way for me to do that."

She'd never heard him less than thrilled about his political future. As long as she'd known him, he'd been sure of his destination. "You sound less than excited."

Maybe he was just tired. Between his position as mayor, the campaign stuff, and the fireman thing, he couldn't be getting much sleep.

"It'll be fine."

"What's wrong?"

He shrugged, his big shoulders moving against hers. Maybe he was feeling pressure from his parents. They'd always done that, even at a distance, with school, then college. His parents had been right in the middle of everything during his run for mayor.

"Are you worried about losing?" she asked.

He shook his head. "Never really think about that."

She smiled. Only Daniel. "What then?"

He lowered his legs, crossed his arms, making his biceps bulge. "I love people. I love this country. I want to make it even better, and there are some policies I want to help change. But it's a big sacrifice. I don't want to be like my parents. I don't want to do it the way they did."

"Do what?"

"Family. Parenting." He shook his head. "I don't know."

"It's a lot of travel, but other politicians manage."

"At what cost?"

She thought of how young Daniel had been when he'd come to live with his grandma. How had that boy felt about being left behind? She saw in his eyes the wounds it had left.

"You wouldn't do that," she said.

"I don't think I'm going to do it at all."

"What do you mean?"

He crossed his ankles and lifted a shoulder. "Marriage, parenthood. I'd rather not do it at all than do it badly."

She frowned at him. "You wouldn't do it badly." She studied his faraway eyes. His strong jawline, now lightly covered in stubble. He was not only handsome, that wasn't even half the equation with Daniel. He was kind and loving and generous. It would be a crime not to pass along all that good DNA.

"Just something I've been thinking about. I haven't signed a bachelor covenant or anything."

"What about that woman you're seeing— Courtney?"

He shrugged. "I ended it awhile back. There was nothing there."

He hadn't mentioned it. It broke her heart to think of Daniel forever alone. Would he give up so much for his future? Would the cost be worth it?

She rolled her head toward him. "You deserve a family, Daniel."

He turned toward her, a wry smile on his lips. "I'll have politics to keep me company."

"Politics won't keep you warm at night."

Something flickered in his eyes. Sadness? They drew her right in and held her there. She didn't like to see him this way. He was always optimistic in his own quiet way. Now she could see some deep ache on his face.

His lips gave in to gravity. He really did have nice lips. Bowed on top and full below. His kisses would be soft and tender, heartfelt. She'd already had a brief taste. Her heart beat faster at the thought.

His lips parted.

She snapped her head forward. She'd been staring at his mouth. Staring at Daniel's lips. Heat climbed her neck and settled in her cheeks, fanning outward. So this was what a hot flash felt like.

He was still looking at her. She could feel it. The space seemed smaller, warmer. One was good, the other not so much.

She pulled her knees up, curling into them as far as she could with her stomach. She unbuttoned the collar of the shirt, needing air. Needing more oxygen to keep up with her suddenly racing heart.

"Jade?"

Breathe in. Breathe out. Look at the door, way over there. Don't focus on the side walls. The encroaching shelves. Plenty of room. Nothing's going to happen.

"You okay?"

Relax. In. Out. In. Out. Nothing's going to happen.

"Look at me." Daniel pulled her chin around, holding it tight, a lifeline. Could he see the panic in her eyes? "You're safe. I'm here."

She focused on his eyes. Those mesmerizing blue eyes. Safe. Daniel. She could do this.

"Nothing's going to happen. You're okay. I promise."

She wasn't in Chicago in her shoebox bedroom. She wasn't drugged. Wasn't alone with—*him.* There was no creaking bed, no heavy weight pressing her into the mattress.

Her eyes drifted from Daniel. He tightened his grasp, drawing her focus back to him.

She filled her lungs. Made her breaths slow. Her heart would follow, right? She couldn't be in safer hands. She knew that. Why couldn't her heart figure it out? She stared into his eyes for a solid minute, letting them calm her. Felt the strength of his grasp and the assurance that he was her protector. Her eyes burned at the thought.

"Better?"

She nodded.

He slowly released her chin, still watching her. She'd never had an irrational fear, and she didn't like it. When had she become such a freak?

"I'm fine."

He seemed to test her assertion with his eyes.

"I am."

Did he know what had caused this? Had he put it together? Probably, but she didn't want to talk about it. He seemed to understand that.

"Why don't we go ahead and get settled for the night. I know it's a little early, but we could both use the sleep."

Sleep was good. Sleep would pass the time. She'd wake up, and it would be morning. They'd be out of here.

He was already up, rooting through the shelves. He pulled down a plastic runner and laid it out at her feet, perpendicular. "It's not much, but it'll keep you off the cold floor."

He looked over his shoulder toward the door, then back to her. "Light on or off?"

There might be a light on in the office, but the door was sealed tight. It would be totally dark. "Would you mind leaving it on?"

"I'll pretty much sleep like the living dead either way." He took his spot on the back wall beside her and patted his leg. "Come on."

"What about you?"

He grabbed a bundle of brown paper towels from a nearby shelf and stuck it between the wall and his neck. "Good to go."

"You can't sleep sitting up."

"Sure I can. Come on."

Eyeing him, she stretched out on the runner, her back to the wall, her head on Daniel's thigh. His warmth felt good against her cheek, her shoulder. Now all she had to do was close her eyes and wait for sleep to come.

Chapter Twenty-Nine

A chill passed over Jade. She turned into the pillow, stretching her arm out, curling into the warmth. Better. Releasing a contented sigh, she drifted away again.

A mild backache nudged her from oblivion. On her side, she kicked out her leg to alleviate the pressure and turned into her warm pillow, snuggling deeper, not wanting to wake just yet. Too early. Sleep.

The pillow moved slowly. Up and down. Up and down.

She frowned, then dismissed the thought. A puff of air hit the top of her head. Had she slept with the fan? She didn't remember turning it on. The air came in regular puffs, synchronized with her moving pillow.

Pillows didn't move. They didn't breathe. She opened her eyes. Her face pressed into her white pillow. She frowned at her pinstriped sleeve, curling around her pillow. Not her pajamas. Not her shirt.

Freezing, her eyes traveled down to her pillow, rising and falling intermittently.

Not. Her. Pillow.

Last night rushed back. Her heart kicked into gear. She was lying on Daniel, and not just her head. She took stock of the rest of her. Her cheek pressed into his chest. Her stomach wedged into his side. Her leg flung over his body.

His breath hitched suddenly. He moved under her, turning toward her. Jade froze. His leg swung over her body, his arm came around her, enveloping her in his warmth. Her head rested on his arm. He tucked her under his chin, gave a soft sigh, then his breaths evened out.

Jade stared into the V of his T-shirt, inches away, her eyes wide. She hardly dared to breathe. This wasn't good. She should move away. But her leg was now trapped between his.

She drew in a slow breath, allowing her lungs to expand fully. His manly smell filled her nostrils. She drew in another. She soaked in the comforting weight of his arm, the steady rise and fall of his chest.

Her internal clock said it was too early to get up. They had nowhere to go. And the floor, beyond his embrace, was cold.

He was asleep. What he didn't know wouldn't hurt him, right? She was warm and comfy, all cocooned. And she was sure she had a couple hours of nighttime left. She closed her eyes and willed her muscles to relax.

* * *

"Daniel?"

The voice hovered on the edge of his consciousness. Daniel fought the pull, not wanting to leave his wonderful dream.

Better than wonderful, a dream come true. Jade was with him, her arms wrapped around him. The sweet fragrance of oranges tickled his nose. He sighed deeply, a smile curving his lips.

"Daniel?"

The voice, louder this time, cut through his dreamy state of slumber. He dragged his eyes open, blinking against the brightness, disoriented. His gaze locked onto a bag of coffee beans and a mountain of filters.

The closet. Jade. He found her tucked under his chin, pressed against the full length of him.

Not a dream.

Crap. Not a dream.

The voice wasn't calling for him anymore. He checked his watch. Seven thirty. Bill Hollis. He couldn't let him leave. He began to ease away from Jade, pulling his arm from her waist, his leg from over hers. Their bodies were as tangled as last year's Christmas lights.

Before he could ease his arm out, her eyes opened. She squinted against the light, blinking.

Then she looked up, her eyes fixing on him. Her lips parted.

He backed off so quickly she rolled forward, catching herself with a hand in the suddenly empty space.

"Sorry." He wasn't sure if he was apologizing for the abrupt movement or for practically mauling her in his sleep.

"Is it morning?" She looked adorable, her hair all tousled, her eyes sleepy.

He remembered Bill and jumped to his feet. "Bill's here."

He pounded on the door, praying the man hadn't given up and gone home. "Bill!" He pounded again. "Bill!"

"Did he leave?" Jade asked, sitting up.

"Hope not." He didn't have another appointment until noon, and even then, it was at the coffee shop.

"Daniel?" The male voice cut through the heavy-duty door.

"We're locked in, Bill. Can you get the key from my desk? Center drawer."

"Oh, good gravy. Be right back."

Thank You, Jesus. Daniel exhaled.

"Dibs on the bathroom," Jade said.

He looked back at her. The intense relief on her face was heartening—and depressing as he realized he'd just gotten as close as he would ever come to having Jade all to himself.

Chapter Thirty

Jade shouldered the phone as she scrounged in her desk drawer for a paper clip. "No worries, Mom. Maybe PJ can come."

"Oh, honey." Jade heard the regret in her mom's tone. "PJ's watching the store for me. Maybe we can move to another Lamaze class, just for this week."

"They're all full. It's okay, Mom. I'll figure something out."

"I thought for sure my appointment was tomorrow. I even had it written on my calendar. You know what? I'll just reschedule."

"No, Mom. You'll have to wait weeks to get in to see him. Your health is too important. This isn't a big deal. We probably won't do anything today beyond introductions. I'll just go by myself."

"Are you sure, honey?"

Jade reassured her mom and ended the conversation, hanging up the phone with a frown.

"Everything okay?"

She hadn't heard Daniel return from lunch. He'd been withdrawn since their lock-in a week ago. Probably feeling awkward about the way she'd climbed into his arms and clung to him like a burr on a dog.

"Mom can't make Lamaze class today. I told

you it was during work hours, right? I tried to get in an evening class, but they were full."

Maybe she should drop out. She'd probably end up with a C-section anyway. She was already scheduled for one since twins were rarely in position for a normal delivery.

"No big deal. You can work until midnight to make up for it."

She smiled a little at his joke, already wondering if it would be possible for Madison to leave the clinic early today. Probably not. Jade would just have to go alone. How awkward. A room full of couples, and her.

Ah, well. It was just one time.

"You have someone to go with you?"

Jade opened the document she was typing for Daniel. "Not really. It's fine. Just one class."

She squinted at Daniel's scrawled sentence on the notebook paper, deciphered it, and typed it in.

"You, ah, want me to?"

She kept typing, her mind on the financial details in the paper, the spelling of the word *accrual*. "Want you to what?"

Accrual basis—what did that even mean? Oh, well. Not for her to understand.

"Go with you. To Lamaze."

She looked up, but he was suddenly busy with the file on his desk. Daniel at her Lamaze class? Helping her breathe and whatnot? Was that weird? Too intimate?

More intimate than being entwined on the closet floor like a skein of yarn? "It's at four."

"I know. My schedule's clear after two."

"I saw all those notes from the building department."

"Nothing that can't wait until tomorrow."

"Aren't you on call tonight?"

"Nope."

Her lips twisted. "This won't help the rumor."

He waved her away. "I don't care about that. No one will know anyway."

She wanted to say yes. The rumor had died down, and he was right. It was only one time and all the way in Louisville. It would be much easier walking into that room with someone. Even if he wasn't a significant other.

"If it's too . . . weird . . . that's fine," he said.

"It's not weird. You're practically my brother."

His fingers paused on the file before moving again. If practicing Lamaze with your brother wasn't weird, then why hadn't she considered asking Ryan when her mother canceled?

"Well, like family, anyway. Sure you don't mind, Daniel?"

"Not at all. Besides, I've been craving brisket from that diner outside Louisville. Maybe we can stop afterward."

"All right then." She finished filing, then stood to stretch. "How was your meeting with Bill Hollis? The ferry situation?"

He twirled toward her in his chair. "He thinks we should buy our own ferry and run it to Louisville and Cincinnati."

"Won't that make the operators of the Cincinnati ferry mad? Your dad seemed to think they have powerful connections."

Daniel shrugged. "Appeasing the Crawfords isn't my job. If Chapel Springs needs a ferry, I'll make it happen. I have a meeting next week with Louisville's department of transportation. They might be interested in partnering."

"That'd be great."

"Not only would it provide transportation to and from work and attract tourists, but it would mean jobs for the community and additional revenue. A win-win."

"Can we afford a ferry?"

He nodded. "Bill found a used old-fashioned ferry that would be perfect. If we can get Louisville to go along, even better."

Brisket was the last thing on Jade's mind as they rushed toward the Lamaze room later that afternoon. They'd left on time but construction on 65 had been nearly at a standstill, and now they were ten minutes late.

A dry-erase board hung on the wall beside the door. *Welcome to Lamaze! Cindy Keating, RN, Certified Instructor* it said in loopy cursive letters.

They entered the large room and came face-to-face with a circle of couples. A blond woman with a pixie haircut and elfin smile popped to her feet.

"You must be Jade! I'm Cindy Keating!" Her tiny frame made Jade long for her own pre-pregnancy body. Not that she'd ever been that thin. Or that . . . exuberant.

"Sorry we're late . . . traffic," Jade said.

"Not a problem! Class, this is Jade McKinley. Why don't you introduce us to your handsome partner?"

"Uh—this is my—uh, friend. Daniel."

He nodded. "Hey, everyone."

They nodded and smiled in return.

"Go ahead and find a spot! I'm sorry we've already done introductions—tight schedule, you know."

After they sat in the padded blue seats, Cindy introduced the other six couples, then settled into the teaching portion.

It took awhile to acclimate to Cindy's enthusiasm. Her cheerleader version of the stages of labor was weird. Cindy knew of Jade's twin status and added particular details just for her. Jade had never heard someone referring to her uterus with such enthusiasm. Hearing intimate details of the labor process in front of Daniel made her squirm. He visibly winced at the mention of tearing perineums.

When Cindy finally finished extolling the virtues of Kegel exercises, she capped her dry-erase marker and pulled a media cart front and center. "Movie time! You all are about to experience a live birth!"

Jade darted a glance at Daniel, but his face gave nothing away.

The lights went out.

"Sorry . . ." Jade whispered.

"No worries. Covered all this in EMT training."

Yeah, but not sitting next to her.

Cindy turned on the TV and grabbed the remote. "This is such a beautiful, no-holds-barred view of the birthing process! Y'all are going to love it!"

"Really sorry," Jade said.

The movie started, and Jade watched silently. Daniel seemed frozen to his seat. She couldn't look at him. Could hardly tear her eyes from the screen. Kind of like a traffic accident. Horrifying, yet mesmerizing.

As the woman's labor progressed, sweat beaded on her forehead. Her face scrunched in pain. A grunt followed, opening to a loud guttural sound Jade had never heard from a human being.

Holy Toledo, what was she in for? A C-section was starting to sound like heaven. Her heart quickened. If she had a regular birth, could she do this? She had not one, but two babies to push out.

There was always a girl's best friend—the

epidural. But she'd heard horror stories about not getting them in time or about the anesthesia not working. Why did moms feel the need to share their horror stories?

Just when Jade thought she couldn't take the movie another moment, the baby was born—a boy. He let out a tiny screech, his face scrunching up just as his mom's had moments before. Jade's breath caught.

The movie played on, finally wrapping up. Cindy flipped off the TV and turned on the lights.

"Isn't that just so . . . !" She palmed her heart, blinking hard. "Gets me every time. We'll be practicing all the breathing techniques you saw as well as discussing pain control options, labor positions, and so much more! But first, let's talk about relaxation!"

A few minutes later, the couples were seated on the floor. After briefing them on relaxation basics, she asked the ladies to contract a muscle.

"All right, partners—it's your job to find the tense muscle—go!"

Jade's eyes met Daniel's. "She gets right down to business, doesn't she?"

He tweaked a brow. "Kind of like a very personal scavenger hunt."

"Ha-ha."

"All right, gentlemen! Keep at it. It's your job during labor to recognize tension and help your partner relax! How are we doing?"

"My partner's not cooperating," Daniel whispered.

"Fine," Jade said. "Choose a limb." She tried to contract her calf muscle and couldn't isolate it, so she settled for her thigh. Unfortunately Daniel started with her arm. He wiggled each of her fingers and worked his way up her forearm, pressing lightly, up her bicep, to her shoulder. His fingers trailed up her neck and to her jaw, wiggling it back and forth playfully.

"That's not a limb," she said, her words garbled.

He started on her other arm, working in the same pattern. She gradually relaxed under his slow touch, had to remind her thigh muscle to remain flexed.

"Keep it up, partners!" Cindy said as she walked the room, watching. "Doing great!"

"You better not be cheating," Daniel said after he'd finished both arms.

"I wouldn't cheat. This is serious business."

Jade's toes were next. He wiggled them until she giggled.

"Stop it," she said, but he made a point of lingering on her ticklish spots.

She sent him a withering look and kicked his hand away.

A moment later, his fingers pressed into the hardened muscle.

"Ding, ding, ding," he said.

"Finally." She relaxed the muscle.

He gave her an ornery look. "My turn next?"

He wanted her hands on him? She smacked him on the chest while a flush crawled up her neck.

His lips twitched. "Fair is fair."

Cindy had them move on to the next exercise while Jade's mind turned Daniel's comment over. She couldn't believe he'd said that. Were things changing between them? She remembered their accidental kiss, their night in the closet.

"We have time for one breathing exercise," Cindy said, bringing her thoughts to the present. "Slow breathing!"

Following directions, Daniel settled behind Jade, straddling her body. Jade leaned forward over her pretzel-style legs, visions of the night they'd snuggled rising again in her mind. She'd told herself it was only because she'd been cold. Only because he'd been softer than the floor. But why had she continued thinking about it every night as she lay in her soft, warm bed?

It was the companionship, the comfort and security of being in someone's arms. She was only human. Of course she craved that. She just wasn't going to get it.

"Ladies, lean into your partner!"

"You heard the lady," Daniel said.

Heat climbing into her face, she straightened her legs and leaned into his hard chest.

"Relax all your muscles! Start at your toes

and work your way up just like we did before."

His arms came around her, his hands resting on his knees. His chest rose and fell. His breath stirred the hairs near her ear.

Relax. Right.

She breathed in his nice, clean, manly smell, soaked in the warmth of him against her back. She liked being in his arms. Was that weird? Wrong? She was having feelings she'd never had before. Stirrings she'd never felt before, not with Daniel.

"Relax," he whispered, his breath tickling her ear.

A shiver went down her arms. "I'm trying."

He smoothed his hands down the pebbled skin of her arms, his efforts to help making it worse.

Focus, Jade. Toes. Calves. Thighs . . .

"All right, ladies, let's start some deep breaths! In through your nose, out through your mouth . . . count to five, partners, nice and slow . . ."

"Deep breath," Daniel said softly. "One . . . two . . . three . . . four . . . five."

She expelled the breath as he counted.

"Again," he said. "One . . . two . . . three . . . four . . . five . . ."

The low tone of his voice in her ear, the rumble of his chest against her back, commanded her attention. He'd been a good partner tonight. No matter how awkward or uncomfortable the exercise, he hadn't complained. He was always there for her. He was going to make someone a fine—

She stopped the thought, remembering what he'd said in the closet. She frowned, her breathing on automatic now. Had he been serious about not marrying?

She understood wanting to do things differently from his parents—and he should. But such drastic measures. Surely he could find a compromise.

That's what Jade had tried to do. She didn't want love, but she did want a father for her babies. Of course, that plan hadn't worked out so well.

The two problems, hers and Daniel's, whirled in her mind, mingling and dancing until they merged.

Her breath hitched.

Daniel peeked over her shoulder, still counting.

She picked up breathing where she'd left off, the idea whipping across her mind like a snapped guitar string.

No. It was ridiculous. She and Daniel getting—

She couldn't even finish the thought. Especially now. Here. Wrapped up in his arms like this, smelling his nice clean scent, hearing his low voice rumbling in her ear.

"Excellent! Great job, everyone!" Cindy wrapped up the class a few minutes later.

Jade and Daniel filed out behind the others. When they reached the hall to the parking garage, they separated from the group.

Jade nudged Daniel's shoulder as they walked

through the garage. "I don't care what anybody says, you're a good man."

His eyes laughed. "I now know more about female anatomy than I ever wanted to know."

"You're welcome."

He chuckled, rubbing the back of his neck. When they reached his car, he opened the door. "Up for some of that brisket?"

"Dinner and a movie," she teased. "Can't beat that."

"I'm pretty sure my retinas are permanently scarred."

The diner was nearly empty, and the service was fast. Between work and Lamaze talk, they kept up a steady stream of conversation. Daniel was easy to talk to. He never ran out of things to say, but he knew when to listen. He was thoughtful and compassionate and giving.

On their way home, the idea that had sprung earlier resurfaced. Jade shook her head, looking out the window as the landscape passed. It would never work. Daniel didn't want that, not with her. Not with anyone apparently. But especially not with her. If he'd thought tonight was weird, how about sharing a bathroom, a bed, a lifetime?

Crazy. Insane.

And yet even as he dropped her off, even as she changed into her pajamas, even as she slipped into her lonely bed, the idea hovered like a pesky mosquito.

Chapter Thirty-One

Jade rapped on Madison's door. Inside, the dogs barked. Their feet scampered across the floor, and the door shuddered in the frame as two big heads peeked through the door's half window.

"Down, guys," Madison said through the door, then swung it open. "Hey, this is a nice surprise. Come on in."

"Hey, Sis." Rigsby and Lulu clambered around Jade's legs. The black lab and border collie threw her off balance, and Jade braced herself against the wall.

"Lulu, Rigsby." Madison grabbed their collars. "Get back." The dogs stood aside, tails wagging, tongues lolling out to the side.

Madison palmed Jade's stomach. "Hi, little ones. It's your favorite auntie."

Jade gave a wry grin. Her sisters had already started competing for the position. "Is Beckett around?"

"He's helping Dad with the tractor. I just got off the phone with Mom. She's loving Lamaze, I'll tell you that. Want something to drink?"

Jade plopped down on the plaid sofa. The dogs followed, settling at her feet. "No thanks. I can't stay long." She scanned the room as she petted the dogs. Pretty blue curtains framed the picture window, a braided rug hugged the wood floor, and family pictures graced the walls.

"I like what you've done with the place. It's looking homey."

"Now that the walls aren't stark white and completely barren?"

Jade shrugged. "He was a bachelor."

Madison took the other end of the sofa with a satisfied smile. "Not anymore."

"No, now he's completely smitten. That man can't keep his hands off you."

"We're mutually smitten."

"I'm really happy for you. Both of you."

Madison had struggled with her twin brother's death for years. It was good to see her come out the other side smiling and content. So worth the embarrassment Jade had suffered when she'd thought Beckett was interested in her.

Madison tucked her feet under her. "So what's up? Not like you to drop by on a Wednesday night."

Jade looked out the picture window at the golden leaves of the oak trees. Fall had come quickly, the leaves changing almost overnight. Time was marching on. She was already seven months, and before she knew it, she'd be responsible for two little lives. The thought always made her lungs feel too small.

"Jade?"

She turned to Madison, wondering what her

sister was going to think of her idea. It had seemed so crazy three weeks ago. But the idea had settled in. Now it felt less insane and more . . . sensible. Or maybe Jade was just kidding herself. She'd lost perspective. That's why she was here.

"I wanted to talk to you about Daniel."

Madison tilted her head. Something flickered in her eyes that Jade couldn't quite decipher. Just as quickly it was gone.

"Ever since the whole closet thing . . . no, maybe it was before that, I'm not sure, but definitely by the time he went to Lamaze with me—"

"Daniel went to Lamaze with you? Why am I just now hearing this?"

"It was so awkward. We had to watch The Movie."

Madison's eyes lit a second before her laughter escaped. "Oh, that is hilarious."

Jade glared. "Anyway . . ."

"Sorry. You were saying."

"I've been wondering about something lately. I wanted to run it by you."

Madison's eyes twinkled. "Are you two secretly dating? Do you have feelings for him?"

"What? No." Sure, her thoughts had run wild once or twice. He was a man, and she was a woman. They spent a lot of time together. It was only natural.

Madison's face fell. "Oh. Sorry. Go on."

"I guess you're actually not too far out of the ballpark. I was . . . well . . . this idea . . . it seemed stupid but . . . I don't know . . . the more I think about it . . . you might think . . . but that's only because—"

"Jade. Spit it out."

Jade took a cleansing breath. "I'm thinking of asking Daniel to marry me."

Madison's lips fell into a straight line. They parted. Her eyes fell at the corners. "I'm confused."

"I know it seems crazy, but—"

"You just said you didn't have feelings for him. Right . . . ?"

"Well, of course I love him. He's Daniel."

"But you're not *in* love with him."

Jade's chin notched up. "Not all marriages start with head-over-heels gushy love. Look at Grandma and Grandpa. They were just friends, matched up by their parents, practically an arranged marriage. And look how happy they were together."

"That was fifty years ago."

"The principles still apply. What? You think we'd stand less of a chance than the couples who marry for love? Just look at Ryan and Abby. They were madly in love when they got married, and look at them now. Game over. Ryan still hasn't recovered."

"They were young."

"Fifty percent of marriages end in divorce."

"Exactly. Marriage is hard under normal circumstances."

"Who's to say what's normal? Years ago arranged marriages were normal, and there were practically no divorces back then. In biblical times—"

Madison popped to her feet and walked toward the window. "You can't do this, Jade."

"Why are you getting upset?" She couldn't see her sister's face but noted the straight line of her shoulders, the crossed arms. "I know it seems crazy at first, but if you'd just listen—"

Madison turned. "You're just scared right now. Worried about motherhood. But this isn't fair to Daniel. He deserves to be loved. Really loved. Not some platonic, watered-down version. And you deserve that too, Jade."

Jade stood. "That's just it, though, Madison. He doesn't even plan on marrying."

Her silhouetted expression was impossible to see. "What?"

"I won't go into it—it's not my story to tell— but I think this would be good for him. He's about to become a national political figure. I would be there for him. What kind of a lonely life would he have with no family? He deserves better than that. I do love him, you know I do. Just not in that way."

Madison's lashes swept down as she studied the floor. "You haven't brought this up to him?"

"No."

Madison's eyes swept back up. "I don't think you should. Think about the awkward position you'd put him in. You're pregnant with twins and feeling the need to give your babies a father, security. I get that, I do, but he's going to understand that too. And he's going to feel pressured to say—"

"No. No, I won't pressure him. I'll let him know I'm fine either way, that it won't change anything. And anyway, if anyone understands what it's like to be raised without a father, it's Daniel. His dad was never there for him."

"And yet he turned out great. You can do this on your own, Jade."

"But why should I when it'll work out so well for both of us?"

"Do you really think you're cut out to be a politician's wife?"

Her back went up. "Hey. I can be personable and charming when I want to be."

"That's not what I mean. All the fancy dinners, all the sucking up and playing nice. It would wear you out. You're very authentic."

"So is Daniel, and he manages."

"Jade, don't do this. Be patient. God has someone for you. Someone who'll love you and your babies. You have to trust Him."

"Maybe *this* is God's plan, did you ever think about that?"

"This is ridiculous."

Jade frowned, her shoulders slumping. Daniel was practically family already. She'd expected some skepticism, but not this.

"I'll think about it. But you can't say anything. Not even to Beckett." Last thing she needed was word spreading around the family before she did anything.

Madison sighed. "I won't."

A few minutes later Jade pulled her car from the gravel drive, her mind unsettled. She hated that Madison had been against the idea. Because the more she'd tried to convince her sister, the more convinced she'd become that it was the right thing for both of them.

She thought about what Madison had said about God's plan. Did God even have a plan for her? The way her life was going, it didn't seem like any kind of plan. More like random acts of trauma.

A terrible thing had happened, and now she had to make her own plans. But Madison apparently didn't understand that. Jade wasn't looking for happily-ever-after, and neither was Daniel. Maybe that's what most people wanted, but the very thought shot terror into Jade's heart. Her relationship with Daniel was appealing. Safe and comfortable. Moreover, her children would feel loved and wanted. They'd grow up secure and well-adjusted. Loved.

Someday they'd know about their birth father, when they were old enough to understand. But they'd grow up with the love of two parents and all the security that went with it. And Daniel would have the family he deserved. She did love the guy. Being good to him would come naturally.

She thought back to the closet, to how it had felt, being in his arms. She could feel that way every night. She'd almost given up on having that. But it was within her grasp. If only Daniel could see the many mutual benefits.

Maybe Madison couldn't see the plan's perfection, but it wasn't her decision. It was Jade's and, ultimately, Daniel's. If he was uncomfortable with it, then that was it. It was over. But if he embraced the idea, it could be the answer to both their prayers.

Chapter Thirty-Two

Daniel lowered the bar to his chest. Blowing out, he pressed the weight up. The loud, driving beat of "Whispers in the Dark" filled his house, bouncing off the walls in a wild cacophony that matched his mood.

He pressed the weight up again, straining, pushing himself. His shoulders burned. A drop of sweat trickled down his temple and into his damp hairline. Despite his fatigue he lowered the bar, sucked in a few ragged breaths, and pushed it up again. A long groan escaped as he strained against the weight, the sound mingling with the insane guitar solo.

He lowered the bar to the cradle, his breaths fast and hard. His pecs burned, and his shoulders needed a rest. But he rose from the bench and lifted the bar behind his head, balancing it on his shoulders.

If he worked hard enough, sweated profusely enough, maybe he could forget. Forget the frustrating meeting with the board of education, forget the unreasonable personalities that had made his left eye twitch, forget the fact that he was cooped up in an office with the woman of his dreams, a woman who had no idea he was head over heels for her.

He closed his eyes and focused on the heavy beat of the chorus, letting it drive him through a set of punishing squats. He'd thought he could handle it. Most days he could. He could keep his eyes, his hands to himself, stay focused on work. He could almost pretend it wasn't killing him.

Then there were days like today.

When everything seemed to go wrong, when it seemed like God was deliberately tweaking his last nerve by dangling the unattainable in front of him 24/7. Days when even a good workout couldn't clear his head or work off the steam.

His thigh muscles quaking, he lifted the bar again and started another set. The song built into a raging mix of driving drums and fast guitar licks, like a fireworks finale, ending with dramatic flair.

The sound of his hard breaths filled the space between songs. That's when he heard the knock on his door.

Daniel lifted the bar over his head, dropping it to the mat. His muscles quivered with fatigue as he walked into the dimly lit living room.

It wasn't late, but October had ushered in earlier sunsets. Through the living room window, the last bit of daylight streaked the sky with muted, fading colors over the river.

"Looking for Angels" began, the music filling the empty spaces of his house.

He reached the door as another knock sounded.

Jade stood on his stoop, her fist still raised. One look at her beguiling smile, one whiff of her spicy, exotic scent, and he wanted to scream at the temptation thrown in his face yet one more time today.

"Hey," she yelled over the music. "Got a minute?"

Her green eyes, all wide and vulnerable, made his jaw clench. This wasn't her fault. "Sure. Come on in."

She brushed past, making the skin at the back of his neck tighten. He pushed the door closed, wiping the sweat from his face with the bottom of his T-shirt. When he turned the music down, the room seemed to vibrate in the virtual silence.

"Skillet, huh? Love the strings. I'm interrupting your workout."

"I was finishing up." He grabbed two water bottles from the fridge. "Drink?"

"Sure."

Normally he would've poured her tea, but tonight he did the easy thing.

"Thanks," she said as he handed her the bottle. She dropped into the corner of the leather sofa.

He took the other end, watching her uncap the bottle and take a sip. Her hair fell away from her face as she tilted her head back, calling attention to her slender neck. Her white filmy shirt was fitted on top and cinched just under her breasts with a wide band.

Daniel looked away, downed a quarter of the bottle. Why was she here? Wasn't it enough that he had to pretend all day?

She set the water on the coffee table. Her toe tapped a beat that was too fast for the power ballad. She clutched her bag to her stomach, and his eyes settled there a moment, on her rounded tummy, guilt pricking him hard. She was pregnant with twins through no fault of her own, living in a—*let's call it what it is*—seedy apartment on the bad side of town, and he was having a pity party about his bad day.

You're a real jerk, Dawson.

He watched her twist her thumb ring. Something was bothering her. Maybe he could stop being so self-centered for two seconds and figure out what it was.

"What's wrong, Squirt?"

She winced a little. He hadn't called her that in months. Wasn't sure why it slipped out now. Maybe the need to keep that barrier in place.

Something was there, bubbling inside. He could see it in her tapping foot, her scrunched brows. He wondered if she was going to quit. The thought made his heart flounder in his chest like a live bass in the bottom of a boat.

Idiot. You were just moaning about too much time with her.

That was probably it, though. She'd gotten a new job, more money, better benefits. Something that didn't bore her to tears. Of course she had to take it. She had the babies to think of. But she was afraid he'd be upset.

"Just tell me, Jade. It's okay."

Or would be once he got through the withdrawal. How would he face his office without her sweet little jabs, her dry humor, her reluctant smile? It seemed inconceivable she'd ever been gone a year. Inconceivable that he'd survived without seeing her, hearing her voice for a year.

His gut clenched tight at the thought of going through that again.

"I, uh . . ." Her eyes bounced off him, settling back on her busy fingers. "I have a proposition."

He frowned. They weren't the kind of words that preceded "putting in my two weeks' notice." Daniel angled himself into the opposite corner of the couch, feeling the need for distance.

"Go on." He wondered if he'd regret the words. There was a humming energy in the room that had nothing to do with the music playing quietly in the background.

She took another drink, not stopping until the bottle was half-empty and crackling with lost volume. A drop of water clung to her lower lip. She blotted it with the back of her hand.

"You can say no." She met his gaze.

The fear he saw there made his mouth go dry.

"I want you to understand that. It won't change anything or upset me in any way. I want what's best for *you*." Her eyes and tone drove home her point. "Okay, Daniel?"

He angled his head away from her. "What are we talking about here?" Even he heard the wariness in his voice. But it was nothing compared to the dread churning in his stomach.

Her eyes clung to his. Not like she wanted to look at him, but like she should. Like it was the right thing, the courageous thing, to do.

Her chin tipped up. "Don't say anything until

I'm done, okay? Just let me get it out, and then you can tell me that I've completely lost my marbles, okay?"

"You're freaking me out."

She gave a wry laugh. "Sorry. I don't know why I'm so nervous, because it's fine either way. There's no wrong answer here so—"

"Just say it, Jade." Before he dropped dead of heart failure. Before he reached out and smoothed away the creases marring her forehead and forgot she was just his friend and employee.

"You know how when we were in the closet you said you didn't want to marry? How your career in politics didn't support the kind of family you wanted?"

His chest tightened. "Yeah . . ."

She started on the pinky ring, watching as she twisted it. "Well, I wondered if maybe something else would work. Deep down, I know you want a family. You saw your mom choose her husband over you to the point that she practically abandoned you here in Chapel Springs. I know you suffered for that, and I'm sorry. She should've stayed. Even if your dad had to be gone a lot. You needed her, and she wasn't there." She looked at him, her hand stilling on her stomach. "I would never do that."

"I know you wouldn't." He'd never thought it for a second. Not even after he'd learned how she'd conceived. His mom wore motherhood like a fancy shawl, but Jade would wear it like a second skin.

"I know you dated that one woman in DC—Courtney?—so I don't think you're completely set against the idea of marriage. I can't help but think you dated her because you can't quite give up on the idea. And you shouldn't. There are so many things you'd miss. Things like companionship and a real home to come back to. What about warm meals, and laughter, and support?"

Was she trying to encourage his relationship with Courtney? Is that what this was about? She was pushing him off on another woman? Swell.

"What are you getting at, Jade?"

She drew in a breath, and he imagined her counting to five. She blew it out just as slowly, and he wished he were counting for her like in Lamaze class so he could speed this up.

She met his gaze. "I'm talking about us. Getting married. You and me."

Everything seemed to stop. His thoughts, his heart, his breath. Even the music paused. Then his throat closed. His breathing resumed, shallow and erratic. His heart made up for lost time.

He'd heard wrong. He had to have. He shook his head as if his ears were waterlogged. But they weren't waterlogged, they were information-logged.

"I—I know what you're thinking."

He nearly laughed. She couldn't possibly. *He*

didn't know what he was thinking. His brain had malfunctioned.

"But just hear me out."

She started on some story about her grandparents, but he couldn't focus. All he could think of was how wonderful it would be to have Jade for himself. To have his ring on her finger. Have her by his side. Quiet suppers and bathroom sink sharing and bickering over closet space. Boat rides and grocery trips and sheet wars. And later . . . school programs, family devotions, Saturday morning cartoons.

He reined in his thoughts with a sharp tug. The images, as wonderful as they seemed, were a lie. Maybe not a lie, but a surface view. Inside, deeper down, was the truth. Jade wouldn't be his. Not really. She loved him, but not the way he loved her. She wouldn't want him physically, the way he longed for her. That sure wasn't part of this "proposition."

The line would be drawn at the bedroom door, and who could blame her? She wouldn't make love to a man she viewed as a brother.

And where did that leave him? She'd be his on paper and before God and man. But her heart would never be his. She'd called it a proposition, but really it was more of an invitation to both heaven and to hell.

If working with her was frustrating, how would it be to live with her? Knowing she was his, but not really? So close to the real thing and light years from what he wanted.

But as close to the real thing as you're ever going to get, Dawson.

He couldn't believe this was happening. *Thanks a lot. Thanks for dangling this impossible temptation under my nose.* He wasn't sure if he was talking to God or to the vague mysteries of the universe that seemed intent upon stealing his sanity.

He could feel the walls closing in, his throat closing up. His clothes felt constricting, the dampness making his skin itch.

He jumped to his feet and walked toward the window where he could see the great stretch of space across the river. The wind rippled the water, dappling it with the last light of the day. His hand palmed the back of his neck, squeezing the tightness.

"You're mad."

"No I'm not," he said automatically. He was frustrated, afraid, confused, tense, and torn. But mad?

Okay, maybe he was mad. Maybe he'd just been offered a choice no man should have to make. A choice of A or B, when he desperately needed C. It was like the "Would you rather" game. Would you rather eat a bucket full of worms or drink a glass of vinegar every day for the rest of your life?

Neither. He wanted neither of these things.

He wanted C. *Why can't I have C, God? Or even no option at all?* He wished he could rewind time and stop the question. He didn't want this choice. It wasn't fair to ask him to make it.

"I didn't mean to upset you. I meant what I said, Daniel. If the answer's no, it's okay. No big deal."

No big deal. Marry her or not. Have the chance of a lifetime with the woman who owned his heart or lose her forever.

"Talk to me." Her voice quivered like the surface of the water. "What are you thinking over there?"

He needed to gather his wits. He wasn't sure he could say no to what she offered. Didn't know if he was strong enough. But maybe he could make her rescind the offer.

When he managed to ease the tension from his face, he turned around, shoving his hands deep into the pockets of his basketball shorts. "I don't even fit the criteria."

"Criteria?"

"Your list. The one you shoved in my face when you asked me to play Cupid." *Tone it down, Dawson.* "I'm not what you want. I'm not thirty, for starters." Why'd he start with the lamest thing on the list?

She waved his answer away. "You're plenty

mature. You're good with kids, you're financially secure, you're rooted in Chapel Springs."

"No, I'm not. My family doesn't live here, they live in DC. And I'll be traveling. A lot."

"But that's okay with me. I'll be home with the kids, waiting for you when you come home."

Unbidden, the image formed, and an ache unfurled in his chest. Him coming up those outside stairs, suitcase in hand, weary from his flight. Opening the door to the sound of laughter, the smell of Jade, the feel of her warm embrace. His eyes hit the floor before she read his thoughts.

He should tell her. Right now. That he *did* want to marry her. That he loved her, and he'd spend the rest of his life proving it, making her love him back.

Then he remembered Cody. Remembered the way she'd trashed him like yesterday's newspaper when he'd professed his love. How she'd avoided him ever since.

Yes, Daniel could tell her the truth, and it would end all this. No proposition. No choice. No Jade.

She'd quit work. They'd become awkward strangers at her parents' house until the discomfort became too much to bear. Then he'd stop going, and Jade would be gone from his life, once and for all.

He could end it all. Right now. She'd make the

decision for him. All he had to do was speak up.

He crossed his arms, and made himself redraw the homecoming scenario with brutal honesty. How, upon his return, she'd lean in for a shoulder hug and pull away too early. How quickly her mind would return to supper cooking on the stove top while his lingered on a brief touch that was destined to go nowhere. How it would feel to have her beside him in bed, only a touch away, and not have the privilege of that touch. He could hardly bear the thought.

He felt her hand now on the bare flesh of his bicep. His muscle twitched.

"Please don't be angry."

She wasn't being fair, and he was going to call her on it. "What about the vows, Jade?"

"What do you mean?"

"The vows. Forsaking all others . . . ?"

She blinked. Those green eyes. Not fair.

"I'd keep them, Daniel. Of course I would. I hope you would too."

"That's not what I—" He palmed his neck, making her hand fall away. Good. He couldn't think straight with her touching him. "You expect me to go the rest of my life without any hope of ever—" His jaws clenched hard. He was just a man.

"Of course not. Our marriage would be perfectly . . . normal in that way." She swallowed hard. Her eyes fell as her cheeks bloomed with color. "I mean, you know, if you wanted it to be."

He turned away, needing space. Needing air. It was flipping hot in here. He was suffocating.

He ran his hand through his hair. "I have to go."

He scanned the room for his keys, seeing his surroundings for the first time in what felt like hours. His shoes in the corner, his couch, his living room. He was already home. He shook his head, trying to clear it.

"*You* have to go." He grabbed her bag off the couch and dropped it in her arms.

"Daniel, I'm sorry."

He opened the front door. "I'll think about it, Jade. I just—you need to go."

She neared, standing too close, and squeezed his arm. "Let's just forget I asked, okay? It's not worth this. I don't want to lose your friendship."

He steeled himself against her touch. "I said I'll think about it." His tone was harsher than he'd intended.

She flinched as she turned away.

He closed the door as soon as she was over the threshold. He was pretty sure he wouldn't think about anything else for days.

Chapter Thirty-Three

Jade remembered Daniel being mad at her only two times. When she'd returned to Chapel Springs after avoiding him for a year and when she was eighteen. He was home from college on fall break, and she'd begged to borrow his car for the homecoming dance. His parents had bought him a new Mustang when he'd graduated high school, and she wanted to surprise Aaron with it.

After the dance, she and Aaron went back the long gravel drive of the Christmas tree farm and parked. Their kisses had become progressively passionate, and his hand inched up her bare thigh, going under her new skirt. He didn't complain when she stopped him, but he tried once more before she finally told him it was time to go.

After she dropped Aaron off, she drove the car back to Daniel's. When he got in, she scooted across the seat so he could drive her home. The interior light flooded the darkness.

She knew she wore a dreamy smile as she greeted him. She looked out over the expansive lawn of his grandmother's estate. She'd spent the evening in Aaron's arms, and all she wanted now was to go home and review every single thing about their night.

She hadn't noticed how quiet the car had gotten until Daniel spoke. "What's this?"

His harsh tone jerked her back to earth. He was pinching a square packet in his fingers over the empty space between them.

"What the heck, Jade?"

"What's—No, we didn't . . . it's not mine."

His eyes narrowed on her, and he seemed more like a dad than a pseudo big brother. She raised her chin a notch. "It's *your* car."

He rolled his eyes. "It's not mine."

"Well, it's not mine either."

"I know it's not yours, it's that boyfriend of yours." A shadow chased across his face, and those blue eyes of his impaled her. "What are you doing, Jade?"

"Obviously not much," she said, grabbing the package. "Since it's *unopened*."

He glared at her for another minute before closing his door. The light went off, hiding the flush she knew had climbed her cheeks. She was stuck with the packet now, and she didn't want to be. She couldn't believe Aaron had brought it. Did he think she was ready for that? Was he? Is that where tonight would've gone if she hadn't curbed his wandering hand?

Gravel spit under the tires as Daniel pulled down the lane, his hands flexed around the steering wheel.

Suddenly she wondered what he'd do with this

private and embarrassing discovery. "You won't say anything, will you?"

Waves of disapproval rolled off him. "You're too young for that."

She didn't like being told what to do, especially not by someone who was continually shoving her youth down her throat. "I *know*."

"Well, *he* doesn't."

"You better not say anything to Ryan." Ryan would tell Mom, or he'd confront Jade and make her wish she could crawl under a rock.

His voice softened. "I won't. Just promise me you won't—do anything. You're better than that, and if he doesn't get that, he doesn't deserve you."

His words warmed her even now as she pulled into the alley behind the office. She was late. She didn't even remember turning off her alarm, possibly due to the fifty times she'd used the bathroom last night. When she finally woke, it was eight thirty. She'd taken the world's fastest shower, throwing her hair into a sloppy updo and grabbing the first thing she'd touched in her closet.

She regretted that now. The top was loose enough on her belly, but the fitted bodice was too snug for her enlarged breasts.

She hoped she arrived before Daniel. She needed a moment to settle in, make some tea, clear her head. The weekend had dragged by. She hated this thing hanging between them. Had wished a thousand times she'd kept her big mouth shut. It couldn't have been more obvious he wasn't interested in her proposal. He'd only promised to think it over to appease her.

She couldn't even blame him. She'd done a terrible job of explaining herself. She'd talked in circles, making little sense. No wonder he'd looked so confused. As she'd prepared for the conversation, she'd tried to anticipate every possible reaction. She'd feared he'd suggest a straitjacket, or even laugh at her idea. She'd suspected he'd be turned off at the thought of being with her physically. But anger had never figured into the equation. He must think her the most selfish woman in the world. Maybe she was.

He'd left Saturday morning for a meeting with his fundraising manager in Indy. He'd been due back last night. She'd thought he might come over or call. She wanted this settled, couldn't stand Daniel being mad at her. She'd nearly texted him several times.

But he'd been pretty clear about needing space. And now they faced a long awkward day together, pent up in the office.

She pulled into her slot, heaving a sigh when she saw the empty lot. Grateful for a few minutes' reprieve, she unlocked the front door, started the tea, and settled in at her desk.

The first message on voice mail made her pause. "Hey, it's me. I got hung up in Indy. I have a meeting that was delayed until Monday. I have a ten o'clock and lunch meeting on the calendar. Could you reschedule those for later this week? I'll be back in the office tomorrow. Thanks."

She listened to the message again, listening for tone instead of content. He didn't sound angry. Almost normal. A little distant or distracted? Maybe he was okay. Maybe she hadn't ruined things between them.

The day dragged worse than the weekend. She rescheduled Daniel's appointments, answered phone calls, and worked on a mailer. The office was quiet without Daniel. Quiet and boring.

By the time she drove home she was exhausted, the mental battle wearing her down. The babies pressed on her bladder, her back ached, and she wanted to climb into bed and pull the covers over her head.

Her rumbling stomach derailed her plan. While she was reheating last night's spaghetti, Izzy called, distraught over some guy. Jade consoled her, talking until dark. When she hung up, she changed into the pink maternity pajamas Mom had bought and stuffed her swollen feet into her fuzzy green slippers.

Overhead, the elephants were performing tricks. Going to bed early was probably futile. She took a long, thirsty drink of water and placed the bottle back in the fridge. She'd regret that last sip in a few hours.

She flipped off the lights and was almost to her bedroom door when a quiet rap sounded on her door. It wasn't late, but it was a work night, and even her family rarely stopped over without calling or texting. Whoever it was knew she was home, since she'd just turned out the lights.

Her heart in her throat, she approached the door and leaned into the peephole, her heart thumping hard.

Daniel stood on the other side, dark head down, eyes fixed on the ground. Her pulse picked up as she leaned away. She drew a steadying breath, unlocked the door, and swung it open.

His head came up, his eyes sweeping down her pajama-clad body.

"Hey," she said.

His eyes stopped at her fuzzy slippers, then darted to his watch. "Sorry. I should've called. You're ready for bed."

She shrugged. "Just getting comfy. Come on in." She opened the door and he brushed past, making a wide path. "Want something to drink?"

"No thanks." He perched on the edge of the recliner, not meeting her eyes. "Sorry to bail on you today. Any trouble rescheduling those appointments?"

She shook her head. "One's on Thursday, the other's Friday."

He leaned forward, hands clasped between his knees. "Good. Good. Any problems?"

She shook her head. "It was pretty quiet. Your trip went well?"

"Yep. Just fine."

The dread that had been building all weekend, swelling throughout today, gained dangerous momentum. So this was how it was going to be. She'd wanted an end to the tension, hadn't she?

She flipped on the lamp and curled into the corner of the sofa, pulling a pillow into her belly as if she could shield herself from his rejection.

It's not like you didn't see it coming, Jade.

She should focus on salvaging their relationship. Getting things back to normal. Was that even possible?

The least she could do was make it easy on him. She wished she'd thought ahead, had something planned. But then she'd done that last time and look how that had turned out. She inhaled deeply, smelling the clean, fresh scent he'd carried in with him.

"Listen, Daniel." She could hear the tension in her voice. "I—I made a mistake. I've been torturing myself with this all weekend. The last thing I wanted to do was put you on the spot or make you feel uncomfortable or like you had to—"

"Yes."

"—Step in and save the day, and I never wanted you to feel—"

"Yes, Jade."

"—Taken advantage of, because our friendship means—" Jade heard his words belatedly. She frowned, taking the pause to breathe because somehow she'd forgotten to do that.

"What?" she asked.

"I said yes." His lips twitched a little as his eyes caught hers. "This makes three times now."

Her breath caught as she stared into his eyes, wondering if she misunderstood. If wishful thinking misconstrued his words. Had she asked a question while she'd been rambling?

"Yes?"

He hiked a brow. "It was a yes or no question, right?"

Now she was really confused. Maybe she *had* asked something. She reviewed her words, but it was all a blur.

"The proposition? Friday? Ringing a bell?"

"You mean . . . *yes?*" The word squeaked out. Yes, he wanted to marry her? Be her husband, the father of her babies, her partner, her lifelong mate?

Something flickered in his eyes. "Unless you've changed your mind."

"But you—when you left—I thought—What happened to—*Why?*"

He studied her for what felt like forever, until

heat flooded into her ears, making them burn. He'd been angry. She'd thought she'd be lucky just to salvage their friendship.

His blue eyes pierced her. "Second thoughts, Jade?"

"*No*. You just seemed so upset . . . I thought—"

Her giddy thoughts and rapid heart confirmed her conviction. She'd told herself all weekend it had been a mistake, but that was only because she thought she'd lost Daniel. But now, with the possibility of this actually happening, she wanted nothing more.

"Maybe I want the same thing as you," he said, finally answering her question.

"A father for your babies?"

His lips twitched again. He settled back in the recliner, tented his hands under his chin. "What you said makes a lot of sense."

"It did?"

"I love the idea of a family to come home to. I just never wanted all the conflict my parents had. Early on, Mom hated Dad being gone so much, and they fought all the time. Then she left me with Grandma and went off with him. I don't want that for any kids of mine. With you, I wouldn't have to worry about that."

"I won't fight you on the travel—I know what your career entails. And I'd never leave my kids."

Our kids? This was going to take some adjusting.

"Exactly."

Her thoughts turned outside this room. "What about—you know, the rumor. Won't this make people believe . . . ?"

"I don't care what people think. If they want to believe the babies are mine, they can. We'll know the truth and tell the truth, that's all we can do."

"And your parents?"

"What about them?"

"They don't like me."

"They don't know you."

She pursed her lips. "They're going to hate this idea."

He left the recliner and sank onto the middle of the sofa, facing her. His knee, touching hers, comforted. The soft glow of the lamp lit his face.

"They're hardly in a position to advise me on marriage. This is our decision, not theirs. What about your family?"

She grabbed the hand that rested on his thigh. It was big and warm. His thick fingers, a hindrance on the guitar, felt sturdy and capable in hers.

"They already think of you as a son. You know that."

"That was before I took their daughter away."

"You're not taking me anywhere. You're already stuck going to all the family gatherings. At least you know what you're getting into."

"I love your family."

She heard the tremor in his voice and knew what he was thinking. She suspected they were more his family than his own were. If something went wrong between him and Jade, he couldn't bear the thought of losing them.

She squeezed his hand. "They love you too. That's never going to change."

"What are we going to tell them?"

"What do you mean?"

He gave a wry smile. "This isn't exactly your typical marriage."

"It is in every way but one. That's between the two of us. I don't see why they have to know details."

"They're going to ask questions. Want to know when we fell in love and how I proposed and what our first kiss was like—I know how your sisters are."

"We've loved each other forever, and I asked you to marry me, and . . . we'll have to see how the first kiss goes." The accidental one didn't count. The heat in her ears flared again. She hoped they weren't the color of tomatoes. She was conscious of his knee against hers, of her hand clasped in his. His touch made her skin hum.

"When will we tell them?" he asked.

She bit the inside of her mouth. At the barbecue? It was four days away, but maybe time was good. Give Daniel a chance to think things through, be certain. She wanted him to be sure.

"Friday? PJ will be home, so we could tell them all at once."

He nodded, his eyes inscrutable. "They're going to ask when."

"A wedding date? What do you think?"

"I assumed you'd want to marry before the babies come?"

Did she? She hadn't given it much thought, had thought it was a moot point. She was seven and a half months.

She shook her head. "I don't think so. I don't want to rush. And I'd really like to fit in a dress that doesn't resemble a tent."

He smiled warmly. "Whatever you want."

He was so good to her. He'd be a wonderful husband and father. She was going to be the best wife he could ask for. She was going to spoil him like he deserved. But first she was going to be sure.

"Daniel, if you . . . if over the next several days you change your mind . . . I just want you to know it's okay. I do love you, and that's never going to change."

He lifted the hand still held in his and kissed the tender flesh of her inner wrist. Gooseflesh skated down her arms.

"I won't change my mind." His words were a pact, the look in his eyes a signature on the dotted line.

She couldn't tear hers away from his. They were so blue, so mesmerizing.

He leaned forward an inch. "Seal the deal?" he whispered.

Her pulse kicked up as her eyes darted to his beautiful lips, so full and nicely shaped. Would they be as soft as they looked? Would it be weird, kissing Daniel for real? Her thoughts flashed back to the accidental kiss, back to their night in the closet. She didn't think so.

She shrugged. "My sisters will ask." She leaned in, meeting him halfway. She was entering territory that could never be taken back. It should scare her senseless. But somehow the thought of not kissing him was worse.

Their lips met tentatively. The lightest of brushes. And yes. Yes, his lips were as soft as they looked. Pliable and warm as they caressed hers in a touch too delicate to make her shiver. Too gentle to shake her all the way to her core. And yet it did.

He made another pass as his scent filled her nostrils. Daniel. Familiar. She wondered if his hair was soft too, how the day's stubble on his jaw would feel against the sensitive flesh of her palm. She fisted her hands in her lap, quaking with restraint.

He pulled away too soon. Could he hear her heart pounding in the quiet? See the flush of her cheeks?

His eyes questioned her.

She worked hard to school her features. "Not bad, Dawson. I think I can give a satisfactory report." Somehow her voice was smooth and calm, not a hint of the desire that flared inside.

* * *

Satisfactory. Less than Daniel hoped for, more than he deserved.

He wished he could step inside Jade's mind. It had been all he could do to pull away when he'd only wanted to deepen the kiss. When his fingers had ached to thread into her hair, skim the smooth planes of her face. He deserved a flipping trophy.

He had to go slow. There was too much at stake. He couldn't scare her away. Already he was afraid his feelings were apparent in the reverence of the kiss, in the way he couldn't tear his eyes from her beautiful face.

He cleared his throat. "You might want to sell it a little harder with your sisters."

"I'll take care of them, don't you worry."

But he did worry. He'd done little else today, this weekend. There was plenty to worry about.

She yawned, covering her mouth, then gave him a sheepish look. Her eyes looked sleepy, her skin pale. Was she getting enough rest?

He patted her pajama-clad leg, needing to touch her again. He could get used to this. "I should let you get to bed."

Someone had to sleep. It wasn't going to be him. He had so much adrenaline pumping through him, he didn't know if he'd ever need sleep again.

She walked him to the door in her cute fuzzy slippers, her purple toenails sticking out. He turned at the door and pulled her into a careful hug, smiling at the way her belly pressed into him. He felt her breath against the curve of his neck and suppressed a shiver.

Voices sounded through the thin walls, someone shouting, an argument. She couldn't feel very safe here. Not after what she'd been through. He didn't want to leave her here alone. His arms tightened.

Soon, Dawson.

He dropped a kiss on her head and made himself let her go. "See you in the morning. Lock up behind me."

"I will. Night."

On the way home, his heart pounded. He could still feel Jade's lips on his, still feel her pressed against him. He'd dreamed of that kiss for years. Tonight it had happened. Better yet, she was going to marry him. She was going to share a life with him.

She was going to be his.

The thought filled an aching hole inside, made his throat dry.

His.

His to touch. His to hold. His to make love to. *Is this really happening, God?* It seemed too good to be true.

She doesn't feel the same as you.

The unwanted thought surfaced, but he pushed it firmly down. He didn't want to think about that. She did love him. Maybe it wasn't quite the same, but it was close enough. The closest he'd ever dreamed of having, and he was going to take it. He'd be a fool not to.

Chapter Thirty-Four

Daniel parked behind Ryan's truck at the McKinley home. He and Jade had come directly from work.

He looked across the car at her. He didn't know which of them he was more nervous for. "You ready for this?"

"Are you?" Jade asked.

"Asked you first."

"They'll be happy for us, you'll see. If maybe a bit confused? We haven't even dated. Maybe we should've dated."

"We work together. We've known each other forever, which is kind of the purpose of dating."

"True." Her head swung to him, her beautiful green eyes widening. "A ring. I don't have a ring."

"We'll tell them we're shopping for one tomorrow. I want you to have what you want, anyway."

"Okay. Okay, that's good."

He reached for the door handle. "Ready?"

She gave him a nod and got out.

Leaves crunched under their feet as they strolled toward the backyard, following the sounds of laughter, the smack of the basketball on the concrete pad. It wouldn't be long and they'd be moving the party indoors for the winter. They'd replace basketball with board games and grilled burgers with roast beef or lasagna. And Daniel would be a part of the family. A real part.

Jade pulled her sweater against the cool October air. Daniel resisted the urge to wrap his arm around her. How quickly he'd begun thinking of her as his. He'd touched her frequently in the office this week. Because she needed to get used to it and because he couldn't help himself.

They were the last to arrive. Ryan and his dad were playing two-on-two with Madison and Beckett on the court. Mama Jo lounged at the picnic table with Grandpa, chatting.

PJ stood on the sidelines cheering Madison on. She made a phantom shot as her sister put up a basket. "Girl power! Oh, yeah!"

Beckett high-fived Madison while Ryan grumbled about a foul.

These people were his family. How were they going to react to the news? He knew they loved him. But Jade was blood. What if they didn't think he was good enough for her?

"Hey, you two!" Mama Jo stepped out from the picnic table and embraced them. "Good week?"

Daniel met Jade's gaze briefly as they nodded. They caught up with Grandpa and Mama Jo until Thomas proclaimed the burgers ready.

All at once, the table was full and tilting to the heavier side. Food was being passed, the conversation turning loud and erratic. Jade's thigh pressed against his, and Daniel couldn't focus on much else.

Would she bring it up? And when? They hadn't discussed it, but surely she'd want to make the announcement.

At the other end of the table, Ryan and his dad talked about this year's crop and the lack of rain, pulling Grandpa and Beckett into the conversation. The girls chatted about a reality TV show. He'd thought Jade was caught up in the conversation until her hand reached for his under the table.

His eyes met hers, an expectant expression on her face: *Ready?*

He tried for a confident smile, gave a slight nod.

Madison and Mama Jo burst out laughing at something PJ had said.

Daniel gave Jade's hand a squeeze, then she released it, grabbing her fork. She clinked it loudly against her glass, cutting through the clamor.

"All right, everyone, I have an announcement to make."

PJ leaned forward. "Oh, goodie, I love announcements." She gasped, her eyes widening. "You're having triplets."

Madison gave PJ a look, elbowing her.

"Sheesh, PJ," Ryan said.

PJ shrugged. "What?"

"For heaven's sake." Mama Jo turned to Jade. "Let the girl talk."

"What's this about, honey?" her dad asked.

"Well . . ." Jade looked at Daniel from the corner of her eye.

In the unnatural quiet he heard her rings click under the table as she fidgeted with them. He took her hand and held it tightly.

"Actually . . . uh, what I mean to say is . . . This is probably going to come as a . . . I know that . . . but this is . . ."

Jade turned to him, panic in her eyes.

"What she means to say," Daniel said, still looking into Jade's eyes, "is that we're getting married." He broke into a grin. He couldn't help it. He was stoked, and he couldn't care less right now who knew it.

The fear in Jade's eyes cleared. Her shoulders relaxed.

Daniel's gaze drifted around the table. Thomas's brows creased as he looked between his daughter and Daniel. Mama Jo's lips lifted, her hands coming to clasp against her heart. Ryan looked like he thought they were being punked. Grandpa helped himself to another ear of corn. Beckett stared at his plate, and Madison—was she giving Jade the stink eye?

"Huh?" PJ said.

Jade cleared her throat. "I know this might seem sudden—"

"Oh, honey, we're so happy for you two. Aren't we, Thomas?"

Jade's dad opened his mouth, closed it again. Oh boy. Not good.

"Wait," Ryan said. "What? When did this happen?"

Jade's hand had grown cold and clammy. Daniel pulled it into both of his, warming it against his thigh. "We've been together a lot, obviously, with work." He met Jade's eyes. "One thing led to another and here we are."

PJ looked between them, frowning. "So you guys are, like, a couple."

"You're quick on the uptake, sis," Ryan said.

"Why didn't someone tell me? You go away to college, and no one tells you anything."

"None of us knew," Ryan said.

Beckett nodded his chin toward them. "Congratulations, guys."

"You're getting married." Her dad finally found his tongue.

"I think you make a beautiful couple. Just beautiful." Mama Jo's blue eyes went liquid. "You've always been like a son to us, Daniel.

Now you'll be our son-in-law. We couldn't be happier, could we, honey?"

Thomas still had that glazed look. "Of course. Congratulations, you two."

"Have you set a date yet?" PJ asked.

Jade looked at Daniel. "Uh, no, not yet."

"But after the babies are born," Daniel said.

"I prefer not to waddle down the aisle."

"Well, wait at least six weeks after," Mama Jo said. "Otherwise it won't be much of a honeymoon."

"Mom!" Jade's cheeks flushed, going adorably pink.

Daniel, conscious of Thomas's gaze, turned his eyes to his empty plate even as his mind went there.

"Let's see the ring," PJ said. "I hope you did us proud, Daniel."

"No ring yet," Daniel said. "We're going shopping for one tomorrow."

"He wanted me to pick it out."

Talk turned to wedding plans. They wanted to keep it small and simple. A church ceremony, close friends and family.

Mama Jo went on about a wedding dress she'd seen in the window at a boutique in town. Daniel's eyes swung to Madison. She wore a tight smile as she listened to Mama Jo. Her eyes flicked to Jade, her jaw clenching. What was with her? Why was she upset with Jade?

Madison's eyes slid to Daniel. They softened momentarily before she looked down. Did this have to do with his feelings for Jade? Madison and Mama Jo were the only ones who knew.

And what if that came up? Right here, in front of everyone? In front of Jade?

An uneasy feeling swelled in his gut. He had to make them promise not to tell Jade. Madison had already promised, but that was before they were engaged. She'd assume Jade knew now that they were a couple.

There was no way he could let Jade find out. He'd become another Cody. There'd be no wedding, no marriage. Jade would never be his. Suddenly he had so much to lose.

He half listened to the conversation, his heart hammering. Why hadn't he warned them in advance? One misplaced word and that was it.

The conversation dragged on. What was it with women and weddings? Endless talk of flowers and invitations ensued, Jade constantly reining them in. *Small and simple, remember?*

Madison slipped away from the table, disappearing into the house with a stack of empty plates. The other women were leaning in, deep in discussion about the wedding party. The men, bored with wedding talk, had resumed their conversation about seed and tractors.

Daniel squeezed Jade's hand. "Be right back."

He found Madison in the kitchen loading the dishwasher.

He set his plate in the sink. "Hey."

She ran a glass under the faucet. "Hey. I guess I didn't get to say congratulations." She spared him a smile.

He leaned on the counter beside her. He didn't have much time. Someone could come in any minute. "Jade doesn't know how I feel."

She set the glass in the dishwasher, pausing to glance over her shoulder at him.

"And you can't tell her."

"*You* should tell her, Daniel."

"She doesn't want me to love her."

"Then why are you getting married?"

He looked her in the eye, his heart beating up in his throat. "Because it's the only way I can have her."

Madison's eyes tightened. The brown in them went soft like melted chocolate. "This is crazy."

"You're missing all the fun." Mama Jo appeared with a stack of plates.

Daniel moved aside as she set them in the sink.

"PJ's trying to talk your fiancée into a four-course reception dinner—she'll cook, of course." Mama Jo seemed to pick up on the tension between them. "What's going on?"

Madison scrubbed a plate, set it in the dishwasher, avoiding their gazes.

"She already knows," Daniel told Madison.

"Knows what?" Mama Jo asked.

Daniel didn't like the stubborn look on Madison's face. "How I feel about Jade."

Mama Jo laughed. "Of course I do. We all do—you're getting married, silly."

Madison shut off the water, crossed her arms. "Jade doesn't know Daniel's in love with her. She's marrying him for—practical reasons."

Mama Jo's face fell. "What?"

"He doesn't want her to know how he feels," Madison said.

"But . . . but why?"

He hated the disappointment on Mama Jo's face, hated that he'd burst her bubble. Daniel took her hand. He had to convince her. This would never work otherwise. "I want to be with her. I want it more than anything. You know I love her."

"Then tell her," Mama Jo said.

Daniel shook his head. "She doesn't want to be loved. Between losing Aaron and—" He caught himself just in time. Jade hadn't told them about being raped. "Jade doesn't want that. She wants a husband, a father for her babies. That's all."

Mama Jo's eyes turned down at the corners. "But that's no marriage."

"We've known each other forever. She loves me. I love her. It'll be enough."

Mama Jo's eyes glossed over. "Will it, Daniel?"

"Of course it won't," Madison said. "You have to be honest with her. Tell him, Mom."

"You don't understand," Daniel said. He had to make them see. "She was going out with Cody, right? Did she tell you why she broke it off with him?"

Mama Jo shook her head.

"He told her he loved her. That's all. That's all it took. She told me she can't handle being in love again, that she won't. That's why she asked *me* to marry her. Because I'm safe. Because—" He clenched his jaw. "Because she knows she'll never feel that way about me."

He swallowed against the hard knot in his throat, fought the sting behind his eyes. He found the familiar linoleum pattern in the floor, tracing the squares with his eyes.

"Oh, Daniel." Mama Jo's voice was filled with heartbreak.

He had to do something. He tightened his hold on her hand as his eyes found hers. "I'll be good to her, Mama Jo. I'll make her happy, I swear it. I'll be the best flipping husband there ever was."

Madison tossed the wet rag in the sink. It slapped against the porcelain. "This is a mistake."

Daniel's eyes cut to hers. "This is none of your business." She wasn't going to ruin this for him. No one was. "It's between me and Jade. She wants this and so do I. The rest of you are just going to have to get on board."

The screen door slapped, and he caught sight of Jade entering. She looked between them. She was too far away to have heard, but their body language gave away too much.

"What's going on?" she asked.

Daniel stepped toward her, smiling, and pulled her into a hug. He forced a light tone. "Nothing. Just talking about the wedding. Please tell me PJ didn't talk you into a four-course meal."

"Uh, no. But I did get sucked into dress shopping tomorrow afternoon."

"But nothing's going to fit," Mama Jo said.

Jade pulled back. "I know, right? I tried to tell her, but you know PJ. She's outside doing back handsprings. You two want to come along?" she asked her mom and Madison.

Mama Jo smiled at Jade, then at Daniel. "Wouldn't miss it, baby girl."

"Sure," Madison said, then turned on the water and resumed washing dishes.

Half an hour later, Daniel and Ryan were called away on a fire run. Mrs. Harper had a grease fire that wiped out half her kitchen. Afterward her old gnarled hands were shaking, and her waxy skin was pale against her floral nightgown. Daniel stayed to settle her down and help her find someplace to stay the night. It was almost midnight by the time he got home.

He'd showered off the smell of smoke and was climbing into bed when the text came in. He smiled at Jade's name on the screen. Everything okay?

Yeah, just a kitchen fire. You should be sleeping.

Tonight went pretty good, I thought. They were surprised, but I think it's going to be okay. On my end at least.

What do you mean on your end?

Um . . . your parents?

I'll handle them. It'll be fine. Trust me.

If you say so.

Grandma loves you. :)

There's that.

Stop worrying and get some sleep.

Yes, dear.

Chapter Thirty-Five

Jade exited the boutique behind her mom and PJ. Her back was killing her, her feet were the size of blimps, and she was done shopping for a dress she couldn't get past her hips.

"Have you shown Jade the cake for the baby shower?" Mom asked PJ.

"She did. It's adorable." Mom was hosting the shower next Saturday. Jade had tried to keep it small, but her mom had an endless circle of friends.

"I can't wait to make it." PJ stopped at the curb. "Hey, let's go to Louisville. There's this great little boutique down from the bakery—"

"Oh, no. I'm so done."

PJ sulked. "Party pooper."

"We'll have time to shop after she's gotten her figure back," Mom said. "We'll leave the twins with your dad and have a girls' day out."

"I'm starving," PJ said. "Let's go out to eat and show off your new ring."

"Sounds good," Mom said.

Jade glanced down at her beautiful ring, a small princess diamond in a band of delicate leaf swirls. "I think I've flashed it around enough for today. Besides, I need to get my feet up. I can hear the water sloshing around in them."

"You look tired." Mom pulled her close. "Let's get you home."

"I'll take her," Madison said. "You two can grab a bite to eat. I told Beckett I'd fry up pork chops for supper."

Jade sank into the cool confines of Madison's car, her back loosening pleasantly at the change of position.

Madison started the car and backed from the diagonal slot. The town was quiet now that tourist season was over. Dry leaves scuttled across Main Street, piling against storefronts, and the afternoon sun dipped low on the horizon.

Madison had been quiet today. Jade wasn't stupid. This ride home wasn't going to come cheap.

"So you're really going through with this."

Jade sighed. "Was it the announcement or the ring that gave it away?"

"Jade. I'm not trying to rain on your parade here, but—"

"Why can't you just be happy for me? Is that too much to ask?"

"Because I can see the train wreck coming from here."

Madison might be older, but that didn't mean she knew best. She had her husband and cozy little home. That was all Jade wanted, and she wanted it for her babies. She set her hand on her stomach. She and Daniel were good together. She could give him a real home, a family. He deserved that.

"This is what we want. That's all that matters."

"I just want what's best for both of you, and this isn't it. You both deserve more than this."

Jade shook her head. Madison was wasting her time. Jade wasn't changing her mind.

But what if she got hold of Daniel? What if he listened? Dread shimmied inside like a thousand leaves under gale-force winds. Daniel seemed to want this as much as Jade. But Madison could be persuasive. What if she changed his mind?

"You need to stay out of this, Madison."

"You're going to want more eventually, you both will. What happens if Daniel actually falls in love one day? What then, huh? What if *you* fall in love with someone else? Can't you see what a disaster that would be?"

"That won't happen." She would never do that to Daniel. Would never betray him like that. "We know what we're doing."

"What about his parents? They're not exactly fans of the McKinley family. They're never going to accept you or us. Have you thought about how hard that'll be for Daniel? With him right in the middle?"

"I'll win them over. When they see how happy I make Daniel, they'll come around."

"You're being naïve."

"And you're being intrusive. Butt out, Madison. I mean it."

Madison was out of line, and the thought of her taking Daniel away made Jade's heart quake. She needed this. She needed him. She hadn't realized how much until now.

Daniel had put it off as long as he could. The dishes were cleared, the leather bill folder perched on the table ledge, his dad's Visa poking out the top. This was his only meal alone with his parents this weekend. The remaining hours would be filled with networking events designed to broaden Daniel's reach. He'd told his grandma about the engagement before he'd left town. She'd been thrilled. His parents were another story.

He'd already broken the news that the transportation department had voted to buy their own ferry. Louisville would partner with them, and the plan would solve multiple problems. His dad hadn't seen it that way. He'd been too upset about messing up the deal with the Crawfords. Neither of his parents would be happy about his next announcement either.

While Mom and Dad discussed details for the next day's benefit auction, Daniel finished his Perrier and thought of Jade. Thought of her beautiful green eyes, her dress-the-way-I-want clothes, her dry sense of humor. He thought of her kissable lips and the tender way she unconsciously cradled her stomach. He wanted a lifetime with his girl, and nothing was going to stand in his way. Not even his parents.

"Mom, Dad." He waited until he had their attention. "I have something to tell you."

His mom fixed that *go ahead, I'm listening* smile on her face while his dad flagged the server and handed him the folder. Dad clasped his hands on the white linen tablecloth and waited.

Daniel drew a deep breath. "I'm getting married."

His mom gave a little gasp. Her ruby lips turned up. "Oh, Daniel! I had no idea things had gotten so serious with Courtney. This is just splendid! Why didn't you invite her along to celebrate?"

"Not Courtney, Mom. I'm marrying Jade."

Daniel glanced at Dad, who gave nothing away. A lifetime of politics had cultivated a convincing poker face. Daniel hoped he never got that good.

"Jade . . . who's *Jade?*" Mom asked.

"Jade McKinley," Daniel said.

Mom's lips flattened an instant before her eyes turned to blue ice. *"No."* She lifted her linen from her lap and slapped it on the table.

Daniel flexed his jaw. "Excuse me?"

"You cannot marry that girl. I won't allow it."

"The girl you brought to dinner?" Dad asked.

Daniel took a short break from Mom's cold eyes. "Yes."

"Daniel, she's . . ." Mom looked over her shoulder and lowered her voice. "She. Is. Pregnant."

Daniel sat back in his chair. "Yes. With twins."

"Twins?" His mom looked away, her cheeks going red, her face struggling for composure. He almost felt sorry for her until he remembered she was standing between him and the woman he loved.

"She *trapped* you. That's what she did." Mom's harsh whisper cut across the barren table.

"That doesn't even make sense, Mom. We've established that the babies aren't mine."

"She is using you!"

Dad set his hand on Mom's chiffon-covered arm. "Victoria. Settle down."

"How can you sit there so calmly when this, this *girl* is trying to ruin him?"

"She's not trying to ruin me, Mom. She

loves me. And I love her. She makes me happy."

His mom rolled her eyes toward the dimmed chandelier hanging overhead. "Talk some sense into him, Allen."

The server set the folder on the table. "Anything else I can get you?"

"No, thank you." Dad signed the bill and slipped his Visa into his wallet as the server left.

Mom's hands were clasped tightly on the table, her rings glittering under the lights. She stared at her glossy red nails.

"I think perhaps we should table this discussion until tomorrow," Dad said.

Daniel looked between them. "Fine." He tossed his own napkin on the table. "But I'm not changing my mind. I'm marrying Jade. The sooner you adjust to the idea, the better for everyone."

When he got back to his hotel room, he checked his phone. He'd missed some texts during dinner.

How'd it go?

Everything okay?

You there?

Hello?

He smiled. It was as close to panicked texting as he'd gotten from her. Was she worried he'd change his mind? That his parents would persuade him to break the engagement? Not a chance. He texted her back.

No worries. The deed is done. Everything's

fine. :) Just got to the hotel. It's late. You should be sleeping.

Like I could sleep. How upset are they? I should've come with you.

It'll be fine. They were just . . . concerned.

Is that code for furious?

It's code for Go To Bed.

I get to sleep in. Are you trying to get rid of me?

Who me?

Can I do anything to help? Call them? Invite them for a visit? Forge an impressive pedigree?

Ha. They just need a little time.

Like an eon or two? Seriously, I know tonight was hard. You've never really bucked them before. You okay?

It was true, he realized. When they'd encouraged him to go to his father's alma mater, he'd given in. When they'd pushed him to run for mayor, he had. When they suggested he ask out some woman who was perfect for him, he'd capitulated.

Even this run for the House. Was it what he really wanted, or was he only following a course they'd mapped out for him? He loved serving the public. Well, most of it. He liked being on a first-name basis with everyone in town. He liked having the authority to make positive changes.

But if he were honest, he didn't like some of it too. He didn't like schmoozing for campaign dollars. He didn't like the thought of representing people whose needs he didn't know, and he especially didn't like the spinning and dishonesty that infested politics.

He thought of his dad's poker face. Was that who Daniel was going to become? It was what his parents wanted. And Jade was right. He'd always gone along with them. Did everyone think he was a total wuss? Was he?

You there?

His thoughts heavy, he replied. They went back and forth for almost an hour, the conversation shifting to their plans for the immediate future. When he finally turned out the lights and closed his eyes, thoughts of Jade filled his dreams.

Chapter Thirty-Six

Jade pulled the nail polish from her bag, admiring the deep purple as she shook it.

Beside her, Daniel tapped out an e-mail on his laptop and clicked Send. It whooshed into cyberspace. "Sure you don't want to go for a boat ride tonight?"

Her back ached at the mere thought. "I can't get comfortable in a bed, much less a boat."

They'd fallen into the habit of having supper together at his place after work. She stayed until bedtime. Sometimes Daniel worked out, sometimes they watched TV. Other times, like tonight, they did their own thing, simply sharing the same space. It was what their marriage would be like, only with two babies in the mix.

She uncapped the bottle of Purple Prose and pulled her foot to the edge of Daniel's sofa. She could barely reach her toes these days. She was eight months, her scheduled C-section only a week and a half away.

Soon she'd be holding her babies in her arms. How would she feel when she looked into their eyes, held their tiny hands? What if they looked like *him?* What if she couldn't love them the way she was supposed to?

She slammed the door shut on that thought. She already loved them. Seeing them, holding them, wouldn't change that. Would it?

Daniel set the laptop on the end table. "What are you doing?"

"Painting my toenails?"

"You're holding your breath."

She finished the big toe. "The fumes can't be good for the babies."

"Neither can lack of oxygen."

She shot him a look.

He held out his hand. "Give me that."

She raised a brow. "Seriously?"

He patted his lap. She handed over the polish and moved her feet onto his lap, turning in her seat.

Her toes were probably going to look like a four-year-old had gotten hold of them. Oh well. She could breathe now, and her knee wasn't shoved into her protruding belly.

She leaned against the stuffed arm, watching Daniel as he bent over her feet. He swiped the polish along her nails in slow, meticulous strokes. His tongue came out, parting his lips.

"This stuff reeks," he said between toes.

"But it's pretty and sparkly."

He smiled briefly before his tongue came out again. His lashes swept down, long and dark against his skin. The light from the lamp cast a golden glow on his skin.

"You're pretty good at this, Mr. Mayor."

"Don't tell anyone."

"I should film it and turn it in to the news. 'Mayor paints assistant's toenails. Details at eleven.'"

"There goes my career."

She imagined him painting her daughter's toenails—presuming one or both were girls. She imagined their wiggling feet, his large hands patiently steadying them while they giggled.

A few minutes later he capped the bottle. They watched a sitcom while her toenails dried. His arm lay across her legs. His hand rested on her bare ankle.

During the commercial, Jade picked up his guitar and played around with a song she'd written in Chicago. She'd built her calluses up over the past couple months.

"Nice melody," he said after she'd played through a verse and chorus. "Kind of haunting."

When the show ended, Daniel held out his hands. She passed him the guitar, shifting her bare feet to the coffee table.

He settled the guitar in his lap, his hand finding home on the neck. "I've been working on something." He started strumming.

A few measures later, Jade recognized the lullaby: "All Through the Night."

He continued, picking gently with his fingertips. The melody floated quietly through the room, the strains soothing and peaceful.

Daniel wasn't a gifted player—he'd be the first to admit it. He worked hard on new songs, and his thick fingers made playing cumbersome. But he had this one down. She wondered how many hours it had taken.

He gave the final strum. The last chord was still ringing out as he looked up at her. "I was thinking about what you said earlier. About the babies being able to hear sounds. If I play this every night until they're born, it'll become familiar. And later it'll remind them of being all snug inside." A flush crept up into his cheeks.

Her eyes stung at the beauty of the thought. At his sweet, selfless nature. How had she gotten so lucky? An aching lump swelled in her throat.

Daniel's face fell. "I didn't mean to make you cry."

She scooted over on the couch. Took the guitar from his hands, setting it on the table. She pulled him into her arms, sighing. "That's about the sweetest thing I've ever heard."

She blinked back the tears, telling herself to pull it together. What was wrong with her? "Plus, these hormones are killing me."

He smiled against her temple. A shiver went down her spine, and she wondered if he felt it. She felt *him*. The warmth of his hand at her back. The solidness of his shoulder against her cheek, the movement of his chest rising and falling against her.

He drew back, his fingers softly pinching her chin. He leaned forward, and his lips brushed hers. Her heart stopped. It was a chaste kiss, soft and supple. Almost over before it began. Not enough.

He drew away. "I hope that's o—"

She clenched his shirt in her hand, pulling him in. She grazed her lips across his, and her heart began beating again.

She felt his surprise in the pause. A heartbeat later, he took the lead. His hands cradled her face, his lips moving against hers in a way she felt to the core. When he deepened the kiss, she barely suppressed a moan.

This was Daniel. It should be weird. Awkward.

But it wasn't. They had sparks or chemistry or something. How could that be? Maybe it wasn't chemistry at all. Maybe it was the pregnancy. The hormones? She hadn't really had a chance to take them for a spin until now.

He pulled her tight against him, her belly pressing into his stomach. She knew her pregnant body was no turn-on. She should pull away before he did.

She drew in a breath, ready to call it. But the clean, manly smell of him filled her nostrils, overriding common sense. Her hands drifted into the hair at his nape. It feathered softly against her fingers. They traveled to his neck, to his jaw. His five o'clock shadow scraped the tender flesh of her palm.

He pulled away, his lips leaving hers.

A whimper escaped her throat. He was leaning back against the sofa arm. She was practically on top of him. Heat rose to her cheeks.

She sat back, looking away. Was he repulsed by her body? Disgusted by her lack of control? They'd practically been brother and sister for so long. There were all kinds of reasons for him to push her away. He'd only offered a chaste kiss, but she'd taken much more.

She squirmed in the silence, needing to know, afraid to ask. But she had to ask. They were getting married. They needed to be on the same page even if that page wasn't pretty.

"Is this—too weird?" she asked. *Say no. Say no.* She didn't think she could take anything else. Where would that leave them?

"No." He curled a finger around her chin, forcing eye contact. "You?"

Did it make her pathetic that she wanted to kiss him again? She shook her head, falling headlong into his blue eyes.

"Good," he said.

On her way home Jade relived the kiss. After she was in bed, she relived it some more. Lying in the dark, she thought about chemistry and hormones and wondered which of the two made her pulse race at his touch. Wondered what would happen when the hormones were gone, and all that was left was an affectionate friendship and a lifetime stretching ahead of them.

Chapter Thirty-Seven

He'd watched Jade all week from the corner of his eyes. Things had changed since their kiss three days ago. Sometimes they brushed past each other by the copy machine. Twice he'd kissed her at the end of the evening. Kisses that had lingered, kisses that had stirred a kind of desire he'd never experienced.

When she'd leave, he'd lie awake, staring at the shadows on his ceiling. Seven weeks and she'd be his. He'd never loved her more. Maybe she didn't love him in the same way, but she did love him. She wanted him. Was it enough? It would have to be.

He couldn't wait to get that wedding band on her finger, to have her as his own. The last week had shown him that the marriage was going to be better than he'd imagined. She actually liked kissing him, couldn't seem to get enough, and heaven knew she was driving him to distraction.

He watched her now, walking to the front door of the office, twisting the lock. Pregnancy had given her cheeks a permanent flush. Her hair had grown long and thick, falling down her back in a glossy brown cascade.

"I didn't make anything to bring to Mom and Dad's," she said as she passed their desks on her way to the back, rubbing the small of her back.

"We can stop by the grocery and pick up something."

"Perfect."

He gathered his things and met her in the back. She was struggling to put on her coat, so he set down his laptop and helped her.

"Thanks." She pulled her hair from under the collar.

He caught a whiff of her spicy fragrance, a tantalizing glimpse of her bare neck. He leaned over and brushed the back of her neck with a fleeting kiss.

He would've been just fine with that. Except the moment his lips met her skin, her breath hitched. She tilted her head, giving him access.

What was a guy to do?

Her breaths grew shallow as he kissed a trail up her neck. She braced herself against the wall in front of her. When he kissed the spot behind her ear, she shivered.

He turned her around and backed her gently into the wall, a hand on each side of her. Then he took a moment just to appreciate her sleepy green eyes, her flushed cheeks, her plump lips. Just a moment though, because her hands came to his shoulders and her fingers wove into the hair at his nape. Then he was gone.

His lips met hers carefully. *Soft, tender, easy,* he reminded himself, conscious of the cruelty she'd suffered. Wanting her to feel safe with him, always.

He cupped her cheek, his fingers threading into her hair. It was as soft as spun silk and smelled of oranges. Her hands slid down his chest and around his waist, pulling him closer.

He deepened the kiss, his other arm coming around her. He was in a dream. He felt this way every time they'd kissed. Like it couldn't be real. Like she couldn't possibly want him this way.

But he hadn't heard any complaints. And now the ragged sound of her breathing was making him downright heady. Heat flared inside, rolling off his skin.

When Jade's hands fell away, he stifled the surge of disappointment. But her lips never paused. She shimmied from her coat. He helped it off her, and it dropped to the ground, one less barrier.

She clutched at his waist, tilted her head into the kiss. The brush of her tongue was nearly his undoing. He couldn't get enough of her. And she seemed to feel the same way. Was it too much to hope that one day she could love him too?

She tugged at his shirt, pulling it from his waistband. His heart found a new gear. Something inside him stirred, hot and dangerous.

"Jade . . ." His tone rang with warning.

"Just want to feel you," she whispered.

The tugging stopped, and her fingers drifted along his stomach. His breath hissed in through his teeth. Her touch wandered to his back, then to his stomach again, burning a trail on his heated flesh.

Jade.

Desire flooded him. He'd never wanted anyone, anything so badly in all his life. He had to stop. He knew his limits, and he was there.

Gathering the scraps of his willpower, he stopped her hands, pressing them to his sides, and broke the kiss. A whimper tore from her throat. It was all he could do to follow through.

"Slow down, slow down, slow down," he whispered.

He set his forehead against hers, closing his eyes, breathing hard. He needed a moment. A long one. And possibly a cold shower. He could still smell her, still feel the heat pouring off her, feel her hands where he'd pressed them to his body.

"You're killing me, woman."

He opened his eyes and found her staring at him. She was breathing hard too, and her hooded eyes made him wish they could fast-forward seven weeks.

"When are we getting married again?" she asked.

He sighed hard. "December 20th."

"Well, whose idea was that?" There was a pout in her voice.

His lips fought gravity and won. "Yours. Something about getting your figure back."

"I meant November. Or tomorrow."

He chuckled, pulling away to see her better. Her lower lip protruded adorably. He'd love nothing more than to kiss it into submission, but he knew better. They both needed to step outside and let a good cool breeze skate over their heated skin.

"We should get going," he said reluctantly. "We're already late." He scooped her coat off the floor and handed it to her, not sure if she'd want it on now.

She pouted, turning her eyes to his. Her mind was clearly not on family or food, and he loved her for it. For that and so many other reasons.

* * *

"Sweetie, you look exhausted," Mom said. "Why don't you go lie down in PJ's room?"

The savory smell of roast lingered in the air. A ruckus sounded in the dining room where the family had gathered for a rousing game of Pictionary. Jade had stepped out to help with the dishes. Since she was the worst artist on the team, no one had complained.

Jade glanced at the mountain of dishes in the sink. "Sure you don't mind?"

"You know I like washing dishes. Go on now. Get your feet up."

Jade heard the game breaking up as she climbed the stairs and passed her old room, now an office. She entered PJ's room and fell onto the quilt, rolling to her side and balling the pillow under her head. Her back muscles screamed as they loosened.

The back door slammed, and laughter sounded in the backyard. The basketball patted the concrete pad. Someone was taking advantage of the weather. They might not have another nice day until spring.

The babies stirred, poking and rolling before settling down and going still again. Jade closed her eyes. Just twenty minutes, and she'd rejoin her family. Meanwhile, she let her mind drift back to the kiss in the office.

Mercy.

She smiled as she thought of Daniel, of the look in his eyes when he'd pulled away. At the way his pupils had swallowed the blue of his eyes. She wanted him so much. Was that normal? Was she supposed to feel that kind of desire with someone who . . .

Who what?

Someone she didn't love? Only she did love Daniel. Just not in that way.

Right?

Her heart pounded so hard the bed shook. Of course she didn't love him in that way. People felt desire all the time without being in love. It was human nature. Maybe it hadn't happened to her before, but that didn't mean it couldn't.

Right?

The only answer was the quickening of her pulse.

A squeak sounded on the wooden stairs. Probably Mom coming to check on her or Dad printing an article for Ryan.

When the footsteps stopped in the office, she decided it must be the latter. But a moment later the stairs squeaked again. More footsteps entered the office. Then voices carried through the thin wall.

"What do you want?" Daniel's hushed voice.

"You have to stop this."

Madison.

Jade clenched her teeth. She'd warned her sister to stay out of this. What if she talked Daniel out of the wedding? Jade sat up. She had to stop her. Her feet swung to the floor, and she cringed as the headboard hit the wall.

"I'm not stopping anything," Daniel said.

"Tell her then."

Jade stilled by the bed, frowning. *Tell me what?* Was Daniel hiding something from her?

"She deserves to know the truth."

"It'll ruin everything." His voice was strained. "I know what I'm doing, Madison. Stay out of it."

Go Daniel, one side of her cheered. But the other side couldn't forget that he was hiding something from her.

"I'm not trying to cause trouble here, Daniel."

Jade missed something as her sister's voice lowered, and the basketball outside dribbled across the pad.

"I love you both," Madison continued. "But you're going to get your heart broken. You're in love—it's not fair to keep that from her. She's my sister. I can't just stand by and let this happen."

Jade's stomach bottomed out. There was someone else? That was the secret Daniel was keeping? Her heart gave a painful squeeze. No, Daniel wouldn't do that. Why would he marry her if he were in love with someone else?

Daniel said something that was too quiet to hear. A sick feeling spread through Jade, making her stomach twist. She needed answers, and there was only one place to get them. She left the room, suddenly not caring about being quiet or eaves-dropping.

Her legs shook as she entered the hallway, doing a U-turn into the office. Daniel and Madison stood just inside the door. Their heads snapped toward her.

Daniel's eyes widened, then a spark of something flashed in them. Guilt? Fear? Were those the eyes of someone who'd lied? Someone she'd trusted?

After a long moment, Madison cleared her throat. "I'll be downstairs." She swept past Jade, giving her tensed shoulder a squeeze.

The stairs creaked. And then silence.

Jade folded her arms, holding herself together. This couldn't be happening. She trusted Daniel. There was no one she trusted more.

He couldn't seem to look at her. He palmed the back of his neck, staring at the rug at his feet. "I guess you—I guess you heard—"

"Who is it, Daniel?" Why did she suddenly sound like a shrew? Why did she care so much? And why did she feel hollow inside?

He looked at her now, his brows creased. "What?"

"Who is she? Who are you in love with?" She

hadn't meant it to come out as an accusation.

The creases disappeared. "No, Jade." He reached out to her.

She flinched away.

"It's not what you—you don't understand."

Oh, but she did. Her heart was breaking into a thousand pieces, which made no sense. *It's the plan. That's all.* Their plan was ruined now. She couldn't marry him if he loved another. That's why the thought cut her in two.

"Who, Daniel?" She thought he could tell her anything. He was her friend, first and foremost. Never had she thought he could keep something like this from her.

He dropped his hand, and she braced herself.

"You," he said, his voice strained. His eyes softened. "You, Jade."

What? He couldn't mean it. But the look in his eyes. Warmth and fear melded together.

Me?

It was hard to argue with that look. Thoughts flashed in her mind. Daniel giving her a job. Daniel taking her to the doctor. Daniel getting angry when she proposed. Daniel kissing her passionately. Daniel painting her toenails. Daniel strumming a lullaby.

"Why didn't—when did—" Her thoughts were scrambled eggs. She couldn't breathe. Her lungs sucked together when she emptied them and refused to inflate again.

"It's okay, Jade. I know you don't feel the same."

It wasn't okay. It wasn't okay at all. His heart was breaking. She saw it in his eyes, and her own was cracking open in response. How long had this been going on? Why didn't she know? She should've known.

His pager beeped.

"Everything's fine . . ." His tone soothed. "Nothing has to change."

But everything *had* changed. He would marry her at his own expense simply because she needed him. Just like he'd given her a job because she needed work. Just like he'd gone to Lamaze because she'd needed a partner.

"Daniel!" Ryan called from downstairs. "Where are you, dude?"

"Did you hear me?" Daniel's tone, his body language was talking her down from the ledge. "I'm not expecting anything from you."

Not expecting anything? She was supposed to marry him. Was supposed to put him first above all else. And she couldn't give him the one thing he needed from her.

Even now the look on his face was about to kill her. A cocktail of emotions, none of them good. She wanted to wash the heartbreak from his face. She wanted to see his eyes sparkle. Wanted to see his lips curl up. But that wasn't going to happen.

She'd never meant to hurt him. Would rather die than cause him—

The thought slammed into her, causing a quake. Everything shook then folded in on her, suffocating. She shook her head. No. It couldn't be true. She couldn't love him. She didn't want to love him. Didn't want to love anyone. That's why she'd picked Daniel. He was safe.

Only he wasn't.

"Daniel! We've got to run. Come on, man!"

How had this happened? She'd been so careful.

He set his hand on her shoulder. The touch burned straight through. "I have to go. Don't—" His eyes pled with her. He dropped his hand, moving toward the door. "We'll talk later."

He slapped the door frame hard on the way out. His quick footsteps pounded down the stairs, and then the room was silent except for the heavy thudding of her heart.

Chapter Thirty-Eight

Jade lay in the dark, a long string of tormenting thoughts winding through her head. A permanent ache had set up residence inside, and no amount of tears had soothed it. How had she fallen in love with Daniel? When? She'd thought her heart was as callused as her fingertips, but it wasn't. Somehow, without her knowing, Daniel had slipped right inside and made a home there.

The darkness that oppressed her when she'd lost Aaron settled over her now, thick and heavy. Her chest felt weighted to the mattress, felt like a boulder rested on her. She couldn't breathe.

This was what happened when she loved.

She saw Aaron's body in the casket, his beautiful skin all waxy, the cowlick he hated sticking up. Felt the darkness smother her with its oppressive weight. A darkness that had taken months to lift enough to allow her to breathe.

She didn't want to be here again.

How could You do this to me, God? Haven't I been through enough? Is this really Your plan for me? Seriously?

How could she have let this happen? She drew in a shuddering breath and blew it out. *Breathe, Jade. Just breathe.*

She wanted to run. She wanted to get in her car and point it away from Chapel Springs and drive until the road ended. She had to get away from here. Had to get away from Daniel and these feelings.

Somewhere under the heavy blanket of darkness, movement stirred. Her hand found her belly and pressed against it. Her babies. She couldn't leave now. Couldn't leave her doctor or her family. She needed their support. Now more than ever.

But she could leave Daniel. She had to. Calling

off the wedding was a given. If she weren't with him, her heart would heal. She couldn't have been in love with him long if she'd only just realized it. She wouldn't hurt forever like she had with Aaron.

Right?

His heart would heal too. He'd find someone who could love him back. Someone who deserved him. Someone normal. Someone not broken.

She only had to separate her life from his to allow them both to heal. How had their lives become so entwined? She closed her eyes against the hot sting of reality. She'd come to depend on Daniel for everything. She'd have to find another job. No way could she go back to that office, sit across from him, pretend everything was the same.

Distance. That's what she needed. What he needed too, even if he didn't realize it yet.

* * *

The accident on 62 took forever. A woman had wrapped her Toyota around a tree, and it had taken the Jaws of Life to extricate her. Her toddler had escaped with mild injuries, but the mother had been medevaced to the hospital with internal bleeding and head trauma. Somewhere a frantic husband and father was speeding through the night, his future teetering on a knife's edge.

Daniel started his car and pulled out his cell.

It was after eleven, but he had to talk to Jade. He hated the way they'd left things. Hated the way Jade's eyes had flitted around the room as if she'd wanted to climb from the nearest window and run far away.

He tapped in a text. **Still awake?** He hit Send and turned on the heater. Everything in him wanted to head straight to her apartment. He had to convince her to marry him still. He couldn't bear the thought of losing her now, not when he'd come so close to having her.

He checked his phone. Nothing.

Come on, Jade. Answer. She'd looked tired tonight, but he couldn't believe she'd be able to sleep. He'd seen the fear. The sooner he addressed it, the better. Letting it fester in her would only make it worse. Even now, she probably had an escape plan. Had probably canceled the church and flowers and invitations.

He hit the steering wheel. The run couldn't have come at a worse time. And Madison. He was so angry at her he wanted to throttle her.

His phone dinged, and his eyes flew to the screen.

Yes, she'd written.

Thank You, Jesus. His heart pulsed as he tapped out a reply. **Can I come over?**

The response came a few seconds later.

It's late, Daniel . . . I'm exhausted.

Talk to me, Jade. I'm going crazy here.

Not on text. Tomorrow.

So you have time to plan your break-up speech?

He hit Send and immediately regretted his words. He dug the heels of his hands into his eyes. Was he trying to chase her away?

I'm sorry. Let me come over. Please?

He ran his hands over his face, anger rattling through him. Anger at Madison, at himself, at Jade for not returning his feelings. It made no sense, but there it was.

A text came in. All right.

He didn't take the time to reply. Just headed toward her place, forcing himself to keep to the speed limit.

When she answered the door, his throat closed up. Under the glaring bulb of the porch light, her eyes were swollen.

I hurt her.

The knowledge was a sucker punch to the gut. He followed her to the couch where she holed up in one corner in her pink pajamas. She hadn't bothered with her green slippers. Her purple toenails looked almost black under the lamplight, and he wished he could rewind to the night he'd painted them. Wished he'd pushed for an earlier date. They'd be married, and it would be too late to back out.

He took the other end of the sofa, wishing he'd given some thought to what he'd say. But when her red-rimmed eyes drifted to him, he didn't have to think.

"I'm sorry," he said.

"For what?" She sounded like she had the world's worst cold. "You didn't do anything wrong."

"I should've been honest with you."

Jade gave a laugh, the humorless kind. Not good.

"This was a bad idea from the start," she said.

His heart pummeled his ribs. "No. It wasn't. It *isn't*. We can still do this, Jade. I still want this."

She shook her head.

She's already given up. Help me out here, God. You haven't brought us this far for nothing.
"Just hear me out."

She closed her eyes. She was shutting him out.

Think, Dawson. "I know where you stand. I'm okay with that. All those reasons you gave me why this marriage makes sense for me still apply. I won't pressure you. I wouldn't do that to you. I know you don't feel the same, and that's okay. I can live with that. I promise."

"We can't do this, Daniel. I can't do this. And it's not fair to you."

She'd already made her decision. He had to talk her out of it. He was good with words. He was a politician, for crying out loud.

He moved over on the couch.

She shrank into the corner, and he stopped on the middle cushion.

"You deserve someone who can love you back." A tear trickled from her eye. "I want you to have that."

"I want *you*. I'll take you however I can get you." God help him, that was the honest truth.

Jade's lip trembled. Another tear slid down her cheek, and he saw something in her eyes that made his stomach clench. "I'm so sorry."

No. His body moved toward her before he had the thought. His hands cradled her face. "Don't do this, Jade. *Please* don't do this."

She closed her eyes, her wet spiky lashes falling against her pale skin. But the pulse in her neck sped, thumping against his little finger. She may not love him, but she wanted him. Her body knew it even if she didn't.

He wouldn't let her shut him out so easily. He lowered his face and brushed her lips, tasting the saltiness of tears. Showing her everything that could be theirs if she only gave him a chance. Her lips moved against his. Hope flowed through him, invigorating him. His pulse synchronized with hers, matching beat for beat. Their lips tangled in a wild dance.

This would always be good, couldn't she see that? It would be enough for both of them. He deepened the kiss, pulling her into him. Her little moan set off an earthquake inside him, and the kiss turned desperate. He loved her so much. He couldn't get enough of her. Would never get enough of her.

He felt her hands on his chest and knew a moment's satisfaction. But then they were pushing him away.

She gave a final push. "No."

He backed away, dread crawling up his spine at the look on her face.

Tears flooded her eyes, spilling over as she stood. She fisted a trembling hand over her mouth. "I can't do this." She worked the engagement ring from her finger and held it out. "I'm sorry. I'm so sorry, Daniel, but you have to go."

She looked ready to come undone, and he wanted more than anything to put the ring back on her trembling hand. To pull her into his arms and comfort her and tell her he wasn't leaving. That he wasn't giving up on them.

But he was hurting her. The realization cut like a knife.

She closed her eyes. More tears. "Please, Daniel."

He stood, numbness flowing though him where there'd been hope only seconds before. He held out his hand. The slight weight of the ring burned into his palm. He folded his fingers around it until the prongs cut into his flesh.

She backed away as he approached the door, putting distance between them. And he knew this was what she had to do. What he had to *let* her do because he loved her. Because he didn't want to hurt her. And that's what he'd done.

She had plenty on her plate without worrying about him. Hadn't she been through enough? One week from today she'd be the mother of twins. She'd need help, but she had her family for that. He was just a burden now.

He looked at her now, makeup smudged beneath her sad, sad eyes. Trails of tears streaking her face. Quivering lip caught between her teeth, holding on by a thread.

Yeah. He was done hurting her. He leaned over, pressed a kiss to her forehead. "Try and get some sleep," he whispered, his voice thick. "Everything will work out, Jade."

Maybe if he said it enough, he'd believe it. He crossed the threshold, and the door shut quietly behind him. The bolt slid into place as she locked him out of her home, out of her heart.

Chapter Thirty-Nine

Jade curled up on the recliner, her eyes fixed on the TV. On the sofa, PJ chuckled at Sandra Bullock as she tried to convince the strangers that she was, in fact, engaged to their comatose son.

Engaged. That had been Jade before last night. She ran her thumb over her naked finger, wondering how Daniel was doing. She hadn't heard from him, not that she'd expected to. She had heard from her family, though, one by one. It had been an exhausting day, one she was eager to see the end of. Not that tomorrow would be better. Right now she wanted to crawl into her bed and pull the covers over her head.

Except *someone* had decided she shouldn't be alone and had conned her into a girls' night in. She gave PJ a long look that went entirely unnoticed.

When was the hurt going to stop? Every time she closed her eyes she saw the look on Daniel's face. Saw the hurt in his eyes, felt the desperation in his kiss. But this was for the best. She was damaged goods, whether he realized it or not. He deserved someone whole. Someone who wasn't too afraid to love him back.

He would change his mind about marriage someday. When he found the right woman, they'd find a way to make his career work. His wife would be one lucky woman.

Jade wrapped her arms around her aching middle. How could she feel so hollow when there were two babies crowding her organs? Pressing on her bladder.

With no small effort, she hoisted herself from the recliner.

"Where you going?" PJ asked without looking.

"Bathroom."

"Want me to pause?"

"No." She'd seen *While You Were Sleeping* three times.

Jade was in the hall when she felt it. First a trickle, then a small gush. She looked down. Dark patches splotched her yoga pants.

A trickle of liquid ran down her ankle. Her thoughts froze. Then she was thinking of everything at once. Of calling the doctor, retrieving her packed bag, calling her family. She was thinking of the babies. Of Daniel.

No, not him.

The babies were coming. Now.

"PJ?" she called. "Um—my water just broke."

The couch groaned as PJ left it. A flurry of footsteps stopped at the hall entry. "But—your C-section isn't for a week."

God love her. "Tell the babies that." Jade smiled, hoping to ease the deer-in-headlights look from her sister's face.

"I'll drive you. Want me to drive you?"

"Sure." Jade pulled up the mental list she'd gone over with her doctor. "Can you clean up dinner while I—" She waved at her wet pants. "Then we'll go to the hospital."

"Clean up dinner . . ." PJ hustled toward the kitchen, the dazed look still there.

Jade changed, made sure the fluid was clear, then met PJ in the living room. Once in her sister's car, Jade called her doctor. She would meet Jade at the hospital.

She couldn't reach her parents, but left a calm voice mail. Madison was in the middle of a vet emergency. She'd come as soon as she finished, but it could be awhile. Ryan promised to call Grandpa and head that way.

"Are you okay?" PJ asked about a dozen times on the way. Each time Jade assured her she was.

The contractions hadn't started. It could be a long night. Part of her hoped for a natural birth, but it wasn't likely. Besides, after the Lamaze movie, part of her was glad. The movie made her think of Daniel. He was supposed to be here. Was supposed be in the room when the babies were born. Was supposed to be their daddy.

She pushed the thought away. Couldn't think about that right now. Had to focus on her babies.

At the hospital, PJ pulled up to the door. An orderly helped her into the waiting wheelchair. Jade checked in while PJ parked the car. A few minutes later they entered the birthing center.

They wheeled Jade into a room where she changed into an ugly gown. She waited in bed while they hooked her up to the monitors. While she was changing, PJ had reached their parents. They were on their way.

A nurse studied the screen. A few minutes later, she checked Jade for dilation. She frowned as she focused on some spot on the wall behind Jade.

Panic bubbled in Jade at the look on the nurse's face. "What's wrong?"

She pulled off the gloves, pushed a button, suddenly fast and efficient.

"What's going on?" Jade asked.

"The cord is prolapsed." The nurse fixed a tight smile on Jade even while she began unhooking the monitors. "Looks like you'll need that C-section after all, sweetie."

Jade tried to remember what she knew about prolapsed cords. It wasn't much. People were suddenly in the room. Her bed was lowered and adjusted. "Are the babies okay?"

The nurses were moving around, quickly but calmly performing tasks.

"Your doctor just arrived and is scrubbing in. We'll have your babies out of there before you can blink twice."

Jade's heart rate tripled while she answered the nurse's questions, her thoughts spinning. She had questions of her own, about a thousand, but everyone was in a rush, and her tongue was stuck to the roof of her mouth.

They pushed the gurney from the room, heading quickly down the sterile hall. Ceiling tiles whirred past.

PJ scurried beside her. Her hand tightened on Jade's. "It's going to be okay. You're prepared for a C-section. They know what they're doing."

Please, God. Let my babies be all right. Jade's eyes stung at the thought of them, all snug inside, depending on her to keep them safe.

But they weren't safe. Something was wrong.

They reached a set of double doors that swung open.

"You'll need to wait here, Sis," the nurse said.

"No," PJ said. "I want to stay with her."

"Sorry, not for an emergency C-section."

Emergency. Jade suddenly remembered covering this in Lamaze.

"She'll be on general anesthesia," the nurse said. "I'm sorry—hospital rules."

Jade squeezed PJ's hand. "I'll be fine. Call the family. Give them an update."

PJ looked down at her, her eyes liquid brown. They were already pulling the gurney through the doors. "I know you will. I'll be right here."

Jade knew a moment of terror when her hand left PJ's. In the OR the staff of uniforms buzzed around her. She'd never felt more alone. They explained what was happening as they darted around under the bright lights, all business.

A mask was slapped on her face. Fear trickled in. What if something happened to her babies? She couldn't lose them. It was her job to keep them safe. What if something happened to her? Who would take care of them? Why hadn't she thought about this before now, when it was too late?

The room blurred, her thoughts became distant and fuzzy. Then blackness closed in.

Chapter Forty

Where was she? Jade couldn't seem to pry her eyes open. Feet shuffled nearby. Something was beeping. That smell. Antiseptic. She drifted off again.

"Jade?"

Something moved against her arm. Her head was full of fuzz, her thoughts thick and unfocused.

"Can you hear me?"

Mom. What was she doing here? Where was she? Curiosity pried her eyes opened. White sheets. Handrails. She looked back to the white sheet, to her belly, barely rounded.

My babies. She palmed her stomach, her eyes flying to Mom. Her heart fluttered like a baby bird's.

"They're fine. Both of them." Mom squeezed her hand. "Two little girls. And they're beautiful like their mama."

Girls. "They're okay? Where are they?" Her eye scanned the room, but they weren't there. Of course not. They'd be in the NICU.

"Your Dad and PJ are with them. We're already head over heels."

"They're breathing all right? They're really okay?"

"The last Apgar scores were excellent."

Jade relaxed into the bed, her empty arms aching. "I want to see them." She wouldn't believe they were okay until they were in her arms.

Mom smiled and squeezed her hand. "Let me see what I can do, Little Mama."

* * *

Daniel clutched the vase of flowers in his hand as he approached Jade's hospital room.

"Go on now." Mama Jo ushered him through the door and backed out, shutting it behind him.

Jade lay against the pillows, sleeping, her dark lashes fanning her pale face. She looked so beautiful, ethereal, even with her hair in disarray, wearing an ugly hospital gown, with dark circles under her eyes.

He walked forward, hardly breathing.

"Jade?" he said quietly.

She didn't so much as twitch. But then she'd been through quite an ordeal, and the anesthesia hadn't worn off. Poor thing was bushed. He'd come as soon as Ryan had called.

He reached out, moved a strand of hair off her face.

She probably didn't even want to see him, but he had to see her. Had to make sure she was really okay. He'd seen the babies too. Two tiny, squirming bundles. They were a lucky pair.

He watched her sleep a moment, watched her

stomach rise and fall. She needed her rest more than she needed to see his face. And he already felt better just seeing her. She'd be okay. She had her family. Her girls. She didn't need him anymore. He set the vase quietly on the bedside table and turned to leave.

* * *

Jade must've fallen asleep, because she was in a different room when she opened her eyes. A nurse was wheeling two bassinets into the room. Her parents and PJ were on her heels.

Jade tried to sit up, but the pull at her abdomen stopped her.

"Hang on, sweetie." The nurse raised the bed until Jade could see the babies cocooned in their hospital blankets, knit caps on their tiny heads.

"Their lungs are okay?" Jade asked. "And the prolapsed cord didn't hurt them?"

"We got them out lickety-split, and they recovered just fine." The nurse picked up one of the girls and set her in Jade's arms. "This one's awake. Her sister likes to nap."

Jade stared down at her baby. Her girl. Her skin was pink and wrinkly, and her glassy blue eyes stared into Jade's with rapt attention.

"Hi there, baby girl. I'm your mama." Her throat closed up. "That was quite an entry you made."

"Aren't they beautiful?" Mom leaned down, the

other baby in her arms. Her eyes were closed, her dark lashes fanning her translucent skin. "Want to hold them both?"

"Yes."

Mom set the other bundle in the crook of Jade's arm. Jade looked between the two. "They're not identical."

Mom propped pillows under Jade's elbows. "No worries about mixing them up."

"Look at her," Dad said. "She's sucking on her lip in her sleep."

Her tiny rosebud lip was tucked in. They were so beautiful, so fragile. Jade couldn't believe they were hers. What a precious gift. Her heart felt so full, she nearly burst with it.

"Okay, we know the names," PJ said. "But which one is which?"

Jade looked at her mom. "How do I choose?"

Mom chuckled. "Don't ask me. Mine were a boy and a girl."

Jade looked between the babies, stopping on the blue eyes that stared back at her. "Well, since your sister is sleeping through this monumental occasion, we'll start with you, little girl."

Jade stared into her eyes. Little muscles puckered between her brows. A deep thinker. The baby blinked, her gaze steady and old beyond her age. "You're Ava." Jade pressed a kiss to Ava's forehead.

Jade looked at the other bundle, so slight in her

arms. "And you, my little sleepyhead, are Mia."

Dad set his hands on their capped heads. His face grew serious. He blinked against the tears, quoting softly. "Children are a gift of the Lord, the fruit of the womb is a reward. Like arrows in the hand of a warrior, so are the children of one's youth."

Her babies' faces blurred under the onslaught of emotions.

Dad set a gentle kiss on each tiny head. "Welcome to the McKinley family, girls."

* * *

When Jade woke next, her mom was by the bed reading a magazine.

"Where are the babies?" Jade's voice sounded hoarse.

Mom held the water jug to Jade's lips. "In the nursery sleeping. Want me to get them?"

"Yeah, I'd like to try feeding them again." Her eyes swung to the flowers on the bedside table as Mom set the jug on it.

She pulled the card from the envelope and read it. *Congratulations, Jade. They are so beautiful. Love, Daniel.* A knot formed in her throat.

"He came in while you were sleeping. He didn't want to wake you."

Jade nodded and Mom left the room to get the babies.

She pictured Daniel standing over her bed, watching her sleep, wishing things were different.

She wondered if he'd held the babies. Wondered if he'd touched her as she'd slept. A knot swelled in her throat as she closed her fingers around the card, curling it into her palm.

Chapter Forty-One

Jade rocked Mia in the chair, patting her back. Ava was already down for the night, and Jade was enjoying a quiet moment with Mia before she turned in.

When Mia let out a soft burp, Jade dropped a kiss on her head and laid her in the crib. She changed into pajamas and headed toward the kitchen.

She could hear her mom fixing a late-night snack. Mom had been staying with her this week, helping with midnight feedings and running errands since Jade couldn't drive yet.

Between family and church Jade had enough casseroles for the next month. The apartment had been overwhelmed with flower arrangements, balloons, and McKinleys. Now, a week later, the flowers were gone, the pink balloons shriveled. Her mom was going home tomorrow.

Jade's eyes drifted to the one remaining arrangement—Daniel's. Daisies, her favorite, bloomed from a vase, a pink bow circling the neck.

"Is she down?" Mom asked, pulling her from her thoughts.

"Out like a light." Jade filled her hospital mug with fresh water. "And I'm right behind her."

"I'll take the feedings tonight," Mom said. "You'd better rest up. You're on your own starting tomorrow."

"We can alternate. I don't want to send you home overtired."

"I have many sleep-filled nights in my future." Mom patted her shoulder. "You, not so much. Now off to bed, sweetie."

Jade gave in. It was useless to argue. She peeked in on the babies on her way by. Their tiny chests rose with each sweet breath. She never got tired of watching them.

There had been some frantic moments when Ava and Mia were both awake and hungry or in need of a change. But mostly they slept. They were so different. Ava had a capful of dark hair, while Mia had just a dusting. Ava's eyes only grew brighter blue, while Mia's had shifted toward green.

Little bits of their personalities emerged. Ava loved her pacifier while Mia preferred her fingers. Ava liked to be watched. If you stared into her eyes it calmed her, and she'd drift away peacefully. Mia, on the other hand, fidgeted under her perusal. She rested easily when Jade's attention was elsewhere.

Jade fell more deeply in love with them each day. Even when she dragged herself from bed for three a.m. feedings, her heart squeezed when she cuddled her girls in her arms, when she watched their delicate eyelids drift shut, when she held their tiny fists in her hands.

She hadn't seen Daniel. She knew he was giving her space, but still his absence hurt. She missed him. She longed to see her girls cradled in his arms like fragile footballs. Longed to hear him calling them Peanut and Nugget. He'd been right. Two girls.

She drew a breath, but the air didn't fill the hollow space inside. Nothing helped except the oblivion of sleep. She left the nursery, her mind turning to more pressing problems.

She'd planned on six weeks of maternity leave, but who knew how long it would take to find a job? Her family had put out feelers. She needed something soon. Her little nest egg would barely cover a month's rent, and now she had the extra expenses of supplemental formula and diapers.

Jade pulled open her nightstand drawer and rooted for her lip balm. As she dug around, she spotted the notes and cards she'd tucked away a year and a half earlier. Her secret admirer.

She pulled out the top one, a new realization setting her pulse racing. Her eyes scanned the typed poem. Had Daniel sent this? Sent all these notes, left the flowers?

She recalled the note she'd received when she returned to town, the one that had been left at her mom's store. The one that had made her freak and spill her fears to Daniel. She hadn't received another after that.

The empty place inside spread outward, swallowing everything in its wake. Of course she hadn't. Because Daniel would never intentionally frighten her.

"Honey, where's Ava's paci?" Mom stopped at the threshold, silently taking in the note in Jade's hand.

"I left it in her crib."

"What's that?"

Jade slipped the note into her drawer and pushed it closed. "Just a note."

She didn't want to think about Daniel, and she wouldn't allow herself to read the notes and poems imagining him as the author.

Mom saw right through her. "He's loved you a long time, you know."

Her heart gave a hard squeeze, and suddenly breathing became a chore. "Don't, Mom."

Jade didn't want to know anything. Didn't want to know how long or when he'd first realized he loved her or how long her mom had known. She didn't want to think about how much she'd hurt him over the years or how much he was hurting now. She couldn't bear the thought.

Mom perched on the bed beside Jade. "Honey,

I don't know exactly what's going on or how you're feeling. But are you sure you and Daniel can't make this work? I was starting to sense that you were falling—"

"No. It's over, Mom." She kept her eyes on the rings she twisted on her finger. Her mom saw too much.

"Are you still in love with their father? Is that it?"

"What? No."

She'd never told the story, and her family had never pressed her. But they would now that the babies were born. They'd think the father should know. And of course under normal circumstances, they'd be right. But these weren't normal circumstances. And there was no reason to keep it from them anymore. Her mom could handle this now. And Jade knew forgetting was an impossibility if they started hounding her about it—and they would.

"I was never in love with him, Mom. We—we had one date and he—" She found her mom's eyes, tried to prepare her before she just spilled it out like yesterday's milk. "It was date rape, Mom."

Mom gasped. "Oh, baby." She pulled Jade into a hug and clutched her tight. "Why didn't you tell me?"

Jade shook her head against Mom's shoulder. This wouldn't change the way they felt about her girls, would it?

"I just wanted to forget it. I didn't want to keep reliving it. I don't really remember much—he drugged me."

Her mom made a deep sound in her throat and looked at her with glassy eyes. "I'm so sorry. I wish I'd been there for you."

"Izzy helped me through it. I wasn't alone. She was a really good friend."

"Did you report it?"

"I didn't even know his last name. He was just a regular customer, and I thought I knew him pretty well. Obviously not. I know I should've reported it. But by the time I felt strong enough to handle it, it was too late. There was no evidence, and I couldn't even give them a name. I just wanted to move past it."

"And then you found out you were pregnant?"

"Yeah." She told her mom about everything from the aftermath to the discovery of the pregnancy. It all seemed so long ago now. "A part of me was so afraid I wouldn't be able to love them." Jade breathed a laugh. "I was so wrong. I couldn't love them more. Sometimes I—" She wasn't sure she wanted to complete the thought.

"What, honey?"

She'd never vocalized what had been growing in her heart since their birth. The fear that spread, consuming her, driving her to check their cribs every time she woke at night.

"I love them so much. Sometimes I'm petrified

of losing them. I watch them sleep and worry they'll stop breathing in the night." She found her mom's eyes. "Will I ever get used to it?"

"Used to having your heart run around outside your body?" Mom shook her head. "Not really. But if you learn to trust God with them, it gets easier. He loves them too. He has a plan for them and for you. You just have to trust that He knows what He's doing. It's not always easy."

She knew her mom was thinking of losing Michael. It had about killed them all when he'd died. Had his death been God's plan? For what purpose? She supposed they'd never know.

Jade didn't know if she was capable of trusting like her mom. She hoped so. Because she didn't want to live her life in fear.

"You've been through so much. You're so strong, Jade."

She wasn't strong. She hadn't felt anywhere near strong until Daniel had come alongside her. Until Daniel had helped her and protected her and—loved her.

Now he was gone, and she was on her own.

Not on her own. She had her two precious girls, and she was going to be strong for them.

Chapter Forty-Two

Daniel shoveled the last bite of turkey into his mouth and chewed without tasting. Across his grandmother's table, his mom and dad chatted about the holiday decorations they were having installed on their DC home.

The chandelier was dimmed in the formal dining room, and centerpiece candles flickered from a nest of pine in the middle of the table. Outside the bay window snow fell diagonally, a thin layer already sticking to the ground. The season's first snowfall. They were expecting three inches, though the first precipitation had come in the form of sleet. He was almost certain to have an emergency call or two tonight. Was surprised he hadn't already.

He wondered if the McKinleys had sat down to their Thanksgiving meal yet. Normally he'd be there, but his parents had flown in this year. He'd purposely told his grandma six o'clock so he'd have a ready excuse when Mama Jo invited him.

He'd been avoiding the family gatherings since the breakup four weeks ago. Mama Jo's feelings were hurt, but what could he do? He'd only make Jade uncomfortable. They needed space. He needed time for his broken heart to mend. Time to get over her. Though on nights like this, when his thoughts turned constantly to her, he wondered if that were a pipe dream.

Keeping busy had been easy enough. With Jade out of the office, his hours were long. The office had been so quiet, so lonely without her. He'd been eager for a couple days off. But now that they'd arrived, he realized the extra time only gave more hours to think of Jade.

He'd moved his weight bench and treadmill back into the spare room. There would be no cribs, no rocking chair in there now. He'd put the equipment to good use this morning when he'd woken to the depressing realization that he had an empty day to fill.

By the time evening had arrived, he'd been relieved for the distraction of family and conversation. But his mom's barely suppressed glee over the breakup made Daniel want to smash his fist through a wall.

"What do you think, Daniel?" Mom asked.

His eyes snapped up. No idea what they were talking about.

"Black Friday," his dad said. "Will it be more profitable this year than last?"

Daniel shrugged. "Hard to say." Couldn't care less, actually.

He'd nearly bought a Christmas gift when he'd been in Dunbar's this week. A snow globe with an angel inside. When he twisted the knob it had played "All Through the Night." He'd had two of them in his hands before he remembered his gifts wouldn't be welcome. Heart as heavy as a boulder, he'd placed them back on the shelf.

"Honey, you're so gloomy," Mom said. "It's Thanksgiving."

Daniel gave a tight smile. "Sorry." His eyes flickered to his grandmother. "The food's delicious, Grandma."

"I'll pass your compliments on to Mrs. Pierson. She was nervous about the stuffing. It's a new recipe, but I think I like it even better."

"It's a beautiful snowy night," Mom said. "We have so much to be thankful for. This lovely meal, our health, your burgeoning campaign fund . . . Dad told me your manager said things are really moving along."

"No business tonight, dear."

"That's a lovely sweater, Daniel," Grandma said. "It looks so soft."

He glanced down. It was the blue one his mom had given him for Christmas the year before.

"I got it at Saks," Mom said. "It's cashmere. Isn't the color beautiful on him? It matches your eyes perfectly, darling."

Conversation turned to Christmas plans. He was supposed to have been married by then. He and Jade would've woken on Christmas Day to celebrate the twins' first Christmas. *Their* first Christmas. Maybe Jade would've hung stockings on the mantel and taken pictures of them with Santa hats. They would've taken the girls to the farmhouse. He would've kissed Jade under the mistletoe that hung over the kitchen threshold while the family passed the babies around.

"So we thought you could come our way this year," Mom said.

The table grew quiet until Daniel realized they were talking to him. Come to DC for Christmas?

"Courtney would like to see you again," Mom said. "We passed on the good news to her."

"Victoria."

"Well, you know what I mean. Good news for *her.* She was elated you were back on the market."

Daniel gritted his teeth. "Thank you, but I think I'll stay here."

"I'm of the same mind." Grandma squeezed his hand. "I'll have you over for a delicious dinner Christmas Eve. How does that sound? We can light a fire in the parlor and play canasta like we used to."

"There are a couple of events it would behoove you to attend, Daniel," Mom said. "Marlin Walters has invited us over for an intimate gathering on Christmas Eve."

"The speaker and his family will be there along with Evan Brewer and Maxwell Worthington," Dad said. "You met them earlier in the summer at the black-tie function. The Crawfords will be there too. It would benefit you to patch up the damage you did with the ferry deal."

What was wrong with these people, networking on Christmas Eve? Didn't they know it was a family holiday? A time to celebrate Jesus's birth?

"I'm sure Courtney would be happy to accompany you. In fact, I already mentioned it to her and—"

"Mom. You didn't."

"Just in passing, dear. You can't continue to sulk around Chapel Springs—"

Grandma stood. "Is anyone ready for coffee? I'll just put on a pot. It'll be nice and fresh in time for pie."

Daniel waited until Grandma slipped into the kitchen. "I don't want to date Courtney, Mom. And I don't want to go to DC for Christmas. This is my home. This is where I want to spend the holidays."

Mom set her napkin on her plate, chuckling. "Well, honey, you'd better get used to being away. When you're a congressman, you'll be gone more than you're home."

Her chuckle was a long fingernail running up his spine. "Well. Maybe I don't want to be a congressman." The words slipped out before the filter caught it.

Mom gasped.

Dad set his hand on Mom's. "He doesn't mean it."

The thought had been there for months, lingering in the back of his mind. Years maybe. He hadn't meant to let it slip. Hadn't even thought it through or prayed about it. But the release of the words had eased tension in his muscles. His shoulders felt lighter, as if a heavy weight had lifted.

He loved being mayor. Why was he chasing after something else when he was content where he was? *Is this right, God? Am I already where You want me?* And why was he just asking now? He'd been aimed at national politics like a precision missile, and he'd never even prayed about it.

He was off course. He felt it in his gut. In his spirit.

"I like being mayor. I love the people. I have a purpose right here."

Mom crossed her arms. "This is ridiculous. You are destined for so much more than this Podunk town!"

Dad leaned in, his blue lasers trained on Daniel. "Do you have any idea how many men would kill for the opportunities you have? You have the skills, you have the connections, you even have the support. Why would you even think of throwing all that away? We've been grooming you for this for years, son."

"You never even asked me if this is what I wanted."

"You wanted to be a politician!"

"I am one. Right here in Chapel Springs."

Mom huffed. Her lips flattened. She shook her head.

"I should've said something a long time ago. It never felt right, but I—"

"This is all that girl's doing!"

Daniel clenched his teeth. "This is my life, my decision." He appealed to his dad. "Being a mayor was good enough for Grandpa. He left a legacy. I'm proud to follow in his footsteps."

"This is a big decision. Take some time, son. Think it over."

"What are you saying, Allen?" Mom's voice rose. "There's nothing to think over." She nailed Daniel with a look. "Do you know what your father has done for you? All the potential you're so carelessly tossing aside? You should be grateful!"

Daniel set his napkin down. "I'm done with this conversation."

"We're done when I say we're done."

"No, Mom." Daniel stood. "I'm done now."

Mom's ruby lips parted before pressing together. His dad sat back in his chair, poker-faced.

"I'm leaving," Daniel said. "Good night."

He slipped into the kitchen to say good-bye

and thank his grandma. He hated to leave early, but his emotions were high. He was going to say things he'd regret.

"Be careful, sweetie." Grandma slid her thin arms around him. "It's probably getting slick out there."

In the car Daniel turned on his wipers as he followed the concrete drive. The snow was coming down in thick flakes, padding the earth with a soft blanket. He tested his brakes at the end of the drive. The wheels slid a foot or so before coming to a stop.

The street was clear of snow. His headlights swung across the pavement as he turned, catching on shiny patches of black. Yeah, definitely a run or two tonight.

He headed cautiously toward his place, his mind back in the dining room. He couldn't believe he'd said it. Couldn't believe he'd stood up to them. But then he'd bucked them on Jade too. Maybe that confrontation had given him the courage to take a stand on his career. He knew he hadn't heard the last of it. His parents wouldn't let it go easily. His mom was as tenacious as a bulldog. His dad had more subtle ways of manipulating.

But he wasn't going back. This was right. He hadn't known how right until he'd said it aloud.

There weren't many cars out. It was early in the evening, and most families were still gathered around the table or stretched in front of the football game letting the tryptophan go to work. That's what the McKinleys were no doubt doing. He should be there, lounging in his spot in the corner of the sofa, Jade under one arm, one of the babies sleeping on his chest.

Needing a distraction, he turned on the radio to check the score of the game. Maybe when he got home, he'd get on the treadmill again. Run until he couldn't focus on anything but catching his next breath.

He didn't see the glare of lights until he looked up from the radio. He turned to the left in time to feel the slam, hear the crunch of metal. His head hit something hard. And then there was darkness.

Chapter Forty-Three

"Look at that snow," Grandpa said. "It's really coming down now."

Jade looked out the dining room window. The flakes were huge. She hoped it would stick. It would give her an excuse to stay in with the girls awhile.

"Beautiful," Mom said.

"Why can't we ever get this on Christmas?" PJ asked.

"We did," Ryan said. "Three years ago,

remember? You nailed me in the head with a snowball as I was leaving to go home."

"Oh yeah."

The snowball had started a boys-versus-girls war. It had ended when Jade stuffed a handful of wet snow down Daniel's shirt. He'd finally called truce.

"Mmmm," PJ said. "Who made the sweet potatoes? These are delish."

"Madison."

"I want the recipe."

"Me too," Mom said. "Though the calories in this alone are putting me over the top for the day."

"Shhhhhhh," Madison said. "No talk of calories on Thanksgiving."

"A couple miles on the treadmill tomorrow, and they'll be gone," Ryan said.

"Hush," Mom said. "No talk of exercising either. It's Thanksgiving, and we have so much to be thankful for."

Dad grabbed her hand and pressed a kiss there. "Like your health."

Mom traded a loving smile with him, then shifted her focus to the babies. "And our beautiful granddaughters."

Madison leaned into Beckett. "Each other."

"A long weekend," PJ said.

"Food," Ryan said, shoving a bite of stuffing into his mouth.

PJ rolled her eyes.

Beside Jade, Ava squirmed in her carrier, then began mewling. Jade set her fork down.

"I got her." PJ scooted her chair back and scooped up the baby. "Speaking of weight gain. Good grief, little girl." Ava instantly quieted as PJ rubbed her back.

Across the table, Ryan's pager went off, quieting the room.

"Oh, honey, no," Mom said. "Not on Thanksgiving."

Ryan checked the screen and pushed his chair back. "Sorry, Mom. The streets are messy. It was inevitable." He pecked her on the cheek on the way out. "I'll try and be back in time for pumpkin pie."

After he left, the family lingered around the table, squeezing in seconds of their favorite dishes. They were in no hurry for dessert, needing time to digest and wanting to wait on Ryan.

The whole meal had felt strange without Daniel. He always came for Thanksgiving, usually with his grandma. Every year he fought Jade over the wishbone. After supper he traded covert smiles with her when Dad jumped from his chair, complaining about some unfair call in the football game on TV. He shot hoops with PJ no matter how cold it was and ended the evening passed out in the corner of the sofa, the newspaper open on his chest.

A distinct odor permeated the dining room. PJ held up Ava and took a whiff. "Ugh." PJ held her out to Jade. "This is all yours."

"I've got her." Mom reached for Ava. "Come on, baby girl. Let's get you cleaned up."

"We're missing the Colts." Dad scooped up Mia and headed for his throne in front of the TV with Grandpa. Madison and Beckett insisted on dish detail. Jade helped PJ clear the table. She was returning to the table when the phone rang.

"Got it," she said, then wondered if it was Daniel calling to wish them a happy Thanksgiving. She wished she hadn't volunteered so fast, but it was too late now.

She covered her ear to hush the rushing of the faucet and Madison and Beckett's banter by the dishwasher.

"Hello?"

"Jade, it's Ryan." His voice was strung tight.

A burst of adrenaline shot through her system. She squeezed the phone. "What's wrong?"

"It's Daniel. He's had an accident. He's being medevaced to Riverview right now."

Her heart hammered, the blood rushing through her veins. "What?"

"He had a car accident. He's unconscious and unresponsive. Tell the others. I'll meet you there."

No. No, God. Not another car accident. This can't be happening. Not again.

She shook her head, another accident, another

trip to the hospital. It had ended so horribly last time. *No, please.* She shook her head.

"Jade? Did you hear me?"

Please, God. Not Daniel. Not Daniel. Not Daniel.

"Jade?"

"Who is it?" Madison asked from the sink. Her face fell. "Jade, what's wrong?"

Get it together, Jade. Think. "Is he—is he going to be okay?" *Please, God. He has to be okay.*

"I don't know," Ryan said.

As the family hunched in waiting room seats, Jade paced the adjacent hallway. Madison and Beckett had stayed behind with Grandpa and the babies. Daniel's parents and Grandma had arrived at the hospital, shaken, shortly after the McKinleys and had disappeared down the hall with the nurse. They hadn't returned with news, and Jade was about to come unglued.

Mom had put Daniel on the prayer chain, and the family's own prayers were constant waves of petition. But Jade had a bad feeling, way down inside. A feeling that kept her feet moving on the sterile tile and made her hands tremble at her sides.

"This is ridiculous," she said. "Why haven't they told us anything?"

"They have to run tests," Ryan said, still in his bunker gear. "It'll take awhile before we know anything."

"What happened?" Dad asked. "Was there another car involved?"

"An SUV was coming down Oak toward Main. He tried to stop, but there was black ice. Plowed right into Daniel's door."

Jade shuddered.

Mom patted the empty chair beside her. "Come sit down, honey."

She needed to see him. Needed to touch his warm flesh and watch his chest rise and fall. What if he didn't wake up? What if he was already gone?

"I want to see him."

"They'll let us back when they can," Dad said. "His parents are with him."

"He's not close to them." His mom was probably demanding that he wake up and stop this foolishness.

Jade rubbed her temple. That wasn't nice. They were scared and hurting too.

She glared at the unhelpful woman manning the front desk. "Can't they at least tell us something?"

Ryan got up. "Let me try again."

Three hours later, they'd been moved to another waiting room. Exhausted, Jade slumped in the chair, digging her fingers in her hair. They'd finally gotten an update from Daniel's father.

Daniel had lacerations from the airbag and a

fractured clavicle, but most worrisome was the head trauma. He hadn't woken yet. The MRI revealed swelling on the brain. The doctors said they'd have to wait and see.

Wait and see. It sounded so easy. So simple. Just wait.

But waiting had become the most difficult thing Jade had ever done. Because the life of the man she loved hung in the balance. She hadn't even been allowed in his room. She wasn't family. Wasn't his fiancée or even his girlfriend.

Hours later, after Jade had gone home briefly to feed the babies, a nurse swept into the waiting room. "You can go in now. Room 423. One at a time, though, and just ten minutes."

"You first, honey." Mom squeezed Jade's shoulder.

Jade rose on shaky legs. Finally. She couldn't get there fast enough. Her heart pummeled her ribs as she walked down the hall, her flats squeaking on the polished floor.

She turned the doorknob and pushed it open. Her eyes caught at the form on the bed. Wires and tubes were everywhere. Machines beeped. The breath left her body in a rush.

Mr. Dawson stood. His eyes were puffy and red. New lines had sprouted across his forehead. Mrs. Dawson sagged in a chair near the bed.

"Is he—is there any change?" she asked.

Mr. Dawson shook his head. "We'll give you a moment," he said thickly, touching her arm. He escorted his wife from the room.

Jade's eyes swung back to Daniel. Her feet carried her to his bedside in a trance. One side of his face was black and blue, his eye swollen. Lacerations marred his beautiful face. His dark lashes swept down over the discolored flesh.

An ache built in her throat, behind her eyes. She reached for his hand and was comforted by the warmth of his skin.

"Oh, Daniel," she whispered. Her throat closed up.

He should be awake, smiling. Throwing snowballs. He should be teasing her and holding her babies and rooting for the Colts.

"You have to wake up." She wrapped her hand around his, wishing she could climb into bed and hold him. "I need you."

Her eyes burned with unshed tears. "Do you hear me? You have to wake up." She watched his eyelids, his lips, for some flicker of movement. But he lay perfectly still except for the rise and fall of his chest. The beeps continued steadily.

"We missed you tonight. There was no one to fight me over the wishbone, and no one else even wanted the drumsticks." Her voice broke.

None of this should've happened. He should've been at the McKinleys', and then he wouldn't have been on the road. There would've been no accident. He wouldn't be lying here unconscious.

Her breath caught in her lungs. If she hadn't broken up with him, this wouldn't have happened. Guilt choked her. Her own heart raced. She sank into the chair Mrs. Dawson had vacated. Her head fell against the cool metal of the bed rail.

She squeezed Daniel's hand. "Wake up, Daniel," she whispered. But there was no response.

"Jade, honey, you need some sleep," Mom said as Jade reached for her coat. She'd come home to feed her girls again. She'd held each of them well past the time they were sleeping before settling them in their cribs.

She wasn't sure how much time had passed. One day? Two? Her family took shifts with the babies. The hospital staff changed. Daniel's fire fighter friends came and went. The *Gazette* called for updates on the mayor. The world around her was moving, shifting, changing.

Everything except Daniel. He remained the same.

She left the hospital when her breasts became engorged and returned after putting the babies down. She felt guilty when she was home. Daniel needed her. She should be by his side. Then she felt guilty when she was with him. Her girls needed her too.

"Jade." Mom grabbed her coat. "I mean it now.

Sleep. You're not doing him any good like this."

"I have to go back."

"When's the last time you ate?"

Jade couldn't think past the fuzz growing inside her brain. "I don't know."

"*Sit.*" Mom led her to the couch and gave a gentle shove.

Jade's knees folded.

"You need to keep up your strength if you want to keep nursing."

A moment later there was a hot bowl of soup in her hands. Jade ladled a spoonful to her mouth. The sooner she got it down, the sooner she could get back to Daniel.

Mom set a glass of milk on the table and settled at the other end of the sofa. Jade was sitting where she had been that night. The night she'd returned Daniel's ring. The night she'd broken his heart.

She'd never told him she loved him. Had never done him that small kindness. What if he never woke up? What if she never got to tell him? Her breath came quickly, stuffing her lungs.

So many things she hadn't done for him. She'd never made her awesome pancakes for him or covered him with a blanket when he drifted asleep in his recliner. She hadn't even played him the song she'd started writing the night he'd played the lullaby for her.

She thought of all the nevers and her heart

caved in on itself, crushing her chest. She couldn't breathe, much less eat. She set the soup on the table.

Losing Aaron had been so hard. But at least she'd done all those things and so much more. Losing Daniel, before she'd given him anything, would be so much worse.

How selfish she'd been. Holding back from loving him because she was afraid. Her depth of love for her girls frightened her too, but would she even think of giving them up now? Of course not.

Yet she'd given up Daniel. She could've made him happy. Even if only for days or weeks, she could've made him happy. But she'd broken his heart instead.

Her lungs closed off, and the ache inside built.

"It's going to be okay, baby." Mom was there, brushing the tears from her face.

Jade shook her head.

"Yes it is. God's got this under control."

"Does He? Sometimes it doesn't feel like it. Sometimes if feels like everything is spinning out of control. Sometimes it feels like He doesn't even care. I mean, Daniel. Of all people. Dear, sweet Daniel."

"Jade."

"It's not fair. Michael, Aaron . . ."

"Don't go there, Jade. Daniel is not Aaron. And we don't know what's going to happen. Look,

God had His reasons, and we don't always understand the why of it. We just have to trust Him. He created all things, He knows all things, and He does have this under control."

At times like this, when the world felt upside down, Jade envied her mom's unshakable faith.

"I wish I could be so sure," Jade said.

Mom wiped Jade's tears away. "You can be. Times like this either cause us to fall away from God or make our roots sink deep. It's our choice. Troubles have a way of doing that, and God knows you've had your share of troubles.

"The same sun that burns a shallow-rooted plant will nourish a deeply-rooted one. I hope your roots burrow down deep. It won't take away your troubles or make things perfect, but it does give you peace and strength through the hard times."

I do want that kind of faith, God. That kind of peace. I'm tired of my life spinning out of control. Of being afraid. Give me courage. I want to believe there's a reason for all this. Some greater purpose, even if I can't see it.

Jade took a tissue from her mom. "You think he'll be okay?"

Mom gave a hopeful smile. "Only God knows. In the meantime we can be there for him. But you have to take care of yourself, Jade. You're exhausted."

"I'll sleep at the hospital." She'd slept in her folded arms when his parents tore themselves from Daniel's bedside. Spent hours slouched in the waiting room chair, head against the wall.

She felt the pull of him now and finished the soup, knowing she had to keep up her strength. Maybe today he'd wake up. Maybe she'd get the chance to tell him she loved him. Maybe it wasn't too late.

Mom stood when Jade finished her soup and helped Jade into her coat. "When PJ gets here, I'll be over."

"Thanks." Jade grabbed her purse. She turned at the door, her heart in her eyes. "I love him, Mom."

Her mom gave her a teary smile. "I know, baby."

Chapter Forty-Four

Pain.

Everywhere.

He tried to move, but his limbs weighed a thousand pounds. He was cold. His heart beeped. And then the fog closed over him again.

Pain. In his head. His shoulder, his chest, his throat. He tried to make a sound, but nothing came out. Tried to move, but the weight held him captive. Too tired. He slipped into the fog, away from the pain.

Then he felt it.

Something soft, like spun silk, on his hand. An angel's voice, whispering softly. He wanted to listen, just a little while. But the fog closed in, and there was nothing again.

He was having a wonderful dream. Jade was there. He couldn't see her. It was dark. But he could smell her spicy scent. Feel her stroking his face. Hear her whispering.

The fog pulled at him. He didn't want to leave the dream. Even though pain intruded. He wanted to see her. Why was it so dark? Why did everything hurt? He could tolerate the pain if he could just see her.

"Daniel, come back," she whispered.

He tried so hard. But then he was sinking again. Back into the fog.

The pain was back. Stronger. His head hurt. What was wrong with him?

A hand clutched his, cool and firm.

"He moved! Allen, he moved!"

Daniel struggled to pry open his eyes. They seemed superglued together.

"Daniel," Dad said. "Wake up."

"Push the button."

"Daniel. Come on, son."

Daniel's eyes fluttered open. He squinted against the bright lights. His head throbbed. His parents leaned over, clutching his arm, his hand.

Metal rails. Beeping. Sterile sheets.

Someone rushed into the room.

"He's awake," Mom told the nurse.

More people came. Uniforms. Why was he in the hospital? He thought back. Thanksgiving. Grandma's table. Snow. Nothing else.

"What happened?" His voice was rusty.

"You had an accident." Mom's eyes were liquid blue. "You're in the hospital. But you're going to be okay now."

How long, he wanted to ask. What happened? Where was his angel? But his mouth wouldn't move, his limbs grew heavy, and he was drifting away again.

* * *

Jade stirred in her waiting room seat. Nurses rushed down the hall. A doctor turned into Daniel's room. Her heart skipped a beat, then went right to double time.

She bolted to her feet. "What's going on?"

Ryan and Mom stirred in their seats, but Jade was already past them. More staff scurried toward the room.

His parents were ushered into the hall. His mom's hand covered her mouth. Her eyes shone with tears. Mr. Dawson pulled her into his arms.

Oh, God, no. Please. I'll do anything. Anything.

Mr. Dawson's eyes caught Jade's. She begged him silently not to tell her what she couldn't hear.

"He's awake," Mr. Dawson said.

"What?" Her feet froze in place. "Awake?"

Mr. Dawson smiled. "Awake."

They wouldn't let her in.

To be fair, they wouldn't let anyone in. They'd been running tests for what seemed like hours, and Jade couldn't sit still. Her wobbly legs ate up the short hallway. The rush of adrenaline had faded, leaving her shaky and exhausted.

But none of that mattered because Daniel was awake. He'd been alert and asking questions, they said. All good signs. She'd spent most of her pacing time thanking God for the good news.

Half of Chapel Springs seemed to be stuffed into the waiting room. Ryan had called the family, and everyone was here except PJ, who'd stayed with the twins. Jade was going to have to go home soon. Her breasts were engorged, but she needed to see Daniel.

Mr. Dawson was speaking with a doctor outside his door, and a moment later he and his wife were ushered into Daniel's room. Jade had never been so jealous of anyone in her life.

She waited as long as she could, but as the day wore on, she had to slip out and feed the twins. PJ had held off on Mia's bottle, and she was getting fussy.

She was slipping into her apartment when her mom called with good news. The CT and MRI looked good. Daniel's cognitive function was normal. Mom and Dad were getting ready to see him. Jade itched to be there with them, but first, her babies needed her care.

After she fed each of them, she placed kisses on their sweet foreheads, a feeling of gratitude sweeping over her, making her eyes water. She had her girls, and Daniel was going to be okay. Her world was turning right side up again.

Thank You, God. Thank You so much. It wouldn't always be this way. Sometimes things turned topsy-turvy. Sometimes everything changed for the worse in an instant. But this time it hadn't, and she was so thankful her heart felt full to overflowing.

She had so much she wanted to tell Daniel. Maybe he wouldn't even care now. Maybe he'd decided her world was too messy for him. Maybe he was done risking his heart for a broken girl. It had been over four weeks since they'd spoken. A lot had happened. Maybe she'd lost him for good.

Chapter Forty-Five

By the time Jade returned to the hospital, the waiting room had cleared out. Daniel was sleeping, with strict orders to be left undisturbed. His parents left to get some rest after Jade promised them she would stay.

Hours went by.

Outside the window, twilight draped over the world like a gauzy blanket. Flurries fell and streetlights flickered on. She looked down the hall to Daniel's closed door, impatience pecking her on the shoulder.

So many others had been in to see him, but she'd missed the window of opportunity. Had he wondered where she was? Did he think she didn't care? That she'd just carried on while his life had hung in the balance?

She had to see him. Just for a few minutes. She wouldn't disturb him. He needed rest, but she had to know he was okay. Had to see him with her own eyes.

She waited until the nurse at the station stepped away and sneaked down the hall, her heart bursting through her chest. She turned the knob and slipped inside, closing it quietly behind her.

The room was dim, the last of the day's light seeping through the window. Get-well cards covered every flat surface. Monitors beeped. The blessed sound of Daniel's breathing punctuated the silence.

She made her way to the semireclined bed. The bruising on his face had shifted toward yellow. The swelling was down, the abrasions healing. Someone had shaved his face. He looked more like her beautiful Daniel. His dark lashes fanned his cheeks. A tuft of hair had fallen over his forehead.

She reached out and brushed it back, loving the feel of it in her fingers. She watched his broad chest rise and fall, so grateful for this fundamental thing.

Unable to stop herself, she laid her hand on his, careful not to disturb him. His skin was warm, his familiar fingers thick and rough. Alive.

They would strum the guitar again. They would steeple under his chin. They would curl around a snowball, dribble a ball, tap out a text.

Would they palm her cheek? Thread through her hair? Catch a tear on her cheek?

She let go of his hand, sank into the chair, and leaned forward, resting her forehead on the cool rail. Stupid. She'd been so foolish to give him up. So afraid to love. She was still afraid. But nearly losing him had taught her something she would never forget. As afraid as she was of loving and losing, she was even more afraid of losing the chance to love him.

Maybe she'd already lost the chance.

The rhythm of the beeping changed. Jade raised her head. Blue eyes stared back. Her own heart skipped a beat. She looked into his eyes, unbelieving as he blinked twice.

Her hand tightened on the rail. "I didn't mean to wake you."

He wet his lips, his motions slow and deliberate.

"Thought I was dreaming." His voice sounded like sandpaper over gravel.

She grabbed his water jug, held the straw to his lips.

She watched as he drank, soaking him in. Watched him reach for the straw, watched his Adam's apple bob with each swallow. The simplest movements, all so wonderful, so miraculous.

His head fell back against the pillow. "Thanks."

She set the jug on the table and regarded him again. Did he realize how bad it had been? How scared she'd been of losing him? How scared they'd all been?

"You had us worried there for a while, Mr. Mayor."

"I heard."

She didn't want to talk about his brush with death. He was alive, his mesmerizing gaze fixed on her. "The waiting room was a zoo. The entire fire department was here, half the church. Heck, half the town. I think they all sent flowers. Your grandma's keeping them at her place."

"I'll open a nursery when they let me out of here."

She gave a wry grin. "You couldn't keep a weed alive."

He smiled. "You know me too well."

She did, didn't she? Knew him and loved him. Loved everything about him. The way he was quiet and introspective, almost introverted. Yet could hold his own in interviews and captivate an audience with an off-the-cuff speech.

She cleared her throat. "Are you cold? You want another blanket?"

He shook his head, wincing at the motion.

"Do you need more meds?"

He shifted. "Maybe you could push that button."

"This one?"

He nodded, and she dosed him with painkillers. "Help is on the way." She hated that he was in pain. She shouldn't have come in and disturbed him when he was resting peacefully.

"Where are my parents?"

"Getting some rest. They've hardly left your side."

He gave a slow blink. He was sleepy. He needed rest more than he needed to hear what she had to say.

"I'll leave you alone so you can get some sleep." She stood, squeezing his hand.

He tightened his hold, surprisingly strong. "Why are you here, Jade?"

She stopped, meeting his gaze. Did he want the simple answer or the complex one? Her thoughts teetered and settled somewhere in the middle. "Where else would I be?"

"Home with the girls." His eyes bore into hers, steady and true. Questioning.

Complex it is, then.

She stepped close to the bed, her heart in her throat, her hand suddenly trembling. Her fingers itched to twist her rings, but he'd captured her hand, and she wasn't willing to give up his touch.

"You want to talk about this now?"

"If it'll keep you in my room."

That was good, right? He wanted her here. Maybe it wasn't too late. Maybe he'd give her another chance. The thought—love, marriage, a lifetime—dangled in front of her, endlessly enticing, just out of reach.

Or maybe he was only lonely for company, no matter who.

He squeezed her hand. "What's going on behind those green eyes?"

"So much."

"Tell me."

It was time to be brave. Time to put words to her feelings. Where to start? Thoughts tumbled around. The last four weeks, the last few days. Unending days. An emotional roller coaster. Just thinking of all the hills and valleys made her head spin.

There was only one place she could start. The place that mattered. The place that had changed everything.

She closed the gap between them, her eyes not leaving him, her heart in her throat. "I love you, Daniel."

His eyes flickered with surprise. Something

else. It slowly faded away as his eyes narrowed. He held her gaze for a long moment, then his eyes went as flat as pool water. He looked away.

Her stomach dropped to the sterile floor, taking hope with it. She had to do something. Say something. Quick.

"I—when you told me—when I found out you loved me, I—" She swallowed hard. "It scared me. Losing Aaron did something to me . . ."

"I know."

But he didn't. He didn't know. "Having you love me scared me to death. I don't know if I can explain it or make you understand how scary love is for me. After I lost Aaron, I just—" She shook her head. "I lived in fear of losing someone I loved again. Of loving like that again."

"I get it, Jade."

"You don't."

He turned his head on the pillow, looking at her. She read the anguish in his eyes, and it gave her the courage to rush on.

"You don't get it. It wasn't just you loving me that scared me. It was *me* loving *you*."

Something shifted in his eyes. Did he understand now? That she didn't just love him. She *loved* him.

"Then you had this accident, and I thought I was going to lose you, just like I lost Aaron. And all I could think about was . . . I never even told you I love you."

374

Something flared in his eyes. Confusion. Questions. Hope. "You love me."

She'd always loved him. He knew that. There was a difference now, a big one.

She came closer until her thighs pressed against the bed. A dozen birds flapped inside her chest, beating to escape. Her palms dampened, her face flushed.

She spoke past the ache in her throat. "I'm in love with you, Daniel. I don't know when it happened, but I realized it that night you came over, the night I gave your ring back. It scared me to death." She blinked away the tears in her eyes. "And I—I thought giving you up would be easier than—"

"You're in love with me."

"I know I hurt you, and I'm sorry. I was hurting too, and missing you so much. But I didn't realize until I almost lost you for good that loving you is worth the risk. That I had to tell you. And I was so afraid I'd never have the chance.

"But I'm trying to walk by faith now, no matter how scary it is." A tear fell. She caught her trembling lip between her teeth. "God brought me you, and I gave you up. And I'm still so afraid. Heck, I'm scared to death right now that you're going to tell me it's too late. That you don't love me anymore and that I—"

He reached up, placed his finger over her lips. "Shhh."

His face blurred. She blinked and her vision cleared. His thumb followed the curve of her lower lip before falling back to the bed as if weighted.

"Not too late," he whispered. His eyes, liquid blue, held hers.

Her heart did a slow roll. "It's not?"

His gaze was steadfast. "I love you, Jade. I have for a long time, and I'm sure not going to stop now."

She let that soak in. Let the love in his eyes soak in good and deep. All the way to the roots. He still loved her. He was giving her another chance. She could do this. She could find the courage to love him, one day at a time. With a man like Daniel loving her, she'd be crazy not to.

Because she loved him so much. Because she dreamed of a lifetime with him, but would settle for however long she got and trust God with the rest.

"I have a head injury."

His strange words pulled her from her thoughts. That last shot of morphine must've kicked in. "What?"

"A moment like this . . . it kind of calls for a romantic kiss, you know? I'm weighted to this bed, and my girl won't lean over and make it happen."

She gave a watery laugh. His girl. She liked

the sound of that. Liked it a lot. So much that she leaned over and touched her lips to his.

He took over from there, brushing her lips softly. He found the strength to brush her hair back, weaving his fingers into it. Everything around them disappeared, dwindled down to the two of them.

Jade set her palm gently on his clean-shaven face, loving the feel of his lips on hers, tasting, coaxing. She'd missed this so much. Missed him. She'd never get enough, if they had ten lifetimes together.

When they were both breathless, she set her forehead against his.

His eyes fell shut. "Listen." The rapid beeping of the heart monitor betrayed his reaction to the kiss. "See what you do to me?"

She took his hand and brought it to her own thumping heart. "Me too."

He sighed softly, his warm breath tickling her lips.

He opened his eyes. "The nurses are going to run in here thinking I'm having a coronary."

"You'd better settle down, then. 'Cause I kind of sneaked in here."

He smiled. "That's my girl." He gave a slow blink, then another, his eyes sticking for a second longer.

She kissed his forehead and straightened. "I should let you rest."

His eyes fluttered shut and stayed. "Go home, get some sleep," he mumbled.

"When your parents get back," she said, but he was already drifting away.

He didn't stir when she brushed the hair from his forehead. She'd leave in a minute. She just wanted to look at him awhile. Let it sink in that he was hers and she was his. That she'd found love despite her efforts to avoid it. That she'd found a man who was worth the risk. That he loved her, had waited for her. Not for weeks or months but for years.

She let her eyes roam over his beautiful, familiar face. His long lashes, his stately nose, his lips, slackening now in sleep. He was breathing easily, sleeping deeply. She looked at the door, considering, then settled into the chair instead. She wasn't going anywhere. Not for a long time.

Epilogue

"Mmmmm, this cake is so good," Jade said.

Beside her on the sofa, Madison cradled Mia on her lap. "Well, you nixed the four-course meal. She had no choice but to pour her heart into the cake."

PJ had spent her Christmas break designing and creating an amazing two-tiered white almond wedding cake.

A flash went off as Mom took another photo. The McKinley home swarmed with family and close friends. White Christmas lights and flickering candlelight warmed the home. The mantel was decked out with stockings and a sprawling garland. An eight-foot spruce crowded the alcove by the staircase.

The Christmas Eve wedding had been perfect. A simple candlelit service at church. Romantic, quiet, and unforgettable. She'd never forget the look in Daniel's eyes as he recited his vows. So full of love and conviction. She tucked the memory away in her heart to revisit later. Since they'd arrived at the farmhouse, Daniel had caught her under the mistletoe twice. The first kiss, just a brush. The second, a lingering kiss that had made her eager for the night ahead.

She scanned the crowd for her husband, smiling even as she thought the word. Husband. He was all hers now. And there he was, chatting with Ryan over by the wall of photos, laughing at some faded memory. They'd already opened presents, cut the cake, mingled with guests. She was ready to get him and go.

He turned just then. Their eyes met and held, and his lips settled into a private smile. He'd gained his strength back in the four weeks since the accident. He looked so handsome in his suit, one hand tucked into his pocket, the other holding a glass of something sparkly. Broad-shouldered and sexy, the look in his eyes made promises she couldn't wait for him to keep.

"Is it hot in here?" Jade asked.

Madison's eyes homed in on Daniel. "You are so in trouble."

Another flash went off.

"Mom," Jade said. "My mouth is full of cake."

"Oh, look, she's smiling!" Madison cooed at Mia, trying to coax another one. Mia had given her first grin to Daniel three days ago when he'd been blowing bubbles.

Mom made good use of the camera, capturing Mia's expressions. "Where's Ava?"

Jade finished her last bite. "The Dawsons had her in the family room a few minutes ago. Ava couldn't take her eyes off the Christmas lights."

Daniel's parents had surprised her these past few weeks. Hanging around Cedar Springs until Daniel was discharged from the hospital. Flying in early to help with the wedding. Apparently Jade wasn't the only one changed by almost losing Daniel.

Mom wandered off to find Ava, and Madison traipsed upstairs to change Mia. Jade brushed through the crowd with her empty plate, stopping to chat with Izzy for a few minutes. Her friend had driven down to stand up with her at the wedding. She looked gorgeous in her red pencil dress, her mahogany hair piled artfully on her head.

The kitchen contained the overflow crowd

and was even warmer than the living room. She set the dish in the full sink and slipped out the back door onto the patio.

The smack of cold air felt good on her heated skin. Her breath plumed in front of her, and her white Victorian boots made prints in the fresh dusting of snow. Fat flakes tumbled down, blanketing the twinkling bushes and sparkling like diamonds under the Christmas lights. It was beautiful and peaceful. The quiet was nice after the busy month.

Between the wedding details, moving to Daniel's house, and playing catch-up at work, there hadn't been much downtime. Throw the twins into the mix, and they'd been lucky to find time to sleep.

Daniel had filled her in on his intentions to give up his run for the House. His memory temporarily impaired after the accident, he hadn't remem-bered telling his parents on Thanksgiving until a few days after he'd awakened. He seemed relieved by the decision, and his parents were coming around.

She and Daniel had also been talking about cutting her office hours or even her quitting altogether. She was thinking about resuming guitar lessons. She had half a dozen students waiting in the wings. Daniel would have to find another assistant, but they both wanted her to be with the babies as much as possible.

She loved watching Daniel with the girls. At first he'd held them awkwardly, as if they might break. But as the days passed, he'd become a natural, walking around with a burp cloth slung over his shoulder and drool marks spotting his sleeve. She'd never dreamed such things could be so sexy.

Jade looked up, watching the flakes fall, feeling the cold wetness on her forehead, on her cheeks. A smile stretched her lips. On impulse she spun around, letting her arms fly out. Her wispy skirt spun around her legs. She closed her eyes and took a few more turns, just because she could.

A few seconds later, arms came around her, stopping her midspin. Daniel pulled her into his chest.

She grabbed his arms, still smiling, dizzy for a moment. "I didn't hear you come out."

"What are you doing?" She heard the amusement in his voice.

"Spinning."

"Why . . . ?"

"Because I'm wearing a twirly dress."

She felt his smile against her temple. "I like your twirly dress." A warm set of lips pressed against the curve of her neck. She sank into Daniel's hard chest, breathing him in.

"Is it time to go yet?" he asked.

They'd booked a suite in Louisville for two nights. Jade couldn't stand being away from the girls any longer. "I don't know which I'm antici-pating more: a full night's sleep or time alone with you."

He dropped a kiss to that spot behind her ear. A shiver that had nothing to do with the temperature shimmied up her spine. "Ah, who am I kidding?" She laughed. "You've been very patient."

"I have. But I'm about to sneak you around front to the car. I want my woman alone." He tightened his embrace and nuzzled her ear with his nose. She looked down at their hands. Their silver wedding bands glimmered under the Christmas lights. They were married. Husband and wife. Sometimes she wanted to pinch herself.

"Did I tell you how beautiful you look tonight?"

"Only about a dozen times."

He turned her in his arms and took her face in his hands, his thumbs brushing her cheeks. Their breath mingled together. "It's true. You're beautiful and amazing, and I love you so much. I'm the luckiest man in the world."

She turned a kiss into his palm. "I love you too. I'm going to make you the happiest husband ever."

"I already am."

The kiss started out soft and gentle, just a brushing of lips. But that was never enough with Daniel. He deepened the kiss, drawing her closer.

She pressed into the solid strength of his chest as his lips played havoc with her heart rate. Her hands slid up his arms and into the soft hair at his nape. She breathed in the clean scent of him.

The back door burst open, letting the party noise out. "All right, you two," Ryan said. "Break it up. The honeymoon hasn't started yet."

Daniel groaned, setting his forehead on Jade's. "Can't a guy have a moment with his bride?" he muttered.

Jade smiled into his eyes, catching her breath. "Mom wants us on the front porch for pictures."

Daniel perked up, looking toward Ryan's retreating figure. "Front porch? As in, on the way to the car? Let's go."

Jade tightened her hold, poked him in the stomach, the rigid muscles unyielding. "Pictures first. Plus we have to say good-bye to everyone, give the twins kisses."

His eyes skated across her face, coming to rest on her lips. "Did someone say kisses?" He lowered his mouth to hers again.

She planted her palms on his chest. "Pictures. Good-byes. Honeymoon. That order."

He tilted his head, narrowed his eyes. "A *few* pictures. *Quick* good-byes. And a quiet honeymoon with limited calls home."

She liked the way he thought. "Deal."

"Kiss on it?"

She smiled. "Happily."

He got his kiss this time. A quick peck that morphed into a long, lingering, breathless kiss. Her favorite kind.

A few minutes later, Ryan stuck his head out the door. "Hurry up, you two. Everyone's getting cold."

"I don't know what he's talking about," Daniel whispered into her ear. "I'm perfectly warm."

Jade tugged his hand. "Come on, Daniel. Let's get this honeymoon started."

The sooner they started their honeymoon, the sooner they started their life together. And Jade couldn't think of anything she wanted more.

Reading Group Guide

1. Who was your favorite character and why? What appealed to you most about Jade? Daniel? Were you frustrated by any of the characters?

2. Jade reaped the consequences of someone else's sin. Has this ever happened to you? How did you handle it? What did you learn from it?

3. Jade decided never to love again because of Aaron's death. Has a bad experience ever affected your outlook on love?

4. Daniel allowed his parents to pressure him into a career he didn't want. Has anyone ever pressured you into something you didn't want? How did it turn out? Did you have regrets?

5. How is Jade like a seed planted on rocky ground?

6. Jade describes the events in her life as "random acts of trauma." Have you ever felt

that way? Do you believe God has a plan for your life?

7. Have you ever felt that your life was spinning out of control? What did you do?

8. Jade's mom said, "Times like this will either cause you to fall away or will make your roots sink deep." Do you agree?

9. What does growing roots in your faith mean to you? How are roots grown?

10. Jade's difficult experiences caused her to change as a person. Only after coming to grips with the pain and dealing with her fear was she able to return to her old self. Have you experienced something similar?

Acknowledgments

Writing a book is a team effort, and I'm so grateful for the fabulous team at HarperCollins Christian Fiction, led by publisher Daisy Hutton: Ansley Boatman, Katie Bond, Amanda Bostic, Sue Brower, Ruthie Dean, Laura Dickerson, Jodi Hughes, Ami McConnell, Becky Monds, Becky Philpott, Kerri Potts, and Kristen Vasgaard.

Thanks especially to my editor, Ami McConnell. Woman, you are a wonder! I'm constantly astounded by your gift of insight. I don't know of a more talented line editor than LB Norton. You make me look much better than I am!

Author Colleen Coble is my first reader. Thank you, friend! I wouldn't want to do this writing thing without my buds and fellow authors Colleen Coble, Diann Hunt, and Kristin Billerbeck. Love you, girls!

I'm grateful to my agent, Karen Solem, who is able to somehow make sense of the legal garble of contracts and, even more amazing, help me understand it.

I owe a debt of gratitude to a few people who helped me with details involving things I know little about: my son Trevor for his help with all things related to the guitar; Tyler Sinclair, my nephew, for his assistance with the political thread; and my brother-in-law Greg Cox for details pertaining to fire fighters. Any mistakes that made their way into print are entirely mine.

To my family: Kevin, Justin, Chad, and Trevor. You make life an adventure! Love you all!

Lastly, thank you, friend, for letting me share this story with you. I wouldn't be doing this without you! I've enjoyed connecting with readers like you through my Facebook page. Visit my website at the link www.DeniseHunter Books.com or just drop me a note at Denise @DeniseHunterBooks.com.I'd love to hear from you!

About the Author

Denise Hunter is the best-selling author of many novels, including *The Trouble with Cowboys* and *Barefoot Summer*. She lives in Indiana with her husband Kevin and their three sons.